Hittin'
IT OUT
the Park

A NOVEL

Dear Reader:

Get ready for a fast-paced voyage in the world of professional baseball with a cast of characters promised to entice fans of the writing duo of Allison Hobbs and Karen E. Quinones Miller. The bestselling authors have teamed up to produce a titillating tale.

Cheryl Blanton and Sexy Sanchez are two women vying for the same catch, Randy Alston, a young Southerner who clinches a $120 million contract to play for the New York Yankees. While Cheryl marries Randy, Sexy insists on throwing a wrench in the wedding vows. The love triangle offers readers plenty of lust, scandal, and sex.

Discover who ends up with the coveted player and what surprising secrets are revealed. The writers build up to an unexpected outcome leaving readers yearning for the next chapter in the trio's lives.

As always, thanks for the love and support shown toward myself and the authors that I publish under Strebor Books. We appreciate each and every one of you and will continue to strive to bring you cutting-edge, exciting books in the future. For more information, please join my Facebook page @AuthorZane, Twitter @AuthorZane, or Instagram @AuthorZane. You can also find my "toys" at Zancspleasureproducts.com and my main web site remains Eroticanoir.com.

Blessings,

Zane

Publisher
Strebor Books
www.simonandschuster.com

ZANE PRESENTS

Hittin' IT OUT the Park

A NOVEL

ALLISON HOBBS & KAREN E. QUINONES MILLER

SBI

STREBOR BOOKS

NEW YORK LONDON TORONTO SYDNEY

Strebor Books
P.O. Box 6505
Largo, MD 20792
http://www.streborbooks.com

ISBN 978-1-59309-610-6
ISBN 978-1-4767-7929-4 (ebook)
LCCN 2014942327

First Strebor Books trade paperback edition March 2015

Cover design: www.mariondesigns.com
Cover photograph: © Keith Saunders/Keith Saunders Photos

10 9 8 7 6 5 4 3 2 1

Manufactured in the United States of America

For information regarding special discounts for bulk purchases, please contact Simon & Schuster Special Sales at 1-866-506-1949 or business@simonandschuster.com

The Simon & Schuster Speakers Bureau can bring authors to your live event. For more information or to book an event, contact the Simon & Schuster Speakers Bureau at 1-866-248-3049 or visit our website at www.simonspeakers.com.

For Kha'ri, Kareem, and Kapri—
You Mean the World to Me.
—ALLISON HOBBS

Maferefun Olodumare
Maferefun Egun
Maferefun Oshun
Maferefun bobo Orisha
I lovingly dedicate this book to both my spiritual and physical family
—KAREN E. QUINONES MILLER

ACKNOWLEDGMENTS

Thanks to all the book clubs and bloggers who have taken the time to post video reviews and written reviews of my work. I also want to thank the many readers who follow me on Facebook and who post so many cute and creative pictures of their Allison Hobbs book collections. All of these efforts make me smile. Additionally, I must thank Charmaine Parker for her patience and dedication in editing this novel. A big thank-you to Sara Camilli for taking on this collaborative project. As always, thank you, Zane for continuing to believe in me. Thank you to my literary best bud, Cairo, whose work I greatly admire and who can have me CTFU with the mere utterance of one word. Thanks, Daaimah S. Poole for being such a kind, sweet, and wise soul. To my BFF, Karen Dempsey Hammond, you are so much more than a friend—you're my sister in spirit and I absolutely adore you. Last but not least, I'd like to thank my writing partner, Karen E. Quinones Miller. I'm thrilled that our combined talents have provided our dear readers with such a delicious and racy page-turner!

Much Love,
Allison Hobbs

I want to start out by thanking The Creator for my life, my talent, and my blessings.

I also want to thank all of the ancestors—literary, familial, and otherwise—who had to endure so much to ensure that I would be able to enjoy the life that I have all these years.

A special shout-out to literary agent Sara Camilli, who for some reason stood by me and encouraged me when other people—whom I thought would—had disappeared. Sara, you are simply the bomb.

And to Zane, whom I've known and admired for years for publishing *Hittin' It Out the Park*. I'm not going to say more about Zane, because otherwise I'd start to gush, and I hate to gush, and I'm going to trust that Zane doesn't like people gushing about her. (Okay, I will say one more thing about Zane…there are SO many people in the literary world who say they always try to help others in this industry; Zane is one of only about five people who doesn't constantly going around saying it, but goes around doing it.)

This is the very first book I've ever written without Evening Star Writers' Group, but even though we never met to discuss and critique my portion of *Hittin' It Out the Park*, it really helped to know I always had the moral support. Thank you, Fiona Harewood, Sharai Robbin, and Akanke Washington. I don't know what I would do without you.

My friends and Prayer Warriors—Fiona Harewood, Victoria Christopher Murray, Jenice Armstrong, Kim Beverly, Johnny Black, Senemeh Burke, Sojourner McCauley, and Makeela Thomas.

I also want to thank the members of the Brothers and Sisters Book Club of Philadelphia/South Jersey—with a special shout-out to Audrey Johnson. Thank you for welcoming me as a member, and thank you for being my friend.

And a thank you to all the readers and book clubs who have read my books and have hosted me throughout the years. I hope you guys never get tired of me—I know I'll never get tired of you.

Just hit me up…I'd love to come out and meet with you. You can always reach me on Facebook at www.facebook.com/karen.e.miller.14. I look forward to hearing from you.

It is important that I take this opportunity to remember, and honor, those who have passed since my last book, but who have meant so much to me: Barbara Wallace, Charles Robinson (Shola Remi), Sherlaine Freeman, Jose Manuel (Oyadina), J. California Cooper, Nelson Mandela, and Maya Angelou—May you all rest in peace. Ibaiye.

I want to thank the health professional who assisted me during my illness and the writing of this book: Brenda Munson Glover and Lynette Lunnon.

Dwayne Ligon, dear friend, thanks for the use of your name. I hope you enjoy your character namesake. <smile>

Of course I thank my family, Joseph T. Quinones and my lovely daughter, Camille R. Quinones Miller. Nice to know you have folks you can always depend on…and I hope they know they can always depend on me.

But I really have to give the biggest thanks to my coauthor, the terrifically talented Allison Hobbs. Thanks, Allison, for your patience and understanding—and most of all, your encouragement and support. I hope this won't be our last collaboration—I enjoyed this one too much!

In closing, I want to once again ask for forgiveness for those whose names I have failed to remember, but without whom my life would not be the same.

Karen E. Quinones Miller

Prologue

April 15, 1997

"I thought you didn't want to know the sex of the baby."

"I changed my mind," Cheryl answered drowsily. "I don't really care; I was only wondering."

The doctor looked down at the teenager and she thought she saw uncertainty in his dark eyes; prompting her to warily tell him: "Dang, Dr. Nehru. Don't worry, there's no chance in hell, I'm changing my mind. You and your wife can keep the baby. I'm only curious, is all."

Dr. Nehru nodded, but indecision still creased his face. A few seconds passed before he pulled a chair close to the hospital bed and sat down. He took one of her hands in his and gave what looked like a forced smile before finally speaking. "Cheryl, you do realize you made the right decision, don't you? After all, you're still a child yourself; there's no way you'd be able to take care of this baby."

The anesthetic she'd been given for the caesarian birth was almost totally worn off, and Cheryl began to feel a little soreness, causing her to grimace as the doctor continued to speak.

"My wife and I can give—"

"Yeah, yeah, I know," Cheryl interrupted him. "Listen, can I have some kind of painkiller or something?"

"Sure." The doctor nodded. "I'll have the nurse come in and give you something in a minute. But I wanted to assure you that—"

"Hey, I only asked if it was a boy or girl; don't freak out," Cheryl snapped. "Make sure I get the rest of the money you owe me, okay?"

"Absolutely!" the doctor said.

"It was a simple question; I don't know why you're making a freaking federal case outta this. It's not like I even really care," Cheryl mumbled loud enough for the doctor to hear. "Shit."

"I'm sorry," he said sheepishly. "It's a boy. We haven't decided on a name yet, though."

"I didn't ask you," Cheryl snapped. "It's your kid; name it what the fuck you want." Her facial expression softened almost as soon as the words were out of her mouth. "I'm sorry. You didn't deserve all that."

The doctor stood up and patted her on the shoulder. "Don't worry about it. You've gone through a lot, and you're bound to be edgy. And of course, you did say you need some painkillers, right? I'll have the nurse give you a shot of morphine."

The sharp aches were worsening, and Cheryl could only give a weak smile and nod in response. The nurse was in the private room less than five minutes after the doctor left, and injected a shot of clear liquid into the IV attached to Cheryl's arm. Thirty seconds later, Cheryl drifted off to sleep, and to dream about the events that had brought her to this point.

"Look, you need money, I can use some extra cash; the plan makes sense," Jackson said urgently. "This cat is going to lay down ten stacks for the privilege of popping your cherry. Hell, ain't that better than giving it away for free to some knucklehead in the backseat of some car?"

Cheryl hated Jackson. Had hated him from the first time she met him, only a few months after her father died and he started dating her mother. And within three years it seemed her hatred was justified. With

Jackson's encouragement, Cheryl's mother became hooked on cocaine, and went through the almost $2 million her father had left them. After the money was gone, Jackson was gone, and Cheryl's mother then turned to crack and alcohol.

Cheryl was fifteen by then, and desperate to come up with money to pay the rent. She had to drop out of the prestigious private school she'd been attending before her father's death and attend public school, but she was also forced to take over as head of the household since her mother was absolutely useless, and was only interested in scoring her next hit, and next drink.

They were evicted from their swanky Upper East Side apartment for not paying the rent, and now the rent on their tiny Harlem apartment was three months' overdue; not knowing what else to do Cheryl had decided to resort to shoplifting. She ventured into Bloomingdale's on Lexington Avenue, stuffed a couple of dresses in her bag, and headed out the door; but almost peed her pants when she felt a hand on her shoulder.

"So you've decided on a career as a booster, huh?"

Cheryl whirled around and found herself face-to-face with Jackson. "What are you doing here? Get offa me," she snarled, yanking away from him.

"I should do exactly that, but I'ma do your little uppity-ass a favor." Jackson gripped her by the arm and propelled her to the back of the store and to the ladies dressing room. "Now get in there, and unload."

"What?"

Jackson stepped closer to her and said in a low voice. "You little idiot. If I saw you putting those dresses in that bag, you think I'm the only one who did? And even if no one else did, the security alarms would have gone off as soon as you walked out the door."

Cheryl looked at him without saying a word, and disappeared into the dressing room. Jackson was waiting for her when she came out.

That's when he made the proposal.

"I know I left you and your mom in a bad way, so let me help you out," Jackson urged. "Look, the cat is offering ten stacks, but I bet I can get him up to fifteen. He's got lettuce like that. We'll split it."

I hate him. He ruined our lives. If I had a gun I'd shoot him, *is what she said to herself, but out loud she could only exclaim:* "Fifteen thousand?"

Jackson nodded. "I think I can get that much out of him."

"And what would be your split?" she asked suspiciously.

"I'm not greedy. I wouldn't even ask for any of it, but I'm in a little bit of a jam, too." Jackson acted as if he was giving it some thought. "How about I take two thousand, and you keep the rest?"

Cheryl's eyes narrowed. "I don't trust you. How do I know you won't keep the whole thing?"

Jackson grinned. "Moi?" he said, pointing to his chest. "You don't trust moi?"

Cheryl sucked her teeth and started walking away. Jackson quickly grabbed her arm again. "Look, you might not trust me, but I trust you. So how about this? The guy pays you, then you give me my cut. Okay?"

Man, Cheryl thought, with thirteen thousand she could pay off the back rent, buy school clothes, and maybe even pay for her mom to go into some kind of rehab program. But, still, she wanted to save herself until she got married. But, wow, thirteen thousand.

"Now, here's the thing," Jackson said, interrupting her thoughts. "If we're going to get him up to fifteen thousand, there're a few things you're going to have to do."

Cheryl's eyebrow and suspicion rose. "Things like what?"

"Well, you're fifteen, right? The younger the cherry, the more men are willing to pay. You're kinda flat-chested, so if you would, well, shave down there, we can probably pass you off as a twelve-year-old."

Cheryl

July 2013

"Would you care for another martini, ma'am?"

Cheryl Blanton leaned her head slightly to the right, and gave a tiny pout, as if the tuxedo-clad drink waiter's offer warranted serious thought. She finally gave a small one-shoulder shrug, and lifted a long-stemmed glass from the solid gold tray he carried.

"Thank you..." Cheryl quickly glanced at the metal nametag on his chest, "Henry." She flashed a quick smile designed to make the older man's heart flutter. "I probably shouldn't, but I'm so bored I might as well get intoxicated." She took a small sip from the glass before giving him a quick wink. "Don't let me get to the point of having to be carried out, okay?"

"I'm sure you have *nothing* to worry about, ma'am." Henry smiled, bowing his graying head as if she had bestowed a thousand-dollar tip upon him rather than a simple off-handed comment. "I can't imagine anyone as beautiful as you being bored very long." He gave another quick nod before backing away into the crowd.

Yeah, well, I hope you're right, 'cause I don't know how much more of this I can stand. Cheryl twirled the drink in her hand and watched the olive do a slow spin, then glanced at her watch. Twelve-thirty. She released a deep breath and looked over toward the corner where she'd last seen her escort. She hadn't wanted to come to the baseball All-Star party at all, but Stephen had insisted.

"*Come on... you never come out with me anymore,*" he had whined. "*And besides,*" he added, when he saw Cheryl was still unmoved, "*there's going to be a lot of celebrities and millionaires there. You never know what you might catch. And wear that short, white lace number— show off those long bronze-colored stilts, honey.*"

Cheryl snorted remembering his words. Celebrities. Yeah, Alyssa Milano and one of the Russian chicks from *Dancing with the Stars* were the only personalities she'd spotted so far. As for millionaires, well, there were none there that she knew or recognized. Besides, there were probably two gold diggers for every possible-millionaire at the party—and she wasn't in the mood to be pushing someone aside to get to a man whose wealth she wasn't sure of.

Stephen was right about one thing, though: the white lace mini was certainly getting her a lot of attention. And it wasn't only her legs that were getting admiring stares. There was something about the combination of the soft texture of her dress, the temperature in the room, and perhaps her naturally sexual nature...but even the slightest breeze made her nipples harden. Looking down, she carefully arranged her long brown hair to cover her 36-Ds.

The drink waiter, Henry, squeezed past her again, and she gifted him a full-tooth smile, and inwardly laughed when he almost bumped into someone because he was smiling back so hard.

Feeling a slight tap on the shoulder, Cheryl turned to face a tall, gorgeous woman wearing a low-cut, skin-tight, gold minidress that left nothing to the imagination. "Oh, de-year!" the woman said in a voice obviously meant to sound haughty. "Flirting with the hired help again, are we, dah-ling? But then class does always find its own class, doesn't it?"

Cheryl struggled to keep a grimace off her face. "No harm in being pleasant, you know." She paused and gave her adversary an up-and-down look. "But then, again, I'm sure you *wouldn't* know, Sheila."

"Shay-EE-lah."

Cheryl let out a tingly laugh. "If it's spelled Sheila, it's pronounced SHEE-luh. Like a female kangaroo." She looked down at Sheila's midsection. "Which is kind of fitting, seeing how noticeable *your* pouch is in that dress."

"Oh, puleeze! This dress is from Armani's—"

"From Armani's summer line," Cheryl interrupted. "I know. I wore it for him at his runway show at Paris Fashion Week last September. But believe me, it doesn't suit you at all." She lightly tapped Sheila's stomach with her Versace gold clutch bag. "So, I'm guessing the rumors I've been hearing about you moving over to plus-size modeling are true. I understand you can make quite a lot of money." She slowly batted her almond-shaped eyes before adding, "And Lane Bryant is always looking for fresh faces, though Ashley Stewart is also an option."

"Cheryl, you can be such a—"

Cheryl rolled her eyes and sighed. "Sheila, if I throw a stick, will you leave?"

Sheila kept a smile on her face as she looked Cheryl in the face and in a honey-coated voice said: "I'd love to continue this conversation, but I've actually spotted someone worth talking to. So, Cheryl, darling, fuck you."

"Of course, honey, and please do feel free to come back and kiss my pretty ass anytime," Cheryl replied, just as pleasantly, twirling her fingers in a 'bye-bye' fashion.

"Slut!" Sheila said, turning around to walk away.

"Ghetto-ass bitch," Cheryl said as she did.

She watched as Sheila sashayed across the room, stopping to strike what she probably thought was a provocative pose in front of a short, but dapper, man who looked to be in his sixties. Having overheard the man talking about the possible ramifications if Yankees third baseman Alex Rodriguez was suspended for steroid use, Cheryl knew he had some kind of professional connection with baseball. Probably a former player, she had figured. *Okay,* Cheryl thought, watching Sheila play with her hair, *obviously she knows he's a millionaire.* She watched in amusement as the man glanced at Sheila, then turned and walked away without saying anything. She wanted to walk over and laugh out loud in the woman's face, but looking at Sheila's hurt expression, she couldn't bring herself to upset her further.

Cheryl started scanning the room, looking for Stephen, wondering—again—how he could possibly think hobnobbing at one of the Major League Baseball's All-Star parties was going to help him land the job interview he wanted. He needed to face the fact that while his family loved him, his friends adored him, and Cheryl, herself, simply cherished him, it would likely be a cold day in Hell before he was hired as a press agent for a major sports franchise. And especially not a media-conscious team like the New York Yankees. Too bad they didn't live in San Francisco, she thought as she started walking toward him. She shook her head. No, he wouldn't even stand a chance of getting hired there.

She waited until the balding middle-aged man with whom Stephen was talking walked off before poking her friend in the ribs and asking, "How's it going, baller?"

Stephen snorted and waved his hand. "Girl, please, I got this."

Cheryl gave a quick glance from side-to-side before stepping closer to Stephen and saying in a low voice, "Hey, hey, hey...what did we talk about on the way over here?"

Stephen's perfectly tweezed eyebrows furrowed. "What?"

"Did you or did you not say, 'Girl, please,' a moment ago?" Cheryl said, pinching his arm.

"Yes, and...oh right!" Stephen rubbed his bicep. "Well, it's no big deal. I doubt anyone heard."

Cheryl placed her now empty martini glass on a nearby table and started straightening Stephen's tie. "Well, let's hope not. Even people who may accept the fact that you're gay may not like you acting like a queen."

Stephen sucked his teeth. "Oh, come on. Saying, 'Oh, girl,' is not acting or sounding like a queen."

Cheryl shrugged. "Not to me...but why give someone arguing against you getting the job more ammunition?"

"Interview, Cheryl, interview. I'm merely trying to get an interview at the moment."

"Girl, please, you know you're getting that." As soon as the word left her lips, Cheryl's hands flew up to her mouth as if to try and force them back in. Eyes wide, she looked up at Stephen, whose amused smile quickly evolved into full-out laughter.

"Now, see, honey, I don't want any more lectures from the likes of you!" Stephen said, finally. "Gonna tell me I can't say, 'girl,' and then you turn right around and call me *girl*."

"All right, all right, I messed up. So, how's the brown-nosing going?"

Stephen leaned his head to the side and smiled. "All insults aside, I'd say I've done very well."

"Oh?" Cheryl raised an eyebrow.

"Yep." Stephen grabbed two glasses of champagne from a passing tray and handed one to Cheryl, then took a sip from the other. "I've been invited to a meet-and-greet at Yankee Stadium next week for the communications director."

"You go, boy!" Cheryl said excitedly. "How the hell did you swing that?"

"Cheryl, girl, you're not going to believe it, but—"

"Eeek!" Cheryl couldn't hold back a scream as freezing liquid spilled over her left shoulder and down the front of her dress. She whirled around, fists balled, expecting to face a smirking Sheila, but instead found herself looking up at a skinny copper-complexioned man with a bad case of acne and a Jheri curl. She blinked her eyes to make sure they were working right. Yes, it was a Jheri curl that he was sporting, even though it was 2013—more than twenty years after that style had played out.

"Oh, Miss, I'se so sorry!" Mr. Jheri Curl spoke, jarring her from her nanosecond stupor. "I was walking and someone musta bumped me, and kinda hard. I hope I ain't hurt ya." His Southern accent was so heavy it was hard to understand him at first.

"Hurt me? No. Soaked me? Yes," Cheryl huffed, almost stumbling as she backed up into Stephen.

"Damn, man. What? You blind?" Stephen grabbed a linen napkin from a table and went to start dabbing at Cheryl but suddenly stopped. "Yo, I mean, what? Did you want to take a picture or something?"

When Cheryl followed Stephen's eyes, her irritation quickly turned to indignation. The cold drink had plastered the short, white lace dress to her body, making her look like a contestant in a wet T-shirt contest, and if Mr. Jheri Curl's expression was any indication, she was the winner, hands down. Her head flew up high, and her back straightened as she took a deep breath, causing her breasts to rise, and heavily heave. Eyes narrowed, she stared at the gaping man. "Oh? I suppose you think this is funny?"

"Huh? Oh! No, ma'am. I'm really very sorry," Mr. Jheri Curl sputtered. "For real. It was an accident, ya know, like I said. Someone bumped in ta me."

"Well, you ruined her dress," Stephen interjected.

"I'll be glad to pay for it," Mr. Jheri Curl quickly responded.

Cheryl's hand slowly made its way to her hip. "This dress happens to be an original Dolce and Gabbana. It cost about three thousand dollars."

"For that little bit of material?" Mr. Jheri Curl's head jerked back. "Get outta here."

"It's called high-fashion, you Lionel Richie wannabe," Stephen snapped.

"Yeah, well, I call it someone sold you 'bout thirty dollars' worth of cloth and thread for a hunnert times the cost." Mr. Jheri Curl shrugged. "But anyways, I weren't speaking about buying a new dress; I was speaking about paying ta get it cleaned." He turned to Cheryl. "Miss, I don't know how many times and how many ways I can say I'm sorry, but I'll pay for the dry cleaning. It can't be but so expensive what to get cleaned."

"Oh, my God, did he really say, 'what to get cleaned'?" Stephen put his hand to his brow and leaned his forehead back in dramatic fashion. "Not only does he look like nineteen-eighties Rick James, he sounds like nineteen-sixties Gomer Pyle."

Mr. Jheri Curl, who Cheryl figured had to be about six feet three, looked down at the five-seven Stephen, with a puzzled look on his face. "Sir, I said I'm sorry. It really was an accident. I'm not sure what you want me ta do, but really, there's no need for name calling."

"Well, if you hadn't—"

"Look," Cheryl interrupted. "Stephen, I appreciate the chivalry, but I'm sure he's not lying, and it really was an accident. Let's get outta here, okay?"

"Fine. Oh, wait. Give me about ten more minutes!" Stephen said hurriedly. "I've got to get Chuck's telephone number."

"What?" Cheryl sucked her teeth. "Who's Chuck?" But Stephen was already scurrying away. "Oh, great," she said under her breath. Here it was she hadn't wanted to go the party in the first place, then she ran into evil-ass Sheila, then she got a drink spilled on her $3,000 dress making her look like a chick from a *Girls Gone Wild* video, and now she couldn't even leave when she wanted because her ride had suddenly decided he needed to track down some "Chuck." Eyes narrowed, she turned to face Mr. Jheri Curl again, prepared to take her entire frustration out on him. "You know—"

"Here you go, ma'am," he said, placing the lightweight jacket he had been wearing over her shoulders. "Let's cover you up."

"Look you—"

Mr. Jheri Curl quickly held out his hand to shake Cheryl's. "Randall Alston, ma'am."

"Okay, then, Randall Alston—"

"Please, call me Randy." He flashed a huge smile. "All my friends do."

"WILL YOU PLEASE SHUT THE HELL UP AND LET ME TELL YOU OFF, DAMN IT!"

The spilling of the drink had only garnered the attention of the people in close proximity of the incident; Cheryl's high-decibel rant, however, caught the attention of almost the entire room. Not only could Cheryl see the people in front of her and to her side, staring, she imagined feeling lasers of heat hitting her back, emanating from the eyes of those behind her.

"Cripes," Cheryl said inwardly.

"Listen, it's really still warm outside even though it's late," Randy said, breaking into her thoughts. "Maybe if we stand outside on the patio for a little while, the warm breeze will help dry you off." He gallantly put his arm around her shoulders and started leading her the few feet to the terrace.

Henry, the drink waiter she had talked to earlier, tapped her on the shoulder as they passed. "Are you okay, ma'am? Can I get you anything?"

She glanced at his tray of martinis, and shook her head. "Wait, yeah. Any chance I can get a double scotch?"

"It would be my pleasure," Henry said, with a nod. "And you, Mr. Alston? Would you like another glass of water?"

Randy gave a sheepish grin. "Uh, no, I don't think I could handle another one."

"So, it was only water, then?" Cheryl asked when they were finally outside, and sitting across from each other at a table off into a corner of the terrace.

"Yep, only water. I don't drink alcohol during the season."

"Good, then I don't have to worry about a stain or smell. Even a clear alcohol like rum or vodka would have meant a dry cleaning bill. Looks like you got off easy." Cheryl smiled up at him. *During the season? Hmm, a ball player, then? Maybe this party wasn't such a waste after all.*

She leaned back and gave her potential prospect a good once-over.

Country, without a doubt, and his hair is pathetic, but once you get past that, and the patch of acne on the right side of his face, this Randy guy is actually kind of handsome. And, face it; he is charming as all hell.

"Wow, this chair is a little wobbly, ya know?" Randy stood up, and quickly pulled a chair from another table to replace the one he'd been sitting on, giving Cheryl an opportunity for a more thorough inspection. She struggled to hide a smile as she looked at the front of his pants. *And he's packing, too.* Now it wasn't only the wetness of the water making her nipples hard.

"So, you're a baseball player? What team?"

"The Scranton/Wilkes-Barre RailRiders."

"Oh!" Cheryl didn't bother to hide the disappointment in her voice. Minor League. Old country Randy Alston was barely making $2,000 a month. Though modeling wasn't half as lucrative as most people thought, she could make five or six times that amount in a good Fashion Week. Ten times that amount if you counted the value of the clothes some designers gave in lieu of cash.

"You probably haven't heard of them," Randy continued. "It's what you call a farm team—"

"I'm familiar with them," Cheryl cut him off. "One of the New York Yankees farm teams, not far outside of Pittsburgh. What position do you play?"

"Third base." Randy smiled. "You've really heard of the Rail-Riders? Get outta here."

Cheryl shrugged. "My father was a sports attorney, in addition to being a HUGE Yankee fan. He knew everything there was to know about the team."

"Was? Your father's passed away?"

Cheryl nodded, biting her lip. "He died when I was ten."

"I'm guessing by the tone in your voice, it still hurts. I'm sorry I brought it up."

"No, it's okay. But, yeah, it still hurts. He and I were...we were really close. I still miss him after all these years. I guess I was what you call a Daddy's girl. As far as he was concerned, I was a little princess. And when you're a kid, you never imagine something's gonna happen to your folks. He was only forty. Who has a heart attack at forty, right?" Cheryl quickly blinked back the tears that she hadn't realized were welling up in her eyes. "But, hey," she said, trying to force a smile. "Such is life. And death. Huh?"

"Hey, hey." Randy leaned over and put his hand over Cheryl's. "You don't have to play down your pain for my benefit or anyone else's, It's okay ta still be grieving."

Cheryl blinked harder, but Randy's soothing words, the warmth of his hands, the martinis, and speaking about her father combined to give her heart a bittersweet ache. She finally gave in, and used her hands to wipe the tears leaking from the corners of her eyes.

Randy quietly moved his chair so that he was sitting by her side. "You okay?"

Cheryl nodded. "I don't know what's wrong with me tonight." She looked up to see Henry approaching them. She felt a small wave of embarrassment, realizing that both he and Randy had seen her minor breakdown. "See, this is your fault," she told the drink waiter with a pout.

"Mine, ma'am?" Henry asked.

"Yes, you were supposed to stop me before I had too much to drink, remember?" Cheryl answered. "Now, look, here I am...a crying drunk."

"Well, ma'am, if you don't mind my saying," Henry said stiffly, placing her drink in front of her, "at least you're no longer bored."

Both Cheryl and Randy started laughing, and though Henry did his best to keep his reserved demeanor, even he eventually let out a few chuckles.

"I brought you another glass of water, in case you changed your mind, Mr. Alston. I hope you don't mind?" Henry asked after he fully gained his composure.

"Not at all, Mr. Reynolds. Thank you," Randy answered, trying unsuccessfully to mimic Henry's clipped tone.

"How do you two know each other?" Cheryl asked after the man had left.

"Oh, we don't really. I only met him for the first time today."

Cheryl looked at him quizzically. "And you exchanged names?"

"Yeah, it's kind of funny, actually." Randy flashed a small grin. "I've never been ta one of these fancy parties before, you know, where they go around serving drinks on a tray, you know? So, I come in with Mr. Archer—"

"Mr. Archer?"

Randy nodded. "He's a sports agent. He's the one what invited me to this party. I couldn'ta afforded no five-hundred-dollar ticket, otherwise."

"So, okay, you came in with Mr. Archer..." Cheryl prodded.

"And so as soon as we come in he's going around talking ta people, and people are talking ta him, and pretty soon I look around and I don't know where he is. So, I'm standing in the corner, by myself, and Mr. Reynolds—"

"You mean Henry?"

"Well, ya know, I'd feel funny calling him by his first name, being he's old enough to be my father," Randy said sheepishly. "So, anyway, Mr. Reynolds walks by with a tray of champagne, and asks if I want one. I say no, and he walks away. About an hour goes by, and I'm still in the corner, by myself, and he comes and asks if I'd like a martini. I tell him no. Another half-hour goes by, and he comes by again. And then he gets kinda close to me and says all proper-like, 'Excuse me, are you sure you don't want anything at all, sir? Perhaps I can get you a special drink from the bar.' So, now I'm feeling a little embarrassed, you know? So I tell him a glass of water will be fine, ya know? But then, when he's about to leave to get it, I ask him if there's a charge for the water."

"Oh, no." Cheryl clapped a hand over her mouth. "You thought—"

"Heck, I ain't never been ta no party where they was giving out free drinks before. And it's an off-payday weekend, so I'm not carrying a lot of cash, ya know?" Randy chuckled. "So, then he looks at me, and his lips get real tight like he's trying not to smile, and he tells me all the drinks are free."

"Oh, poor Randy," Cheryl cooed, between chuckles.

"When he gets back he's smiling and all, and I'm feeling like I know him by now, so I introduce myself, ya know? And then he tells me his name, and bam, I done met my first person at this high-falutin' party."

Cheryl took a sip from her drink. "Well, you know Mr. Archer."

Randy snorted. "I probably know Mr. Reynolds better than I know Mr. Archer."

"I thought he was your agent?"

"Mine? Nah. I wish he was, though." Randy let out a sigh. "He's got some pretty big names on his roster."

Cheryl's brows furrowed. "I don't get it, then. Why did he give you a ticket to this party?"

"To tell you the truth, I don't know." Randy shrugged. "He showed up in the dugout last week, and was talking to our manager. After he finished he came over and tapped me on the shoulder and asked me if I'd ever been to New York City. I told him no, and he said that Nike was giving a party that I might want to check out, ya know? Told me the date, gave me his card, and said for me to call his office to have them send me a ticket. They mailed me the ticket, I caught the bus up from Scranton this morning, and here I am."

"And here you are."

"And here I am." Randy gave a slight chuckle, his eyes lowering to the table, before shaking his head. "Yep. Here I am."

"Hey, what's wrong?" Cheryl gave him a slight nudge. "You okay?"

"Yep, I'm okay," Randy said, hurriedly looking up again. "I was kinda hoping, well, ya know, that this invite mighta meant something."

"Something like what?" Cheryl asked, although she was sure she knew what he meant. It was the dream of every Minor League player to make it to the majors. Randy would be no exception.

"I don't know. Well, I thought he was, ya know, scouting me or something." Randy started chewing his lip. "I been with the Rail-Riders for almost three years now. Went there right outta high school. This is the final year on my contract. It woulda been nice if a big-time agent was interested in finding me a spot in the majors. But when we bumped into each other when we were coming in, it was obvious he didn't even recognize me, ya know?"

"Oh, wow."

"Don't get me wrong, I had a great time, and all," Randy added. "And I always knew making it to the majors would be a long shot. But always, in the back of my mind, I kinda hoped the only way I'd be returning to Eufaula was to visit family."

"You what?"

Randy grinned. "Eufaula. You-FAH-luh. It's in Alabama. About two hours south of Atlanta."

"Small town?" Cheryl wasn't sure why she was interested, but she found she was genuinely so. After gleaning that he was only about twenty-one, made less than $30,000 a year, didn't have a car, and really no prospects, she had definitely excluded him as potential boyfriend material—even if he did have a nice package. Still, there was something touching about the young man sitting next to her. She was charmed by him.

"Eufaula's not too small. About thirteen-thousand people." Randy laughed when he saw the expression on Cheryl's face. "Okay, maybe to you that's very small, but I'll have you know Eufaula is the biggest town in Balfour County."

"Is that so?" Cheryl giggled.

"Oh, here you are!" a catty voice called out behind them.

Cheryl closed her eyes for a few moments and shook her head a couple of times, hoping that by the time she looked up the owner of the voice would have disappeared. No such luck. "What's up, Sheila?"

"Nothing." Sheila leaned her weight on her left leg, slowly jutting her right hip out provocatively. "I noticed you out here, and thought I'd walk over so you could introduce me to your boyfriend." She glanced at Randy, then gave Cheryl a smirk. "I simply love his hair. How long have you been seeing each other?"

Cheryl didn't miss a beat. "About three weeks." She leaned her head on Randy's shoulder, and smiled as he put his arm around hers. "Sheila Arlington, I'd like you to meet Randall Alston. Randy, dear, this is Sheila."

"How do you do?" Randy nodded.

"Randall Alston?" Sheila frowned. "Should I know that name?"

Cheryl sighed, then turned and looked at Randall. "You have to excuse her, babe. Unlike me, Sheila is one of those really dumb fashion models who doesn't know anything about sports, politics, or...," she gave a slight shrug, "or really anything at all besides clothes."

Randy nodded, then gave Sheila a quick and disdainful up-and-down look and said with a smirk: "Nice dress." He squeezed Cheryl's arm. "So, babe, what were we talking about?"

Yes! Yes! Yes! Cheryl wanted to raise her arms in victory. She had no idea that Randy could be that witty and that cold. And she liked it.

Sheila stood there, a dumbfounded look on her face, for a few seconds, before flipping her hair over her shoulder and slinking off.

"I can't believe you said that!" Cheryl said as soon as she was sure Sheila was out of earshot. "That was so cool!"

"I can't believe I been sitting here talking to a fashion model," Randy said, both amazement and admiration evident in his voice. "I should have known, though, because you are really beautiful, ya know. And I been dying ta tell you that all night."

"Aw." Cheryl waved her hand dismissively.

"Wow!" Randy gushed. "Have you been in any magazines?"

"Well…" Cheryl started counting off on her fingers. "I've been in *Glamour, Ebony, Cosmopolitan, Self,* and I've made the cover of *Essence, Cosmopolitan,* and…" She stopped and looked at Randy and grinned. "And one day, hopefully, I'll make the cover of the *Sports Illustrated Swimsuit* issue."

"Ah!" Randy let his head dramatically fall to the table. "I wouldn't be able ta take it."

Cheryl laughed.

"Oh, no, I'm so serious!" Randy said, straightening back up in his seat. "Man, you know what I would do if after I get back to Eufaula I one day see your lovely body on the cover of *SI*?" Randy shook his head. "Man, I don't even know what I would do, ya know?"

They both started laughing, and Cheryl impulsively reached over and gave Randy a hug. What a sweetheart.

"But tell me more about you," Randy said.

"Like what?" Cheryl smiled.

"Well, like, how about your name?" Randy grinned. "I know you're a model. I know you wear three-thousand-dollar dresses. And I know you're beautiful. But, heck, girl, I don't know your name!"

"Oh my goodness, you don't! I'm sorry! I'm Cheryl. Cheryl Blanton." She offered her hand, and Randy pulled it to his lips and kissed it.

"Nice to meet you, Cheryl. And how old are you?"

Cheryl frowned. "It really is impolite to ask a lady her age."

"Aw, nah, sorry. But you look so young, yet you act so mature, you know?" Randy flashed the sheepish grin that Cheryl had already begun to admire so much.

Cheryl gave a tingly laugh. "No, that's okay." *Okay, he said he's been with the team almost three years, and he went there right after graduating high school, so...*"I'm twenty-four."

Randy grinned. "We're about the same age. I'm twenty-one."

Cheryl could see the insecurity behind the smile. *He's hoping I won't say he's too young for me. Aw, isn't that sweet?* She gave a little giggle. "You only recently became legal, huh?"

They both laughed.

"And, hey listen, I really want ta say thank you." Randy lowered his eyes and put his hand over Cheryl's.

"For what?"

Randy gave a half-smile and a small shrug. "Only thank you, okay?"

Cheryl nodded. Intuitively she realized he was expressing his gratitude for her claiming him as her boyfriend when Sheila tried to zing him. She leaned her head against his shoulder again. "Well, thank you, too."

"For what?"

"I simply wanted to thank you, okay?" Cheryl didn't care whether or not he knew what it was she was thanking him for, because honestly, she didn't know herself. But she hoped he realized the thanks were sincere. Usher's love song "Here I Stand" was playing in the background. "Oh, don't you love this song?" she asked, snuggling closer to him.

"I never really listened to the words before, but I like it now," Randy answered, stroking Cheryl's hair. "It's the way I feel about you."

"Boy, you don't even know me," Cheryl said with a laugh.

"I know. But I'm not lying. It's the way I feel," Randy said solemnly.

"What time do the buses to Scranton stop running?"

"It doesn't matter. I went ahead and got a motel room. I plan on catching the noon bus tomorrow."

"Okay." Cheryl stood up, and slowly removed the jacket he'd given her from her shoulders. She lifted Randy's chin so that he was looking into her eyes. "You've wasted your money because you're staying with me tonight."

Randy's eyes widened, and Cheryl could see his Adam's apple do a quick jig. "That would be fine. You ready to leave now?"

"I am," she answered in a husky voice.

"Well, then so am I." Randy got up so quickly his chair fell over backward. He looked down at it, then at Cheryl, and they both laughed.

"Smooth, ain't I?" he said, bending over and picking it up. "Don't even answer that." He put his arm around her waist, and they walked back into the ballroom, and toward the exit.

"There you are, Randy! I've been looking all over for you. Glad to see you made it."

"Oh, hello, Mr. Archer."

"Mr. Archer? Please! Call me Danny!" The man who had dissed Sheila a few hours earlier slapped Randy on the back. "Enjoying yourself?"

"Well, yes, I was, but, uh, we were about ta leave."

"We?" Danny looked at Cheryl as if noticing her for the first time. "Yes, of course. Well, I'm glad you were able to make it. How about you give me a call next week? Let's see if we can get together for lunch?"

"Uh, sure!"

Randy was still shaking his head as he and Cheryl climbed into a taxicab. "I can't believe it. He ignored me all night, then all of a sudden, he's telling me ta call him by his first name and asking me ta lunch." He pulled Cheryl into a hug and kissed her forehead. "Girl, ya know, I think you're my good luck charm."

At her apartment, Randy complimented her décor, but Cheryl didn't bother to waste time with small talk. She took him by the hand and led him to her bedroom. Like a gentleman, he took a seat in the lilac, wingback chair and folded his hands in his lap.

Tickled by Randy's good Southern manners, she laughed aloud and then eased out of her damp dress and winked at Randy. He stared, mouth agape, at the sight of her large, firm breasts and rose-colored nipples.

"Gosh!" He ran a shaky hand down the side of his face.

Cheryl reclined on the bed and then propped herself up on an elbow. "Are you gonna sit there and stare or are you gonna come and join me?"

Fully dressed, Randy stood and woodenly crossed the bedroom. Smiling teasingly, Cheryl patted the mattress. He sat at the edge of the bed, back erect, his fingers interlaced with his hands once again resting upon his lap.

Acting out the role of a teasing vixen was fun and Cheryl vamped it up, squeezing her breasts and stroking her nipples. Unable to take it any longer, Randy moved closer to her and gently nudged her back until she was lying on the bed. He hovered over her and hungrily put one of her breasts in his mouth, swirling his tongue around the tip.

His warm breath tickled her breast and a sudden rush of warmth filled Cheryl's body. "Don't stop," she uttered as she pulled him on top of her. Showing him what she really wanted, she wrapped her long legs around his waist and ran her hands over his body as she lifted his shirt over his head. Though he appeared slender, his chest and shoulders were strong and athletically muscular. Cheryl traced her finger over his skin, feeling every bulge of his sinewy muscles, and sighed at the magnificence of his sculpted torso.

She bit her lip to keep from crying out as Randy continued to lick, suck, and devour her nipples that were now as hard as diamonds. Her nipples were her weak spot, and she could easily lose control if Randy kept up his expert tongue game. She hadn't expected such masterful ministrations from a country boy.

Diverting his attention away from her breasts, she lifted up to meet his mouth, and began kissing him ravenously. Although she could feel his burgeoning erection through his pants, Randy seemed content to kiss for hours. Cheryl, however, wanted more. She wanted to get inside his pants and fondle his pulsing manhood. The thought of his hot flesh pushing inside of her and scorching her insides caused Cheryl to grow moist with anticipation. The moisture escalated to a dripping wetness that spread between her legs and leaked to the crotch of her panties.

She reached downward, struggling to unzip his pants and liberate his manhood without pulling her lips away from his. With a great deal of effort, his pants finally fell halfway down. She then yanked at his briefs, freeing his dick that was heavy and thick with desire.

Torn between sucking his dick and stuffing it inside her overheated pussy, Cheryl was relieved when Randy finally took some initiative and eased her panties over her hips. Next, he parted her legs, getting a close look at her moist sex. He grunted appreciatively as he parted her labia. He inserted a finger, and then lowered his head and sucked on her swollen clitoris.

Cheryl arched her back as he slid his finger in and out while tugging on her clit with his lips. She writhed and thrashed as the dual pleasure became unbearable, pushing her to the edge of sanity.

Without warning, he withdrew his finger and drove his tongue inside her creamy, hot box. She gave a sharp intake of breath. Excitement building, she widened her legs and then wrapped them around Randy's neck.

Cheryl squealed and writhed. Randy's tongue game was everything. In fact, it was so good, Cheryl found herself nearing a climax from his mouth alone, but she wanted more. Attempting to back away from his thorough tongue lashing, she moaned and pleaded for him to give her some dick. Desperately, she pulled him up to her, kissing him passionately, and tasting her own salty juices on his lips.

Grasping his dick, she guided it inside her, her eyes becoming wide with bliss as she realized how well he fit inside her. She held on to him, tight, as he moved with smooth, swift motions. He kissed her neck, nibbled on her ear as he slid in and out of her juicy, tight clutch.

On the brink of orgasm, Randy murmured desperately, "Baby, I'm sorry. I'm about to cum."

"It's okay. Give it to me, Randy," she responded in a husky voice.

He clenched her shoulders and squeezed his eyes shut as he speeded up his thrusting, giving her every inch of dick, and filling her with exquisite pleasure.

In tune with Randy, Cheryl could feel the familiar shuddering as a climax bubbled up inside her. Randy continued to plunge into her, and she half-moaned and half-screamed as waves of pleasure overtook her. Randy came quickly after Cheryl, and they clung to each other, sweat pouring, hearts pounding in unison.

"Girl, I've seen it, but I ain't believin' it." Stephen stood outside the living room with his arms crossed, watching Cheryl walk back toward her bedroom. "Was that really the Lionel Richie-looking, Gomer Pyle-talking, country bumpkin that you walked to the door, roomie?"

Cheryl yawned and gave a full stretch. "Yep, that was him. He was having a bad night, so I decided to take him home and grant him a pity fuck. But then he got some good news right as we were leaving the party, so it turned into a congratulations fuck."

"Oh! A congratulations fuck, huh? I've never even heard of that. How was it?"

"Good enough for him to ask me to marry him." Cheryl picked up the remote from a coffee table and clicked on the television.

"Well, you go ahead, girl. I want details." Stephen walked over and sat down on the couch, then patted the cushion next to him for Cheryl to do the same.

CNN has recently learned that the Yankees have decided to bring up two players from farm teams to play out the rest of the year, in preparation for a possible 100-game suspension of third baseman Alex Rodriguez next season due to his steroid use.

"Oooh," Cheryl said, slowly sinking down onto the plush, velvet couch. "Oh, it was good. And something tells me it's gonna get even better. Believe it or not, he'd never eaten pussy before last night. But, I'll tell you, the man's a natural."

"Really?" Stephen put his hand to his mouth as if surprised. "Do tell me more!"

"Stephen, wait." Cheryl said excitedly. "Did you hear what the announcer said about the Yankees?"

"I wasn't paying attention. What did he say?"

"He said the Yankees are bringing up a couple of third basemen from the minors to play out the rest of the season."

"Well, that would only make sense." Stephen took a sip of his coffee. "Alex Rodriguez can appeal his suspension all he wants, but there's no way that fine Latino is going to be playing next season. The Yankees have to bring up a couple of minor leaguers so they can get some experience playing behind Jayson Nix."

Cheryl nodded. "Nix has had a good year on third, and the Yankees are going to be banking on getting Rodriguez back as soon as the suspension is over, so they probably aren't going to try to spend any really big bucks bringing in a free agent."

"Right. So they bring in a couple of guys now, see who's best, and decide who they'll sign for next season to play behind Nix."

"Okay, listen to this," Cheryl said animatedly. "Randy is a third baseman."

"Who's Randy?" Stephen looked puzzled.

"You know him better by young country bumpkin." Cheryl rolled her eyes. "Anyway, he plays for the Yankees farm team in Scranton."

Stephen sat up straight. "Uh-huh. And?"

"And it turns out that all of a sudden he's being courted by a big-name sports agent."

"Uh-huh, uh-huh," Stephen said eagerly. "And?"

"And did I mention that he asked me to marry him?"

"Girl, stop!" Stephen jumped off the couch, spilling his coffee onto the hardwood floor. "Oh, now look what you've made me do. Please don't tell me he was serious, and you better not be telling me that if he was serious that you're considering doing it. And puleeze don't tell me you're marrying the next Alex Rodriguez." Stephen stopped abruptly, as if a thought suddenly hit him. "Girl, young country bumpkin is a might too ugly to be replacing that handsome-ass Alex."

"If he makes it to the majors—even if he only makes the league minimum of four hundred thousand—he can afford to get a good haircut, and a whole bunch of Proactiv." Cheryl leaned back, and crossed her legs; a satisfied smile on her face. "But let's see what happens in the next few months before we start shopping for a wedding dress."

Sexy

July 2013

Sexy Sanchez sent an alluring smile in the direction of the tall guy with the intense blue eyes and the interesting tats on his arms, signaling him to follow her. He looked like a hot rocker type with his five o'clock shadow and carefully tousled, golden hair, molded into disarray with hair product.

For most of the evening, he'd been on lockdown with his girl-friend's arms wrapped possessively around his waist. When nature called, and the clingy chick had finally disentangled herself and gone downstairs with one of her tipsy friends to use the restroom, Sexy was ready to make her move.

All the restrooms in the house were crowded, and Sexy banked on having sufficient time to snag the hot rocker. Growing impatient when the guy didn't budge from the door frame he was leaning against, she beckoned him by crooking her finger.

Me? he pantomimed, pointing to his chest.

She nodded, turned around, and pranced along the corridor.

It was typical July weather, and despite the air conditioning, the body heat inside the overcrowded party had the temperature soaring. Sexy decided to leave the confines of the crowded frat house where the rowdy celebration was being held and relocate to the quiet and spacious rooftop.

As she headed for the backstairs that led to the roof deck, she bypassed a twerk contest between three white girls who should have been ashamed to bring attention to their deficient derrieres, but were too intoxicated to care. When white girls competed in impromptu twerk-offs, there was always an overabundance of alcohol involved.

Continuing her trek down the hallway, she looked over her shoulder and couldn't hold back a smug smile. As expected, the hot rocker dude was following her like an obedient sheep.

Upon closer inspection, he was dreamier looking than she'd realized with fine-boned features and sensual lips. He seemed like the overly confident type who could have his pick of women, and she'd observed numerous girls shamelessly trying to divert his attention away from his girlfriend throughout the night.

But Sexy wasn't merely *any* woman. Among her group of friends, she was the only ethnic chick, and she was often referred to as being uncommonly good looking—an exotic beauty with an olive skin tone, large doe-shaped eyes, and dark flowing hair.

Tonight, Sexy looked extra-hot in a crop top embellished with beads and sequins and she was rocking a teeny-tiny pair of denim, cut-off shorts and ankle-strap stilettos that showcased her perfect pair of long, shapely legs. People often mistook her for a runway model, which she thought was hilarious. Becoming a brainless model was not the occupation she aspired toward. When the day came that she had to consider employment options, she was certain she'd lean toward a career in the CIA or some sort of corporate espionage. In the meantime, she'd continue living off handouts from her parents and the kindness of strangers.

A slew of bangles and bracelets decorated both her wrists and jangled musically as she sauntered along and turned a corner, striding past a room that was crammed with kids gathered around a giant bong. One girl was bent at the waist, her long hair nearly sweeping the floor as she giggled at a private joke that only she could hear. Another moron with orange crumbs around his mouth was digging his orange-tinted fingers inside a bag of Cheetos, his jaws working overtime as he crunched on the snack while waiting for his turn to hit the bong.

Drugs had never interested Sexy. She preferred being clear-headed when manipulating and outmaneuvering her idiot friends, her stupid family, and brain-dead society in general. No one was shrewder than Sexy, and she delighted in proving that fact at every opportunity.

Excitement coursed through her as she heard his footsteps climbing the stairs behind her. She pushed the door to the rooftop open and the evening breeze blew through her hair.

Holding a frosty bottle of Coors Light, Hot Rocker was right behind her. "Wow! This is so cool," he uttered, looking around and then staring up at the star-filled sky.

"It's an amazing view; I figured you'd enjoy it," she said, taking his hand and leading him over to the lawn furniture. She plopped down on a wicker loveseat and motioned for him to have a seat next to her. "My name is Sexy."

"Perfect name for you."

"Sexy Sanchez," she added with a provocative smile.

"Cool name. Are you Puerto Rican??"

"No." She gave a shrug. "I'm strictly African American, as far as I know."

"You have an exotic look, like you could be mixed with Middle Eastern blood."

"So I've been told. And what's your name?" she asked, abruptly changing the uncomfortable subject regarding her heritage.

"Ryan Bellevue." He looked around. "You must party here a lot."

"What makes you say that?"

"How'd you know about the secret stairway leading to the roof-top?"

"I make it my business to know a lot of things," she said in a mysterious tone.

"I've sort of had my eye on you all night," Ryan confessed.

"I know. That's why I lured you away from your girlfriend."

His blue eyes sparkled in amusement. "You didn't have to lure me. You could have asked."

"That wouldn't have been any fun," she replied, reaching out and examining the bronze, medieval pendant that hung from a leather cord. "Interesting piece of jewelry," she commented.

"I'm a history buff and rabid collector of historical artifacts."

Sexy groaned inwardly. Ryan was providing too much informa-tion. She couldn't have cared less about his personal interests. She let out a sigh of indifference as she released the pendant.

"Want a sip?" Ryan slanted the beer bottle toward Sexy.

"Sure, if I can sip it from your finger," she said in a sultry tone of voice.

"Oh, wow!" He chuckled nervously, and then inserted his index finger into the mouth of the bottle.

Grasping his hand, Sexy guided his dripping finger to her mouth and drew it inside, closing her eyes and murmuring, "Mmm."

"Damn! You're wild! Who are you and where have you been all my life?"

"Shut up and kiss me." She took the beer bottle from his hand and set it on the ground. Snuggling close, she looped her arms around Ryan's neck and pressed her lips against his. As her tongue snaked inside his mouth, her hand slid between his legs. She caressed the erection that strained against his jeans.

He broke the kiss and stared at her through eyes that were heavily lidded with lust. "You're so beautiful. Man, I want you so bad," he said hoarsely.

"What would you like to do to me?" she whispered, her lips curved in a taunting smile.

"Make love to you," he whispered.

"Make love? You can do that some other time."

Panic surfaced in Ryan's blue eyes. His forehead creased. "Why not now?"

"No time for lovemaking, I want you to fuck me."

"Oh, yeah! That's exactly what I want to do." He groped her, hastily feeling her breasts and rubbing her inner thigh.

The wicker loveseat was too small and wasn't sturdy enough. They'd have to get down on the dirty floor of the roof or stand up. Opting to stand, Sexy rose and Ryan immediately leapt to his feet. Sexy led him to the concrete ledge that bordered the roof. She stepped out of her shorts, and he dropped his jeans.

Already wet with anticipation, Sexy didn't require any foreplay. She grasped Ryan's hand and guided his fingers to the warm, sticky moisture between her legs. "See what you do to me?"

"Oh, damn." His chest heaved as he struggled to penetrate her in the awkward standing position.

Actually, it wasn't Ryan who had her so hot and bothered. It was the idea that she'd snagged another woman's man with hardly any effort. Ryan's girlfriend was probably looking for him at that very moment. *Your man is preoccupied, dumb bitch, so stop trying to hunt him down!* The idea of the girlfriend searching the frat house in vain filled Sexy with so much excitement, goose bumps began to spread up and down her arms. And her pussy reacted by going from slightly moist to heavily drenched.

"Ooh! You're so wet," Ryan said between gasping breaths.

"Don't talk. All I want you to do is fuck me," she urged with a note of steel in her voice.

Backing her against the concrete wall, he thrust himself deeply, grunting as he slammed into her. Sexy clung to him as he rammed her over and over. A sly smile formed on her lips. She'd won the bet she'd made with her roommate, Arielle, who claimed Ryan was known to be unreasonably faithful and would never cheat on his girlfriend.

As Ryan grunted and groaned, Sexy thought about the hundred bucks and lunch at Chipotle that Arielle owed her. Her nitwit roommate could have saved herself some money had she listened when Sexy told her that no man remained faithful once she'd set her sights on him.

Fussing with his hair, trying to get it back to its original windswept look, Ryan asked Sexy if she had a mirror.

"Sorry. No," she replied as she dug around in her clutch, fingers deliberately glossing over her compact mirror. She wanted Ryan to look disheveled, as if he'd been fucking on the sly, and she wasn't about to assist him in making himself presentable.

"There isn't any lipstick on my face, is it?" he asked, wiping at imaginary red streaks.

"You look fine," she assured him. "You should go down first and I'll stay up here for like, another five or ten minutes," she suggested, pretending to be helpful.

"Thanks, I appreciate it." The lust that had been in Ryan's eyes was now replaced with guilt. "My girl is probably looking for me, so I'd better get back to the party. I, uh, suppose I'll see you later," he said sheepishly.

"Yep. See you later," she said nonchalantly, fluttering her fingers.

Sexy had heard that Ryan's girlfriend was a jealous bitch who was known for creating scenes even when there was no reason for her to be suspicious of Ryan. Eager to witness the big blowup, Sexy didn't plan on waiting around on the rooftop—not even for two extra minutes. As soon as she heard the door to the stairs open and close, she checked her reflection in her compact mirror. She reapplied lip gloss, brushed her hair, and then bounded down the stairs while simultaneously texting Arielle: *Cough up my money and meet me in the kitchen.*

Beer was stocked inside the fridge as well as multiple coolers in the frat house kitchen. There were so many people jam-packed inside the room, Sexy was only able to distinguish Arielle by her ghastly, purple-tinted hair.

"Pay up, bitch," Sexy demanded with laughter when Arielle approached her.

"Where's the proof, whore?" Arielle retorted.

With a smirk on her face, Sexy searched through her purse and pulled out Ryan's medieval pendant. "What do you think about this?" Sexy taunted, holding the pendant by the leather cord.

"Wow, I'm impressed."

"As you should be. Now, hand over the dough, and don't forget lunch tomorrow."

"I don't have any cash on me, but we'll stop at the ATM tomorrow—on our way to Chipotle." Arielle eyed Sexy with admiration. "How was he?" she whispered conspiratorially.

"Quick." Sexy and Arielle burst out laughing. "There was nothing spectacular about him. Ryan's merely another notch on my bedpost." Sexy pulled out her phone and took a picture of the pendant and then began tapping the screen.

"What are you doing?"

"Tweeting about my conquest and posting the evidence on Instagram."

"Ohmigod, you're so malicious."

"I know." Sexy smiled and returned her attention to the screen of her phone.

From the corridor, Sexy and Arielle could hear Ryan's jealous girlfriend accusing him of cheating, while Ryan proclaimed his innocence.

"What's that insecure bitch's name?" Sexy asked Arielle.

"Cyndi Waters."

"Thanks." Sexy tapped the screen a few more times. "She'll find out that I fucked her man when she follows me back on Instagram."

Valentine's Day – 2014

"Oh, my God, you are unbelievable."

Randy had been saying it all morning, but Cheryl couldn't hear it enough. After all, she agreed with her new husband. So, once again she leaned over in their king-size bed and rewarded him with a kiss and a "Thanks, babe."

"Uh-uh, thank you!" Randy said, running his fingers through her disheveled hair. "I thought my Valentine's Day present to you couldn't be topped. But, boy, was I wrong."

Cheryl glanced over at the five-carat pink diamond ring lying on the night table beside the bed. She had expected jewelry—most husbands gave their wives jewelry for Valentine's—but the trinket had exceeded all of her expectations. "Honey, believe me, I'm not complaining." She moved closer so that their naked bodies melded into each other, then wrapped her arms around his neck for an even more soulful kiss, when her Valentine's Day present to him popped up from under the sheets.

"Good morning!" the gorgeous, raven-haired woman said in a cheery voice, making Cheryl wonder how long she'd been awake. "Oh, man, what a night. Right?"

Cheryl watched as the woman scooted up to snuggle against

Randy's back, and noted with satisfaction that when she did, Randy moved closer into Cheryl. And when the woman tried to once again snuggle against him, Randy actually sat up in the bed and leaned against the headboard, pulling Cheryl up with him.

"Morning," Randy said with a self-conscious smile.

"Actually, it's afternoon." Cheryl pointed to a digital alarm clock on the night table. "It's almost one-thirty."

Cheryl watched as the woman languidly edged the sheets from her body, slowly exposing a pair of 38DD's, a remarkably flat tummy, a voluptuous set of hips, and an incredibly full round butt.

"Well, then," the woman said, trailing her hand down to her pubic mound, and then playing with her clitoris, "anyone up for some afternoon delight?"

Cheryl glanced at Randy and noted the slight hardening in his expression. "No, I think we're good, Vonda," she said sweetly. "But thanks for a wonderful night."

Initially, surprise spread across Vonda's face, but the woman quickly composed her mouth into a little pout, and then in a baby-doll voice said, "What about you, Randy? You feel like a little playtime with me?"

Cheryl's eyes widened as a wave of rage rushed over her. "Look," she said, leaning over Randy to get closer to the woman. "Didn't you hear—?"

"My wife said, we're good," Randy said, cutting her off. "Baby," he said turning to Cheryl, "Do you want to call a car service to pick her up, or would you like me to take care of it?"

"I got this, babe." Cheryl pulled Randy into a long kiss; opening her eyes, though, to glare at the woman over his shoulder. "You wanna go hit the shower, Randy? Maybe we can go to Havenwood for a post-Valentine's Day lunch. I want to show off my new ring," she said when they broke the kiss.

Cheryl waited until Randy wrapped himself in a plush burgundy robe, and disappeared into the bathroom before jumping out the bed, and pulling the sheets off Vonda. "Okay, up and out! Thanks for the night, but your services are no longer required."

Vonda tugged back part of the sheet to partially cover herself as she got up. "You've got some fucking nerve trying to treat me like some kind of whore. Please remember, you approached me. I did you a favor, sleeping with you and your husband."

"First off, you did me no favor. I may have approached you, but you are getting paid five thousand dollars for the night, bitch. So, in my book that does make you a whore." Cheryl stood over the woman, not caring that she was totally naked in her fury. "Secondly, I wouldn't be treating you like the gold-digging whore that you are if you didn't make a play for my husband."

"Oh, please," the woman said, yanking on her clothes as she talked. "So, big deal, I asked him if he wanted to go another round this morning. You didn't mind last night when I was sucking his dick and you were eating my pussy, now did you?"

"Last night was last night." Cheryl walked over and grabbed her new ring off the night table and put it on. "When I said enough was enough this morning, you should have left it at that. But no, you have to try and establish your own little relationship with him." Cheryl sat on the edge of the chaise lounge and crossed her long legs. "That shit doesn't fly, bitch."

"Well, it wasn't anything personal, and I'm sorry you took it that way. I wasn't making a play for your man." Vonda was dressed now, and was pulling her purse strap over her shoulder. "You don't need to get me a car service; I'll catch a cab outside."

Maybe the woman wasn't trying to cozy up to Randy to try and establish a side relationship—but why chance it, Cheryl thought as she watched through the window as Vonda climbed into a taxi.

There was no way she was going to lose her new husband, whom she loved, and the new lifestyle that she loved just as much.

No, she reasoned, she wasn't a gold digger; after all, it wasn't money that made her take Randy home that first night. It was quite plain he didn't have any. She didn't even know he had the potential to make it to the upper economic stratosphere until after she had turned him out. If she hadn't decided to grant him a pity fuck, she wouldn't be living in a $2 million condo in trendy SoHo, wouldn't be driving a Maybach that matched his, nor would she be sporting a five-carat pink diamond that likely cost a cool $2.5 million.

True, they had pretty much gone through Randy's $5 million signing bonus. But that was okay, she reasoned; with a five-year contract with the New York Yankees, there was plenty time to put money away in savings. And since that five-year contract was worth $120 million, there was also plenty of money to save.

Cheryl still couldn't believe her luck. After Randy left the apartment she shared with Stephen that morning, he texted her three to four times a day and called her on the phone every night for an hour-long conversation—each ending with another marriage proposal.

"Cheryl, I know we haven't known each other long, but I ain't never felt like this about anyone," he begged each night. "It's so hard to believe that someone as together as you would even want to talk to someone like me, ya know? I don't want to lose you, girl."

It took two weeks of his pleading before she consented to rent a car and drive down to Scranton to watch one of his games. It was a ninety-degree August day, so she wore a white halter top and tight linen pants, and her hair was swept into an up-do, with a thin wisp hanging down either side of her face. Randy made a big deal of introducing her to all of his teammates before the game, and the envy on their faces was evident.

"Boy, you'd better be sure to hit a home run today in honor of this fine young filly," his coach told Randy after shaking Cheryl's hand.

"Coach, I think I'm going to have to hit two," Randy responded. And he did.

It wasn't until after the game was over that he found out that Danny Archer—the sports agent who had given him the tickets to the party—had been watching from the owner's box. "Randy, you're exactly the kind of kid I want on my client roster," Archer said, slapping him on the back. "The kind of kid I need on my roster. Sign with me, kid, and I'll guarantee you a spot on one of the majors."

"See," Randy told Cheryl after he signed on the dotted line, "you really are my good luck charm."

Two days later, the baseball commissioner announced that Alex Rodriguez would be suspended for the rest of the 2013 season, and the entire 2014 season.

Cheryl attended four more of Randy's games in Scranton before the big news came in September. He and a third baseman from another farm team were being sent up to the New York Yankees.

"Can you believe it? I can't believe it," Randy excitedly told Cheryl on the telephone. "They're only signing me for league minimum, and only for the two months left in the regular season, but that's still more than ten times what I make now, ya know?"

"Baby, I'm so proud of you!" Cheryl gushed appropriately.

"I know you are, babe. That's why I love you!" He waited a beat before adding: "Will you marry me, now?"

Cheryl emitted a heavy sigh, before giving the response she'd rehearsed for the past two days. "I don't know if that would be fair to you, Randy."

"Huh? What are you talking about?" Randy demanded.

"Big things are happening for you. You're young. Do you really want to get tied down now, Randy?"

Randy was quiet for a moment, then finally said: "I don't get it. You know how I feel. I love you, girl."

Cheryl took a deep breath. "I know how you feel right now, but what about when all this money starts rolling in, and all the girls are all over you? Are you going to be thinking, 'Damn, look at what I'm missing?' I don't want that. I don't want you to resent me. And I damn sure don't want you cheating on me."

"What you talking about, Cheryl?" Randy pleaded. "Man, me getting a shot at the majors is exactly that...a shot. We don't know if I'ma get a real contract. And all these girls you talking about... where are they now? They ain't sweating me now, so why would I pay them any mind later? I ain't stupid, Cheryl. You've proved you want me for me, ya know? I ain't even trynta to be thinking about someone who wants me only 'cause I mights gots some money."

"Babe, that's what you say now—"

"Marry me, Cheryl."

"Randy—"

"I love you, Cheryl. Marry me—"

"Randy, I'm going to have to hang up—"

"Cheryl, I love you. Tell me you're gonna marry me—"

Click.

Cheryl looked up to see Stephen standing in her bedroom doorway, eating strawberry Häagen-Dazs ice cream from the carton. "I guess that was the young country bumpkin, huh?"

"I'll thank you to not call my possible multimillionaire husband a 'young country bumpkin,'" Cheryl said, walking over to Stephen and sticking a finger in the carton.

"Fair enough. How about I call him 'young country boy'?"

"That'll do," Cheryl said, making another finger scoop.

"So, how long are you going to make 'young country boy' wait?"

"I don't know yet," Cheryl answered after she swallowed.

"What are you waiting for?"

Cheryl shrugged. "I'm not in a hurry."

"Bet you'll be in a damn hurry if he gets a ten million-dollar contract," Stephen said, taking another spoonful himself.

Cheryl laughed.

"Okay, now here's the big question," Stephen said, waving his spoon in the air. "When are you going to give young country boy a makeover? My God, every time I see him I want to buy a pair of hedging shears and whack that shit off his head. I get the heebie-jeebies every time I think about the mess he must leave on pillows. Ew!"

"Uh-uh," Cheryl said, wagging her finger. "No makeover yet."

"But—"

"Trust me...I know what I'm doing."

"Well, make sure you give him some diction lessons, too." Stephen made a face, then added, "Ya know?"

Cheryl rolled her eyes and sighed. "Oh, God, why does he have to say that every other sentence?"

Since the Yankees were already mathematically out of the pennant race, Cheryl knew there was a good chance that the coach would put Randy and Arnold Vare—the other third baseman who was getting a tryout—into a few games, so he could check them out. As luck would have it, however, it was Vare who was given the first shot while Randy rode the bench.

"He made an unbelievable catch in the seventh inning," Randy told Cheryl at the 40-40 Club, where he went with other players after the game. "It's a shame they lost, but if he keeps playing like that, I might not even get a shot at showing what I can do, ya know?"

"Hey, stop worrying!" Cheryl lightly kissed him on the cheek. "I have faith in you, babe."

"Yeah, but if I don't get a chance to show what I can do—" Randy repeated.

"Shush!" Cheryl put a finger against Randy's lips. "I have faith that you will."

Randy shook his head, though a smile finally began to find its way to his face. "I love you, Cheryl."

"Good! Keep that thought." She patted him on the cheek. "I'll be right back."

The ladies room was only about four yards away, but Cheryl's strut toward it garnered a lot of attention. Maybe it was the Yankees team crop top, or the low-rider jeans, but by the time she made it to her destination, she had been approached five times—twice by celebrities whom she recognized.

Cheryl emerged from the bathroom stall in time to hear a petite blonde, who was putting on lipstick in the mirror, tell another woman: "Wow, did you see who arrived and was looking good? The guy that plays on the TV show, *Law & Order: SVU.*"

"Shit! I thought that was him! I'm on it." The second woman turned and ran out of the bathroom, without drying her hands or even turning off the faucet.

"Oh, no you don't, bitch! I saw him first," the platinum blonde said, scurrying after her.

Yeah, tonight is definitely a gold-digger's payday, Cheryl thought grimly, looking in the mirror. *So why am I sitting on a bar stool consoling a guy who might never make more than $30,000 a year when I can be pushing up on someone already worth millions?* Unable to answer the question, and unwilling to ponder it further, Cheryl headed back into the club. As she was passing a group of woman huddled together, she heard one say, "Ew, who's that guy there? I hope he's rich, because he's sure ugly as shit." Cheryl didn't need to look and see to whom the woman was pointing; the look on Randy's face let her know that he had both heard and seen.

Without missing a stride, Cheryl walked up to Randy's bar stool, positioned herself between his legs, and drew him into a long soulful kiss—so long and passionate that it elicited first giggles, then laughter, and finally applause from the people around them.

"Thank you," Randy whispered in her ear when she finally released his lips.

"I love you," she whispered back in response. It didn't matter to her if it was true or not; he needed to hear it, and she figured it wouldn't cost her a dime to fulfill that simple need.

The next day the coach once again put Vare in the game, and he once again did a magnificent job on third base, making an extremely difficult out in the first inning. But then in the bottom of the inning, the centerfielder was hurt while sliding into first base. Cheryl's heart almost stopped when it was announced that Randall Alston was coming in to replace the player. Randy trotted out to first base, to no fanfare since no one had heard of him, but that wasn't to last long. As soon as he got there, he started edging toward second as if to steal. Derek Jeter was at the plate, and the pitcher should have been focusing all of his attention on that homerun hitter, but couldn't since he was continually being forced to throw to keep Randy honest. And the crowd loved it. Finally, one of the pitcher's throws to first was too low and bounced off the first baseman's glove. The man on third stole home, and not only did Randy steal second base, he also stole third.

But that was only the start. In the fourth inning—his first time at bat—Randy hit a grand slam home run that put the Yankees up by three. Then, when Randy was playing defense at the top of the fourth, he made an unbelievable catch. As soon as the ball was hit, he began backing up, and within milliseconds was at the warning track—the ball only now beginning to curve downward. It seemed that the ball would go into the stands, giving the batter a home run, but Randy made an incredible leap at the fence and grabbed the ball. The hometown crowd went wild, and so did the pitcher on the mound as well as the relief pitchers sitting in the bullpen.

For the remainder of the season, Vare got virtually no playing time, and Jayson Nix and Randy alternated at third base. Randy was batting an amazing .410 and hit an astounding nine home runs in thirty at bat, and the New York media was having a field day. Randy's name was all over newspaper headlines, radio talk shows, and television sports broadcasts. But it was the Yankees home finale that Randy put on his best performance, hitting three back-to-back home runs and committing two steals.

Two months later, Randy—now sporting a well-trimmed buzz-cut instead of a Jheri curl, long sideburns and a light beard that covered his acne, and a razor-thin mustache that gave him a deb-onair look—stood at the head of a conference room at Yankee Stadium. Danny Archer and the Yankees owner stood with him at the podium as the Yankees general manager announced that the team had signed Randy to a five-year, $120 million deal.

When it was Randy's turn at the microphone, he thanked Almighty God, he thanked his mother, his grandparents, and he thanked the good people of New York who had shown so much support for him. Then he looked at Cheryl, who was standing in the back of the room, near an exit, and took a deep breath: "I also need to thank a woman who has been in my corner since the first magical day we met. A woman who has been with me through my ups and downs. A woman who believed me when there were times I didn't believe in myself. A woman who didn't care how much money I had in my pocket, but only how much love I had in my heart."

Cheryl's breath quickened as Stephen, who had been handing out press kits to the reporters, suddenly appeared at her side.

"Cheryl Blanton." Randy walked toward her with a bevy of reporters crowding around him. When he was right in front her, he fell to one knee, and pulled out a beautiful diamond solitaire ring. "Will you marry me?"

Under the circumstances, how could she say no?

The sound of the shower being turned on full blast pulled Cheryl out of her reverie. She shook her head and smiled; since his physical makeover it always took her husband a good twenty minutes to prepare for a shower. First he had to trim the sideburns, then his beard, then tweeze his mustache—it took him almost as long to get ready in the morning as it took her. But it was worth it; the man looked damn good. And she was delighted when the daily speech lessons she encouraged him to take had tamed his diction so much that his heavy Southern accent actually sounded a bit sexy, rather than corny. Yes, she had turned him into a man worthy of being her husband.

And, of course, she looked good enough to be married to a handsome multimillion-dollar baseball star. She turned to look at herself in the full-length mirror. Boobs still high and firm. Stomach still sporting the muscle-tone that made bikinis all the more attractive. Butt and thighs as toned as ever. Yeah, she looked good, she decided. Very good. You would never be able to tell she'd had a child. Luckily, like her mother, she looked years younger than her actual age. In fact, she was able to model for teen magazines, though never for full-body shots because of her voluptuous chest.

But, she began chewing her bottom lip, *will I be able to pull this off forever? What if Randy finds out that I'm actually nine years older than him? Will he care?*

Worse, she thought dismally, what if he found out about the baby she'd given up?

He'd made it clear, from day-one, that he wanted to start a family right away starting with a Randy Jr. And Cheryl was in total agreement. Most people thought that models made fabulous money, but the reality was it was only supermodels like Joan Smalls and Jourdan Dunn who were pulling in ten or twelve thousand for a photo shoot. Sure, Cheryl was averaging a good twenty thousand or so a month, but she was quite willing to give up an uncertain quarter of a million dollars a year to please a husband who was making a contractual $24 million. But they'd been married four months, and she hadn't missed a period yet. Once, when her period was two days late, Randy had run out and bought a pregnancy test, and it almost made her cry to see the disappointment in his eyes when the stick refused to turn blue.

How would he react if he knew that I had a kid, a boy no less, and gave him up? There's no way he'd want anything to do with me, the way he values family.

Her body shivered, involuntarily, though the windows were closed and plenty of heat was coming from the room's ceiling and floor vents.

"Well," she said aloud, pointing to her image in the mirror, "It's only a matter of time, no need to worry; you are going to give your baby a baby." She moved to put on a robe, so she could get herself a cup of her favorite coffee—Ethiopian Fancy—but then thought the better of it. Despite not having a child to keep her husband happy, she still knew how to keep him dumb and grinning with lust.

"Hey, babe," she said, entering the bathroom without bothering to knock. "How about I join you for some post-Valentine's Day shower fun?"

Randy's grin answered for him.

Cheryl slipped inside the shower and stood behind Randy. With an arm wrapped around his waist, she lathered his back with mint-scented gel. She worked her way down to his firm butt, thighs, and calves. While kneeling on the floor of the shower, she gently grasped his ankles, turning him around as she began washing his feet. Ducking her head, she kissed his foot and licked between his toes. The soft moan that emanated from Randy spurred Cheryl to move on to his other foot and lavish it with special attention.

Moving upward, she poured gel into her hand. The tingly sensation of the mint gel along with Cheryl's hand stroke had Randy thrusting so fiercely inside her soapy, closed fist, his dick began to pulsate. Not wanting him to climax too quickly, Cheryl withdrew her hand and said, "Do me."

Following Cheryl's lead, Randy positioned himself behind her. He soaped the back of her neck, her back, thighs and magnificent ass, and while still standing behind her, he concentrated on soaping up her breasts. Kneading and squeezing them until Cheryl was purring. "I love your big, titties, babe," he murmured.

One hand caressed her soapy breasts and the other stroked her satiny-smooth ass cheeks. He slid a hand between her thighs and she parted them for him, allowing him access to her plump, slippery pussy lips. His bold caresses made her jerk and shudder as he teased her pussy lips open.

"Do you want me, baby?" Randy asked hoarsely.

"I want you in the worst way." Cheryl couldn't hide the need in her voice as she spread her legs wider.

Randy let out a grunt as he bent behind her and slid his dick forcibly into her tight, plush depths. He took a deep breath, braced himself, and gave it to her nice and slow. But when Cheryl began pushing back with her ass, wordlessly demanding to be fucked harder and deeper, Randy gave her exactly what she wanted.

"You've got the best dick in the world," Cheryl proclaimed.

"Damn, you feel good. I don't need nothing else except this tight pussy of yours."

"Randy!" Cheryl's voice cracked as Randy drove into her. Every stroke of his dick was a hot lash of mutual pleasure. "You're hitting my spot, babe. Making me cum," she said, choking out the last word right before her body began to convulse.

"Baby, you're too much. I wouldn't be surprised if we made a baby in that shower," Randy said after he finally caught his breath. "I don't know what I did to deserve you, but I thank God I did it." A grin suddenly appeared on his face. "And man, that Valentine's Day present. Whew!"

Cheryl giggled and threw a towel at him, then began drying herself with another one. "You should have seen your face when Vonda walked in the bedroom wearing nothing but a big red bow. Priceless!"

"Yeah, you got me good that time, I gotta admit," Randy said with a laugh. He walked behind Cheryl and grabbed her into a hug. "I never know what to expect from you, Cheryl; you're full of surprises. You got us doing role-playing, having sex in cars, having sex in elevators, in public...and now even bringing another woman into our bedroom. Wow!"

"Hey," Cheryl patted her husband's cheek, "I gotta keep my man happy. You are happy, right?"

"What do you think?" Randy nuzzled Cheryl's neck.

"So, do you think it's something you'd like to do again?" Cheryl asked slowly.

"Well, I mean," Randy stammered. "Are you serious? You wouldn't mind?"

Cheryl gave a little laugh. "Okay, here's the deal. It's not something I would say we do every day, or even every month, but if you ever find there's a woman you really, really wanna 'do,' let me know and I'll see what I can hook up."

"For real?" Randy asked excitedly.

"For real. But," Cheryl added, "the deal is you can't ever have sex with another woman unless I'm involved. Is that a deal?"

Randy's expression turned somber, and his voice lowered as he pulled Cheryl firmly into his arms. "Baby, I'm not stupid. You don't ever have to worry about me cheating on you." He gave her a lingering kiss, then looked deeply in her eyes and said in a sincere voice: "Cheryl, you're the woman I love, the woman I married, and the woman who's going to be the mother of my children. I'll never do anything to hurt you."

March 2014

S itting up in bed, Sexy scanned her Instagram page, smiling at the selfies she'd taken. She was addicted to posting selfies on her page, and she narrowed an eye as she scrutinized the images. The close-up of her cleavage looked hot, and judging from the amount of likes and favorable comments, her Instagram followers agreed. But there was always a hater. Some chick with the screen name, BeyondBeauty, posted: *You get what you pay for & your low budget tatas don't impress me.*

Sexy gazed sneeringly at BeyondBeauty's profile pic, her discerning eyes zooming in on the hater's abundance of obvious, store-bought hair. Quickly tapping the screen, Sexy shot back: *From head to toe, everything about me is authentic and certified. Can you say the same, weave-head?*

"Boom! Take that!" Sexy shouted out loud.

On the other side of the bed, her roommate, Emma, groaned irritably and pulled the covers over her head. "Stop yelling; I'm trying to sleep."

It was one in the afternoon and Emma would probably sleep another two hours or more. Sexy, on the other hand, was a morning person. Even when they partied until dawn, Sexy was awake before noon, no doubt the effect of her structured upbringing. Her controlling and success-driven father always rose at precisely five in the morning and expected the rest of the household to be up an hour later. Her highly organized mother, who was passionate about keeping up appearances, would have fainted if she saw Sexy's current living conditions.

Sexy perused the room and rolled her eyes. After a stupid argument over nail polish remover, Sexy had moved out of Arielle's place and was now crashing with Emma. But Emma's place was a pigsty, with heaps of clothes and other miscellaneous piles of junk scattered everywhere. Sexy tried to keep the place neat, but it was a wasted effort. Emma was an unapologetic slob and no amount of complaining, coaxing, or even picking up behind her was going to change her slovenly ways. Besides, Emma paid the rent, and the lease was in her name, so it wasn't as if Sexy could kick the girl out.

Until Sexy found a way to support herself, she had to deal with her living situation. The home she'd grown up in was an elegant stone colonial in a prestigious suburb, thirty minutes from Philadelphia. Now she was reduced to sharing a crammed, one-room studio in the gloomy basement of an outdated apartment building. The only good thing about living in a dump was the location. Residing in downtown Philly provided a new adventure every day. Being in the heart of Center City was so different from living in her boring, elitist neighborhood in Bryn Mawr, Pennsylvania.

A hunger pang drew Sexy's attention away from Instagram. She checked the mini-fridge and scowled at the contents. Nothing but old, moldy food. The only items that looked remotely edible were the six hard-boiled eggs that Emma had picked up at the deli yesterday in preparation of jump-starting yet another low-carb diet.

With food on her mind, Sexy changed from yoga pants and a

tank top into a tight-fitting club dress, stilettos, and a waist-length jacket. She flaunted her shapely body at every opportunity, and the frosty March weather didn't deter her. She got a kick out of the way men gawked at her each time she exited the apartment.

She sashayed down Ninth Street, heading for her favorite deli. Tires squealed and car horns honked as men whistled at her, trying to get her attention. She ignored the catcalls and kept walking with her head held high, and wearing a smug smile. The way she always caused a commotion, one would think that she was a celebrity. It was a shame she didn't have any talent. Maybe if she made a sex tape, she could get rich and famous and wouldn't have to rely on her parents' generosity any longer. It was something to think about.

Greeted by irresistible aromas when she opened the door to the deli, her stomach rumbled and her mouth began to water. Last night at the party she and Emma had attended, she'd dined on chips and dip and other snack foods, and she was ready for something of substance.

"I'll have a meatball sandwich with mozzarella," she told the woman behind the counter, who gazed at her with her mouth turned down in disapproval.

"Anything to drink?" the woman asked disdainfully.

Accustomed to being hated on by other women, Sexy smirked at the deli employee, and then said, "Pepsi, a Red Bull, and...oh, yeah, give me an order of fries." She turned to go have a seat at one of the small café tables.

"Excuse me, Miss."

Sexy turned back around. "Yes?"

"You have to pay first."

"Since when? I never heard of that policy."

"Since now." The woman folded her arms defiantly.

The jealous-hearted bitch was simply trying to give her a hard time, and Sexy refused to feed into her petty little game. With a shrug, she dug out her debit card from her purse and handed it over. Sexy supposed she should have been appreciative that this hater was taking orders at the counter instead of being in the back cooking the food. She seemed capable of mixing in rat poison with the meatball sauce.

Another stab of hunger reminded Sexy that she was close to starvation, and the cashier-bitch hadn't even processed her order. "Hey, why're you taking so long with my debit card?"

"It's not working."

"What do you mean it's not working?"

"The bank declined it for insufficient funds."

"That's bullshit. I have more than enough money in my account to pay for a damn meatball sandwich," Sexy said, her voice rising.

"Talk to your bank," the cashier said, sounding self-satisfied and vindicated for some perceived wrong.

Sexy wanted to slap her, but in a civilized society, the only thing she could get away with was snatching the card out of the woman's hand and storming out of the deli. Standing outside, she immediately called her mother and screamed into the phone, "What's going on? Why isn't there any money in my account?"

"Good afternoon, Amanda, dear. It's so nice to hear from you," Clarissa said in the fake, cheerful tone that Sexy hated.

"What are you trying to do, Mom—cause me to die of starvation?"

"That wouldn't be an issue if you were home with your family where you belonged."

"Being home wasn't working. You know it. I know it...we all know it."

Clarissa sighed. "With you running wild in the city, your father and I don't rest easily. We made an agreement and you broke it."

"Aw, Mom. Why do you insist upon treating me like a child?"

"We agreed that you'd check in with us once a week, yet we haven't heard a peep out of you in almost three weeks. We've called and left messages, to no avail. The only way to find out if you were dead or alive was to cut off your cash flow."

"Now that you know I'm alive, can you please put the money back in my account?"

The sarcasm in Clarissa's voice turned into a whine. "How long is this rebelliousness going to go on, Amanda? After giving you the best of everything from exclusive prep schools to European vacations, your father and I never dreamed you'd turn out like this. How did we fail you?"

"You didn't fail me, Mom. I'm a work in progress."

"Are you still staying with that dance student on Lombard Street?"

"No, we had a fight and I'm crashing with another friend."

"Someone more responsible than a dance student, I hope."

"Yeah, she's a future rocket scientist, Mom," Sexy said irritably.

"Watch the attitude, young lady. I'm your mother and I have every reason to be concerned about you. A well-bred young lady shouldn't be roaming the streets the way you do."

"You make it sound as if I'm a hooker, working the track or something. God, I'm not roaming the streets. I live in a safe place with a friend."

"What's your friend's name? And where exactly do you live?"

"Her name is Emma. You don't need the address because I'm in the process of hooking up another crib."

"'Hooking up another crib'! Do you hear yourself, Amanda? You sound like someone from the streets—not someone from a well-educated and prominent family. How long is this going to go on? Your continual shameful behavior has broken your father's heart and it's left me utterly mortified. What kind of future can you possibly have if you don't finish your education?" Clarissa began to cry, emitting little sniffles and murmurs of anguish.

Growing bored with the conversation, Sexy said the words she knew her mother wanted to hear. "I'm not stupid, Mom. I know I need to finish school, and I plan to. But I need to have a fun summer before I allow myself to be shipped off to that snippy school in London."

"It's for your own good."

"I know," Sexy grudgingly admitted.

"Before I transfer the money back into your account, you have to promise that you'll keep up your end of the bargain."

"I promise to check in at least once a week."

After groveling on the phone, pleading for money like a common beggar, Sexy needed more than food. She needed a couple new outfits to make her feel better. One of her booster friends—a chick named Brianne—had a few Prada pieces that she wanted Sexy to check out. Sexy was an unapologetic clothes whore and now that she no longer had access to her parents' credit cards, she had to get her designer wear the best way she could. Needing cash to pay Brianne for her stolen goods, Sexy trekked to the nearest ATM.

A man stood at the machine making a transaction and Sexy stepped back a few feet, giving him privacy. From behind, she admired his broad shoulders beneath his jacket. And his firm ass looked hot in his sweat pants.

He has a nice body, but I bet his face is ugly as sin.

Standing out in the open on the pavement, her very presence once again began to cause a commotion, attracting lots of attention.

Horny male passersby appraised her leeringly, and rubbernecking motorists, unable to keep their eyes on the road, had to slam on their brakes to keep from rear-ending the car in front of them.

Sexy shrugged. It wasn't her fault that she had it like that.

When the guy at the ATM turned around, Sexy drew in a long breath. Not only was his body hot; his face was cute as shit. Playing coy, she glanced at her phone and pretended not to notice him.

"Hey, lovely lady; what's good?"

"Ain't shit," she responded nonchalantly.

He looked her up and down. Stroking his chin, he smiled approvingly. "What are you about to get into?"

"I was about to withdraw some cash and take myself out to lunch."

"No need to touch your funds. Why don't you let me treat you to a meal?"

"I don't even know you," she said with her top lip turned up, pretending to be offended.

"Allow me to introduce myself. I'm Yusef Rawls." He said his name with emphasis, as if it should ring a bell, which it didn't.

"Hey, Yusef; my name's Sexy Sanchez." She watched him closely, eager to see his reaction to the alias she'd given herself after leaving her family and striking out on her own.

"Sexy, huh?"

She nodded and smiled seductively.

"Damn, baby. Sexy, you are!" Laughing, he gestured to the shiny Jaguar that was parked at the curb. "My chariot awaits you."

Sexy would have been satisfied going to Five Guys for a burger, but wanting to impress her, Yusef took her to a fancy restaurant—the kind with folded linen napkins, polished silver, and white tablecloths. She had suffered through far too many brunches, lunches, and dinners with her pretentious mother in upscale places such as this, and she was extremely disappointed.

Unbeknownst to Yusef, he'd lost a point for bringing Sexy to an establishment that reminded her of the so-called privileged life she'd escaped from and was trying to forget.

The maître d' greeted them and as he led them to their table. Sexy pointed to a cozy little booth in the rear. "Is that table reserved?" she asked.

"No, would you prefer to sit there?" the maître d' inquired with a practiced smile.

"Yes, thank you." Sexy returned his phony smile.

Seated across from Yusef, Sexy perused the menu. Finding nothing remotely appealing, she fought the urge to fling the stupid menu across the room.

Yusef reached over and lightly caressed her hand. "See anything you like?"

"Nothing on the menu looks familiar." She gave him a puzzled expression. "I think I might be out of my depth. Do you mind ordering for me?" she asked, pretending to have no experience with fine dining.

"Sure, baby. I'll order for you." With brows furrowed, Yusef began studying the menu on Sexy's behalf. "How about the Crabtini for your appetizer?"

Sexy wrinkled her nose. "What's that?"

"Lump crabmeat mixed with vinaigrette and served in a martini glass."

Crabmeat served in a martini glass sounded ridiculous, but Sexy widened her eyes and beamed at Yusef as if intrigued by such a unique idea.

Pleased with himself, Yusef smiled back. "In my business, I meet a lot of gorgeous women, but they're all so fake. You're a natural beauty, and I dig that. I also like how down to earth you are. The average, gold-digging chick would have ordered the most expensive thing on the menu, but you gave me the option to decide how much I wanted to spend. That was very considerate."

"Thanks, I try to be thoughtful." She picked up her glass of water and took a sip. "So, what exactly is your business, Yusef? I hope you're not in the drug game."

Yusef pretended to choke. "Baby, I'm all the way legit. I love myself too much to be out in the streets dodging bullets and risking a lengthy prison sentence."

"So, what do you do for a living?"

"I play ball. I'm Yusef Rawls, and I pitch for the Philadelphia Phillies," he said, leaning back in his chair, looking extremely pleased with himself.

"Can I be honest?"

Yusef gestured for her to go ahead.

"No disrespect. I'm sure you're like, a local hero or star or something, but I've never heard of you. I don't know anything about baseball."

"It's all gravy, baby. I'm glad you don't know anything about me. A high-profile cat like myself has to beware of groupies with hidden agendas. I made a move on you, and to be honest, it was refreshing to hit on a gorgeous woman instead of getting hit on by the kind of chick who's looking for a meal ticket for the next eighteen years."

"It must be difficult not knowing who likes you for yourself and not your image."

"It's not difficult. I can spot a gold digger a mile away."

Sexy leaned forward, and said with a giggle, "Look in my eyes and tell me what you see—a gold digger or a sincere and trust-worthy person?"

"I can't play that game," Yusef said, frowning and shaking his head.

"Why not?"

"Because I'm blinded by your beauty. My brain is telling me to enjoy this lunch with you and then lure you back to my place to hit it and quit it." Yusef placed a hand on the center of his chest. "But my heart is telling me to make you wifey."

"Umm. Listen, Yusef. I guess I should be flattered and everything, and I hate to burst your bubble, but you've mistaken me for one of those gold-digger chicks you were talking about. I don't care who you play ball for, I don't know you that well, and quite frankly, my only interest is in having lunch and possibly letting you hit it. What makes you think I want to be *wifey* to you or anyone else?"

Speechless, Yusef gaped at Sexy.

"You're full of yourself, you know that?" she said as the server brought their appetizers to the table.

Yusef waited until the served left before responding. "I believe you politely put me in my place without even raising your voice." He broke into a smile. "And now I want you more than ever. I need a take-no-shit woman in my life." He gazed at Sexy with a love-sick expression.

"Look, I have to be honest with you. I'm going away to school in September. I'll be attending my mother's alma mater in London."

"London, England?" Yusef's voice went up an octave and he looked distraught.

Sexy nodded. "So, I'm sure you can understand that I'm not look-ing for anything long-term. I'm simply trying to get through the spring season and have an amazing summer that I'll never forget."

"All I can ask is that you let me be a part of your memorable summer," Yusef said with an earnest expression.

Sexy raised her water glass. "Well, let's toast to Sexy and Yusef's amazing, unforgettable summer!"

Sexy laughed as they performed the ritual of clinking glasses, but Yusef seemed lost in thought and didn't crack a smile.

After they finished their entrées, Sexy ordered a slice of Chocolate Sin Cake for dessert, but Yusef seemed to be brooding and said he didn't want any dessert.

Sexy thought it was comical that a grown man was so accustomed to having his way that he was throwing a silent tantrum merely because Sexy had no interest in becoming his *wifey*. Deciding to toy with him, Sexy held up a forkful of cake. "Wanna taste this?" She twirled her fork in the air and licked her lips provocatively.

"Stop playing." A slight smile tugged at the corners of Yusef's mouth.

Sexy inserted the fork in her mouth and moaned, "Mmm. It's so chocolaty and sinfully sweet." She ate the chunk of cake and licked the chocolate icing from the fork. "Baby, why don't you taste it?"

Yusef couldn't help from chuckling. "Why are you deliberately fucking with me, Sexy?"

"I want you to taste some of this deliciousness."

"Yeah, all right," he muttered.

She rose from her seat and slid into the seat next to Yusef. She fed him cake, murmuring, "Is it good, baby?" Before he could respond, her hand slivered beneath the table and fondled the stiffening lump inside his pants.

"Oh, yeah. It's real good," Yusef whispered as Sexy unzipped him and withdrew his erection, stroking it up and down.

Yusef had his head back and his eyes closed when the server reappeared. "Is everything okay? Can I get you anything else?"

"We're good, aren't we, hon?" Sexy asked Yusef.

"Yeah, yeah. We're good," he said in an impatient tone.

The server departed and Sexy sped up her hand stroke.

"Ohmigod, this is freaky. I can't believe you had my dick in your hand while the server was standing right there."

"Shhh. Be quiet and enjoy it."

Yusef was quiet for a few moments, but then he emitted a croaking groan that turned heads in the restaurant and triggered laughter from Sexy.

Cheryl

March 2014

"I thought we had a deal! What do you mean he wants seventy-five thousand dollars?"

Stephen threw his hands in front of his chest and backed away from Cheryl, who was slowly approaching him, nostrils flared, and fingers furled. "Sweetie, I'm sorry, I really am. Believe me, I called him every name but the child of God, but what else am I gonna do? Threaten to kill him or something? Let's be real."

Cheryl's eyes narrowed as she backed Stephen into a corner and started jabbing him in the chest with her finger. "But we had a deal! Did you remind him we had a deal, Stephen? I paid him five thousand for that birth certificate, passport, and social security card eight years ago, and now he wants me to pay him seventy-five thousand?" She stopped and looked at Stephen, then took a deep breath, as if trying to compose herself, then suddenly shouted: "SEVENTY-FIVE THOUSAND?"

"Calm down, girl! Please, it's not my fault. I'm as shocked as you." Stephen patted her on the back while leading her to the couch. "Let me get you something to drink. Iced tea. I'm not getting you any wine in the mood you're in."

"So he simply called you out of the blue?" Cheryl yelled out to

Stephen who disappeared into the kitchen. "How did he even get your number? You've changed it like three times in the last three years."

"True." Stephen came back with a tall glass of iced tea, and placed a coaster on the living room table. "But he got it from Raphael."

"I never did like that bitch, Raphael."

"Be nice, Cheryl." Stephen sat down next to Cheryl, and put his arm around her. "It's not Raphael's fault. He didn't know what Jocko was going to do."

"So, he calls you out of the blue, and says he wants seventy-five thousand dollars?"

Stephen let out a large sigh. "That's right. He saw the press conference, where Randy proposed to you, and the bastard obviously started seeing dollar signs floating in front of his eyes."

"Damn." Cheryl chewed her lip, while deep in thought. "But the press conference was in October. Five months ago. Why'd he take so long to get in touch with you?"

"He was in the joint."

"He was in jail?"

"Yep. He was busted on federal fraud charges back in August. Got caught up in some kind of sting operation for some Mafia or so-called mafia gang or something," Stephen explained. "He's been on Rikers Island for the last eight months. I suppose it took him this long to make bail."

"Mafia? Gangs?" Cheryl looked up, and shook her head. "Damn, Jocko was that deep into organized crime?"

"Girl, that man ain't no joke. Never was," Stephen said, shaking his head for emphasis. "When I told you I was going to give you the hook-up, I gave you the real hook-up, 'cause that's what I do. 'Cause that's how I roll."

Cheryl was twenty-three, and had recently graduated from Lehman College with a bachelor's degree in psychology. She was applying for a job as a social worker at a group home when she first met Stephen. He was sitting in the waiting room filling out an application right along with her, but he was obviously peeking at her paper.

Light-skinned with curly hair, Stephen was dressed preppy-style from his cardigan and bow tie down to his loafers.

"Look," Cheryl finally said, with much attitude, "Is there a problem?"

"I beg your pardon?" Stephen said in very proper tone.

"I'd like to know why you're busy eyeing my paper," Cheryl snapped.

"Oh, please." Stephen rolled his eyes. "It's not like this is some kind of chemistry test. I don't need to steal answers from you, Miss."

"Then keep your eyes off my application."

"Yeah, whatever." Stephen snorted.

Cheryl's interview was over in less than ten minutes—it took that long for the resident manager to tell her that they were only hiring people with master's degrees at the moment, but he would keep her application on file. She wanted to tell him that he should have put that in the job listing, but held her tongue.

She hadn't spent all of the $35,000 she had received for giving up the baby eight years earlier—because she had received a full academic scholarship that included room and board, she didn't have to spend any for college—but she had put a good dent in it. Like her mother, she was a fashion fiend, and although she did a lot of her shopping at designer outlet stores, it still cost a lot of money to look as good as she did.

Regrettably, the first $3,000 worth of clothes went to waste;

maybe it was having the baby that made her growth hormones kick in, but between the ages of fourteen and eighteen, she had shot up an amazing six inches. She was five feet five inches when she started high school. She was five eleven the day she entered college. And after living in the dorm for one semester, she couldn't bear to continue living with two other girls, one of which was bulimic, causing their dorm room to perpetually reek of vomit.

Cheryl couldn't bear her living situation, and so she decided it was worth the money to move into her own apartment. Moving into a safe and nicely maintained building wasn't cheap, and she'd spent a lot of money on rent and living expenses for the next four years of college. Then, when her mother died only three months before Cheryl's graduation, Cheryl spent another $5,000 on her funeral. Andrea Blanton was a full-fledged crack-addict and alcoholic by the time of her death, and her face was so ravaged by her lifestyle, Cheryl opted for a closed-coffin funeral. But it turned out it barely mattered since only Cheryl and the funeral director bothered to attend the services.

Depressed after getting turned down for the social worker job, Cheryl stopped at a nearby lounge and took a seat at the bar. She was drowning her sorrow with her second mojito when the guy who'd been stealing glances at her application entered. Upon spotting her, his eyes lit up and he smiled as if they were old friends.

He took the seat next to her and said, "From the looks of things, you didn't get asked back for a second interview either."

Cheryl rolled her eyes at him and turned up her lips. She was in a bad mood, and there seemed to be no reason why she couldn't take it out on him. "Still trying to put your nose in my business, are you?" She turned her back on him.

The man snorted, then tapped her on the shoulder. She faced him, ready to tell him she was going to call the manager, but before she could say anything, he picked up her hand and shook it. "My name is Stephen Rogers."

Cheryl was startled by his audacity, but also amused. "Well, since it seemed you were trying to memorize my job application, you already know my name."

Stephen nodded, while simultaneously waving to get the bartender's attention.

"Nope, I didn't get asked back." Cheryl shook her head woefully. "And I'm getting so low on cash, if something doesn't turn up soon, I'm gonna be living in a homeless shelter." She was exaggerating, of course, but the mojitos were working on her, causing her not to care.

"Okay, well, here's the thing." Stephen leaned in and lowered his voice. "I have a way for you to make some quick cash, if you're interested."

Cheryl immediately stiffened as an image of her mother's last boyfriend flashed in front of her eyes. She was fifteen when he'd said almost the exact same words, and convinced her to sell her virginity to a stranger, and then bilked her out of the money.

"Could you do me a favor and get the fuck out of my face?" she said through clenched teeth.

Stephen's jaw dropped. "Hey, you know what? You could have simply said no. There's no reason for you to start getting ghetto. Damn."

"Boy, you don't even know what ghetto is," Cheryl snapped.

"Oh, you're putting on a pretty good display," Stephen retorted.

"Shit, you should be glad this is all I'm doing." Cheryl sneered. "You come sitting next to me—uninvited—and then you're going to proposition me? I shouldn't be going ghetto on your ass; I should be going homicidal on your—"

"Proposition you?" Stephen's eyes widened and his mouth dropped again. "Girl, ain't nobody in this bar propositioning your skinny ass."

"Oh, no? So you don't want to fuck me, you just want to pimp me out, huh?" Cheryl smirked. "Sorry, been there, done that. Now, if you don't mind, please get the fuck out my face."

Stephen sat up straight in his chair, and tapped his right index finger on the bar as he looked Cheryl directly in the eyes. "Oh, I'll get out your face, but not before I set your rude ass straight about a few things. I don't pay for pussy, and I sure as hell don't pander pussy." He paused for a moment, and then pursed his lips together before adding stiffly, "I don't even like pussy."

"Man, if you don't—" Cheryl's head jerked back slightly. "Wait. What?" She looked at him quizzically, and right at that moment, he raised his left eyebrow, a movement that—coupled with the last two minutes of conversation—Cheryl found outrageously amusing. So much so that the smile she didn't have time to hide turned into a giggle, and then full-out laughter.

Stephen gave her a disdainful glance and turned in his seat, but in less than a second Cheryl could see the beginning of a grin. "Okay, so I've outted myself," he said, shrugging. "There're worse things than being gay."

"Damn, the way you put that makes me think that you don't really believe there're worse things than being gay," Cheryl said, a little surprised at his tone.

"Yeah, whatever." Stephen shrugged his shoulders. "Let's not even get into that."

"No problem." Cheryl took a sip of her drink, and then looked at him suspiciously. "So, you're not after my luscious body. What is it that you want, then?"

"I'm tempted not to tell you," Stephen said sullenly. "I think I've changed my mind." He took out a ten-dollar bill to pay for the drink the bartender placed in front of him.

"You *think* you've changed your mind?" Cheryl gulped down the rest of her mojito.

"I'm not sure." Stephen rolled his eyes. "You are really an obnoxious b—...witch, so I don't see why I should tell you about an opportunity for you to make two thousand dollars for two days' work."

"Are we talking legal?" Cheryl's eyes widened. She could use the extra money. And maybe it wasn't a one-time shot. Was this an opportunity to make two thousand bucks every week?

"Yes, it's legal." Stephen crossed his arms over his chest. "You're about, what, five feet eleven? Size four?"

Cheryl nodded.

"D cup? One hundred and fifteen pounds?"

"One hundred and twelve." Cheryl's eyes narrowed. "Are you sure this has nothing to do with sex?"

Stephen uncrossed his arms and leaned his elbows on the table. "Honey, in a way, everything in life is about sex. But what I'm talking about is a modeling gig."

"Modeling?" Cheryl chuckled. "You're kidding, right? What are you, a recruiter for one of those scam agencies that has you spend hundreds of dollars for head shots for a portfolio, and then they never find you any work?"

"Nooo." Stephen pursed his lips again. "But I'm going to forgive you for asking since I know that does happen a lot."

"Oh, gee, thanks."

"A model friend of mine overbooked, but she really doesn't want to cancel either of the two bookings because it'll hurt her reputation in the industry. She's almost exactly your size, weight, and proportions," Stephen explained.

Cheryl waved for a waitress and ordered another mojito. "What makes you think I know how to model? You've known me all of what...twenty minutes?"

Stephen waved his hand. "First of all, it's not rocket science. I've watched you walk; you have natural grace, and all. But the beauty of this particular gig is that it's fit modeling."

Cheryl ran her tongue over her bottom lip. "Fit modeling, huh?"

"Yes. It's for two different local boutique lines. All you do is go in, and try on clothes—"

"I know what fit modeling is. A designer uses fit models to see how their garments look on an actual woman rather than a mannequin, to check for comfort, fit, and flow."

Stephen looked surprised, but then nodded. "Good, then you know it's only three hours top, each day. And both gigs are paying fifteen hundred dollars."

Cheryl raised an eyebrow. "So it's three thousand dollars, then, not two thousand, right?"

Stephen crossed his arms again. "Well, you'd have to give my friend something since she's the one who booked the gigs, and I think I deserve a little something-something."

"So I'm supposed to give up thirty-something percent?" Cheryl snorted. "Yeah, right."

"Is it that much?" Surprise was evident in Stephen's voice, making it obvious to Cheryl that he hadn't done the math. "But, yeah, whatever, it's only right," Stephen argued. "You wouldn't be making anything at all if she didn't make the booking and I didn't tell you about it."

Cheryl put her drink on the bar and propped her face on her arm. "Did she ask you to find someone?"

Stephen shook his head. "No, but I was on the telephone with her before I walked into the job interview, and she told me her problem. Then when I saw you, I couldn't help notice the resemblance in your body type. That's when the idea came."

"Okay," Cheryl said slowly. "So, how about you call girlie back and tell her you came up with a great idea. You ran into an old friend who does modeling, and she's free...whatever days it is, the bookings are... and that you convinced her to help you out."

"What?"

Cheryl shrugged. "Make it clear that I'm doing it as a favor to you because I was planning on going on vacation or something. Then tell her you did it out the goodness of your heart, and I'll go ahead and give you fifteen percent, but only on the condition that you see if you can hook me up a few more times."

"Hmm...not only a little nasty, but also a little crafty, aren't we?" Stephen said thoughtfully. "But really, do you have any modeling experience?"

"My mother used to do high-fashion runway before I was born, so she taught me how to walk when I was a little girl—"

"So that explains how you knew what fit modeling is," Stephen said, "But if you're serious about modeling, why don't you go ahead and sign up with an agency? With a shape like yours you could probably land a couple of swimsuit jobs, even if you're a little over the hill."

"Over the hill?" Cheryl raised her eyebrow. "Oh. Okay, that's why you were peeking at my application, huh? To check out my age?"

Stephen grinned.

"Well, I'm NOT serious about modeling," Cheryl said. "To be truthful, I never considered it until now. But I do need money, and this might be a quick way to make some money, so...hey!"

Stephen shrugged. "Yeah, you're right. Too bad you're getting in the game so late." He looked at her intently, stroking his chin. "You know you really look younger than twenty-three; I bet you could easily pass for sixteen."

Two weeks later, Cheryl was $2,550 richer, Stephen was $450 happier, and they had already become the best of friends. Modeling was a breeze for the beautiful and statuesque Cheryl, and with some urging from Stephen, she decided to try to make it a full-time career.

"But, girl, you can't go into a modeling agency saying you're twenty-three," Stephen said one day when they were lounging in his East Village apartment. "All the top agencies want the young fresh sixteen- and seventeen-year-olds. Honey, you've got to lie about your age."

Stephen was what was known as a "down-low brother," an African American gay man who pretended to be heterosexual, but his language had relaxed quite a bit since he had become close to Cheryl, she noted with amusement. At least when they were alone.

"I thought about it," Cheryl responded, while flipping through the latest copy of *Vogue*. "But when you sign up, they ask for your social security card and photo ID with full name and birthdate. I've already checked into it."

"Well, I might be able to help you out with that."

Cheryl looked up from her magazine. "Oh? You're printing driver's licenses in your bedroom now?"

"Oh, no, girl, I have much better uses for my bedroom." Stephen grinned. "But I do have the hook-up."

"Man, you always have the hook-up!" Cheryl said excitedly. "Okay, what's the deal?"

Stephen's friend Jocko wanted $10,000 for a birth certificate, social security card, and passport. Amazingly, Stephen managed to get him down to $5,000. Cheryl held her breath when she first presented the forms to the modeling agency, but exactly as both Stephen and Jocko had assured her, no one knew the difference. And like that, Cheryl had shaved six years off her life.

It meant that today, everyone except Stephen thought she was twenty-four. This also meant that everyone thought she was only three years older than her husband—not nine.

But now Jocko was threatening all of that. And if Randy found out she'd lied about her age, he might start trying to dig into her past to find out what other lies she'd told. *Good Lord, what if he actually found out I gave up a baby boy when I was fifteen? He'd hate me.*

"Stephen, I can't let Jocko spill the beans." Cheryl stood up from the couch, and started pacing back and forth.

"Girl, I know." Stephen sighed. "You're going to have to come up with the money. Think you can do it?"

Randy was in Tampa with the Yankees for spring training, but even if he were in town, Cheryl knew she'd have no trouble getting the money from the bank. They had joint savings accounts, and he never asked her to explain her spending. And if he did, she could come up with some excuse—like extra spending on the surprise birthday party she was throwing for him when they got back in town in a month. Still, how many more times would she be forced to sneakily withdraw money to pay off Jocko?

Cheryl grimaced. "Yeah, I won't have a problem getting the money, but here's the thing, Stephen: I give him this; how do I know he doesn't come back for another taste from the pot?"

"You think...oh shit. I didn't even think about that." Stephen fell silent.

"Yeah," Cheryl said after a minute or so, "well, it's something to think about." She stood up and reached for her handbag. "So, yeah, call him and tell him I said, okay. Don't give him my telephone number or anything, but I'll get his contact info from you later, and we'll make the arrangements."

Stephen slowly rose from the couch, a suspicious look on his face as he followed her to the door. "You've got a plan, don't you?"

"Maybe, kinda sorta, we'll see." Cheryl kissed Stephen on the cheek. "And don't forget we have to go shopping for something to wear for Randy's surprise birthday party next month."

"Ooh, girl, I can't wait." Stephen rubbed his hands together. "I've been looking forward to this for weeks."

Cheryl laughed and lightly tapped his face. "Well, fair warning, I've invited all his teammates and even some of the Yankees brass, so you'd better be on your best behavior at the party."

S exy posted selfies on Instagram wearing a bikini while posing on the balcony of the riverfront apartment she now shared with Yusef. She received mostly favorable comments, but there were a slew of nasty comments from her ex-roommate, Emma, and Emma's hateful friends.

Perhaps it had been rude and inconsiderate of Sexy to pack up and leave without giving Emma a heads-up, but Emma had a lot of nerve being upset when she had been the queen of inconsideration with her sloppiness and hoarding habits.

It was a no-brainer to vacate the pigsty she'd been sharing with Emma, and move into Yusef's luxury condo when he'd made the offer.

With Yusef's training and travel schedule, Sexy often had the place to herself. Additionally, he gave her a generous allowance that spared her from having to check in with her mother in order to continue receiving the measly stipend that her stingy parents granted her.

Sexy was so pampered by Yusef, she wasn't sure if she'd be willing to give up the good life to attend school in London. Her parents would croak if she broke her promise, and refused to return to school. But life with Yusef didn't require an elite education.

Decisions. Decisions. Did she want to be obligated to her parents or Yusef? She concluded that she'd rather be indebted to Yusef.

Being a kept woman and playing the role of wifey was a hell of a lot more appealing than being under her parents' thumbs.

Whenever Yusef traveled with his team, Sexy treated herself to burgers and pizzas and all sorts of greasy fast-food. But when he was in town, they dined at only the best restaurants, and it had become a ritual for Sexy to jerk him off with her hand concealed beneath the crisp, white tablecloth at the conclusion of their meal.

Tonight, Yusef had invited a teammate and his wife to join them for dinner, and Sexy was looking forward to seeing the couple's shocked and embarrassed expressions when they realized the naughty behavior that was taking place right under their noses.

Smiling as she relaxed in the Jacuzzi tub, Sexy bolted upright when Yusef burst into the bathroom. "Dinner's cancelled."

"Why?" she asked, disappointed. She enjoyed desecrating snobby restaurants by leaving behind a linen napkin filled with semen.

"I got traded to the Yankees," he said in a shocked tone. "I have to pack my things and go to Tampa early tomorrow morning to join them for the last few weeks of spring training."

"What about me? Are you taking me with you?"

"Not right now. I have to get acclimated with the team and I don't need any distractions."

"Oh, I'm a distraction?" she said with a hand on her hip, obviously indignant. "If that's how you feel, we can put the brakes on this relationship right now. In fact, I'm packing my shit and moving the hell out. I refuse to allow you to treat me like I'm an inconvenience." She stepped out of the tub, yanked a towel off a hook, and wrapped it around herself.

Yusef caught her by the arm before she stomped out of the bathroom. "I'm sorry, Sexy. You're not an inconvenience and I'm sorry I gave you that impression. This is all so sudden, my head is spinning. All I'm asking is that you bear with me for a little while. After I'm down there for at least a week, you're welcome to join me."

He reached inside his pocket. From his wallet, he withdrew his Platinum AMEX card. "My agent pulled some strings and got me and my plus-one an invitation to Randy Alston's surprise birthday party next month. Take my card and buy yourself a hot, new dress. Randy's married to a gorgeous model, and I want my new teammates to see that my girl is as fashionable and beautiful as Randy's wife."

"Who's Randy Alston?"

A look of disbelief covered Yusef's face. "Are you serious? You don't know who Randy Alston is?"

Sexy shrugged again.

"He's the top third baseman and the highest-paid player on the Yankees roster." Sexy gave another shrug and rolled her eyes toward the ceiling. She didn't know or care anything about the Yankees or any other sports team. With a sigh, she grudgingly accepted the credit card. "I'm still mad at you, Yusef, but I'll attend the stupid party with you on one condition."

"Anything...name it," Yusef said with a lopsided smile.

Sexy dropped the towel. "I want a farewell fuck. It has to last all night long. You can't stop until my body's numb and I'm speaking gibberish because my brain is fried. Got it?"

"That's not a problem, baby. You know you can get it whenever you want," Yusef said, tearing off his clothes.

A month later, Sexy and Yusef took a limo from his Upper Manhattan hotel to Birdland, a premier jazz club in the theater district where Randy Alston's surprise birthday party was being held.

"You haven't said one word about my dress. Don't you like it?" Sexy inquired.

"I love it, but don't you think you went a little overboard on the cost? Four-thousand-five-hundred dollars for a skimpy little dress that you'll probably never wear again seems a little reckless." There was an edge in Yusef's voice.

"Oh! So, that's what you're upset about. You've had a stink attitude ever since I arrived in New York, and I had no idea it was about the money I spent on the dress." Nostrils flaring, Sexy pointed a finger at Yusef. "With all the money you make, I can't believe you're concerned about the cost of my dress. You told me the chick who's throwing the party is a fashion model, and in so many words, you emphasized that you wanted me to outshine the bitch, so why're you making such a big deal over the money I spent?"

"Can you lower your voice? Let it go for now. We'll talk about it later on when we get back to the hotel."

Sexy folded her arms in defiance. "I'm not talking about shit, later on. I don't even know if I want to go back to the hotel with you. In fact, I don't think I want to be bothered with this dumb-ass party."

"Don't be like that, baby. I shouldn't have said anything. But I figured if our relationship is going to work, I had to speak to you about exercising some boundaries when you're running up my credit card."

Sexy gave Yusef a contemptuous look. "You have issues, dude. You think every woman is a gold digger who's out to beat you. I bought this dress to make you proud to have me on your arm, but since you wanna lecture me about responsibility, you can tell the limo driver to turn this shit around and drop me off at the train station."

"What are you saying?"

"I'm saying I want to go back to Philly and return this fucking dress."

"Come on, baby. Get a grip. Why're you blowing this thing out of proportion? I only made a comment, and there's no reason for you to ruin our evening. Look, I don't want you to return the dress. My bad for even bringing it up."

The driver glided up to the curb in front of the club and Yusef caressed Sexy's arm. "Let's go in the party and have a nice time," he said in an appeasing tone. "This will be the first time I get to mingle with the other players in a social environment. I don't want there to be any tension between you and me. Okay?"

"Hmph! You're the one who caused the tension, so don't blame me!"

"I know. I know. I'm an idiot. Do you forgive me?"

She sucked her teeth. "I hate you," she whispered.

"No, you don't. You love me as much as I love you," he whispered in her ear. "And I'm gonna show you how much I love you when I get you in bed tonight."

Sexy looked hot and she knew it, and she was accustomed to being appraised and admired back home in Philly, but she found it a little odd that glamorous New Yorkers—both men and quite a few women—were ogling her like she was a juicy piece of meat.

And Yusef was such a hypocrite. With all that talk about the cost of her dress, he grinned with delight with his prideful eyes darting to her revealing dress each time he introduced her to one of his teammates. She got the impression that Yusef wanted every man at the party to check out the skin she was showing and to lust over her.

Annoyed with Yusef, Sexy took a trip to the restroom to get away from him for a few moments. Inside the restroom, two attractive women were checking out their reflections in the mirror, touching up their makeup, and gossiping.

"That heifer needs to be working for the Secret Service the way she keeps close tabs on her man. She's practically joined at the hip with Randy, and it's not a good look. Cheryl needs to lengthen the leash on her husband—at least for tonight."

"I know, right? It's his birthday, after all, and she should get from up under him, and give him some breathing room," the other woman chimed in with her mouth turned down in disapproval.

"Birthday or not, she's so afraid of losing her Mega-Millions Man, I doubt if she'll let him out of her sight for one minute, tonight."

"We can't put all the blame on Cheryl, though. I heard that Randy's nose is so wide open, the groupies don't stand a chance. Word on the street is that Cheryl has him so whipped, he won't even sign autographs for good-looking women unless Cheryl gives him permission."

Sexy approached the mirror, and the two chicks looked her up and down sneeringly before departing the restroom.

Haters! Gazing at her image, Sexy reflected on what she'd over-heard about the birthday boy. *So, he earns mega-millions, does he? I wonder exactly how much? I bet a man making big bucks wouldn't complain if his woman bought a forty-five-hundred-dollar dress.*

She hadn't met Randy Alston or his wife, yet, and after over-hearing the gossip about their marriage, Sexy was eager to meet the couple. She didn't care how gorgeous his wife was reported to be, Sexy highly doubted if Randy's wife or any other woman at the party looked better than she did.

Loving a challenge, Sexy smiled maliciously as she made a bet with herself that she could not only get Randy's attention, but could also steal his heart away from his stupid-ass, jealous wife.

When Sexy exited the restroom, Yusef was waiting outside the door. "Why'd you stay in there so long? Randy and his wife just arrived and we missed shouting out, 'Surprise!'" Yusef said with a note of hostility in his voice.

Sexy shot him a disapproving look. "I don't give a shit about shouting, *surprise*. What are we, six-year-olds? Goddamn!"

Yusef relaxed his facial muscles. "Nah, nah. It's not like that. It's all good. But I want to introduce you to Randy and Cheryl before this place gets so packed and you can hardly have a decent conversation." He ran a caressing finger down the side of Sexy's face. "Schmoozing with the Alstons can't hurt. So, be extra polite to his wife."

Holding Sexy's hand, Yusef led her over to where Randy and Cheryl were holding court. Cheryl's beauty couldn't be denied. She was dressed elegantly in a silk ivory dress with a long slit up one side, and she carried herself with the dignity of an aristocrat, Sexy noticed with disdain.

But Cheryl's demeanor and haute couture didn't intimidate Sexy. After years of ritzy prep schools, and a lifetime of being under the tutelage of her socialite mother, Sexy had been well-groomed and was completely aware of proper etiquette at social gatherings. However, after observing the way Randy's eyes traveled over her body, Sexy decided to forget about social graces. Presenting her slut-side would be the quickest way to get what she wanted.

"Hi, there," she said with a sultry smile when Yusef introduced her to Randy. Randy actually blushed, and his wife inhaled sharply, obviously livid.

"Sexy Sanchez? What's that, your stripper name?" Cheryl blurted as she possessively hooked her arm into Randy's.

Sexy laughed. "I'm not a stripper, and although Sexy's not my birth name, I had it changed legally for obvious reasons."

Cheryl opened her mouth and then closed it. Blinking rapidly, she steered Randy away from Sexy and Yusef, and began greeting other guests.

"What was that all about? Why'd you embarrass me like that?" Yusef asked angrily.

"What?" Sexy asked with a shrug, and then left Yusef standing alone as she meandered over to the bar. She sipped champagne and plotted on her next move. If that Cheryl bitch thought she was going to keep her husband away from Sexy, she had better think again.

Sexy glanced to her right and there was Randy, conversing with an older white man with silver hair and tanned skin. Sexy assumed the man had money and power, judging by the way he was able to have a discreet conversation with Randy without Cheryl hovering over them. In fact, Cheryl was on the other side of the room, chatting with a handsome, curly-haired dude who was a bit sweet, according to Sexy's gaydar.

Making her move, Sexy sauntered up to Randy and the silver-haired man and said, "So, we meet again."

"Yeah, I suppose so," Randy said nervously. "Mr. Jeff Roberts, this is Miss, uh, Sexy Sanchez. Miss Sanchez, meet Mr. Roberts, one of the owners of the Yankees franchise."

"Nice to meet you, Miss Sanchez," the older white man said, smiling and gazing at Sexy leeringly. He patted Randy on the shoulder. "I could only stop by for a few minutes. My pilot is waiting to fly me to Miami. Anyway, happy birthday, Randy and many more."

"I'm honored that you stopped by, sir. Have a safe flight to Miami."

"I'd like to have a very turbulent flight with you," Sexy said suggestively after Mr. Roberts walked away.

"I don't think Yusef would approve of that."

"I don't give a damn what Yusef approves of. I think you're hot, and I want you. Do you want me?" Sexy boldly asked, twirling her hair.

"Absolutely, I do. But, it's not that simple. I have a wife and—"

"What your wife doesn't know can't hurt her."

"I don't keep secrets from Cheryl. I'll tell you what. Let me run this by her and I'll get back to you."

Randy strode across the room, leaving Sexy with her mouth hanging open. Was dude actually going to ask his wife if he and Sexy could fuck around? Sexy had experienced some weird encounters, but this was by far the strangest shit she'd ever been involved in. And what was even weirder was that instead of telling Randy to kiss her ass, she was patiently sipping champagne and waiting for him to get his wife's permission to fuck her!

Cheryl

The enormous ballroom was packed and booming; athletes, models, millionaires, and the rest of New York City's beautiful and powerful people were on their feet singing along with Young Jeezy and DJ Greg Street who were turning it up with one of their hit singles from the "Seen It All" album.

More than $600,000 was spent making Randy's twenty-second birthday one he would never forget—even the Yankees' brass had kicked in a hundred thou toward the surprise bash for their superstar—but for Cheryl, the night had soured a few minutes after the loud chorus of "SURPRISE" had ended when she and Randy walked through the door.

Surrounded by dozens of friends and teammates slapping Randy on his back and wishing him well, Cheryl was still able to spot the little hoochie mama from about thirty yards off. The little bitch looked like a stalking tiger with a clueless, innocent antelope in its sight. Having worn the look herself in her single days, Cheryl's antennae instantly went up as Yusef introduced her and Randy to the slut who called herself Sexy Sanchez. Not taking any chances, she steered Randy away from the girl after only a few minutes.

But now Cheryl gritted her teeth, watching the little slut slinking over to Randy and Jeff Roberts, and then making an obvious play for Randy as soon as Jeff walked away. *I knew she'd be after him as soon as she thought the coast was clear. I shouldn't have left Randy's side for one damn second.* She tried to control her breathing, but there was no controlling her racing heart. There was no doubt about it, that skanky bitch was trouble.

Though some ten feet away, she could clearly see the expression on Randy's face, and it was clear that Sexy-babe was pulling no punches. He looked as if someone had just grabbed his junk and given a seductive squeeze; not many women could make a man sport that look simply by talking. She herself had done it to men many times—and it looked like Sexy had the same provocative talent.

"Yeah," Cheryl whispered to herself as her husband walked toward her as if in a stupor, "this one's going to be trouble."

"Hey, babe, I can't believe you did all this for me." Randy pulled Cheryl into a warm embrace and followed with a soft kiss. "And how did you manage to keep it secret? I really thought we were only going out for a quiet dinner."

Cheryl patted her husband on the cheek. "It wasn't easy, but it was worth it. You should have seen the look on your face when they yelled, 'Surprise!' And as a matter of fact, you will get to see it. Stephen said he got a good shot of your expression."

"Oh, Lawdy, I can imagine what it looks like." Randy laughed. "I don't think I even wanna see it."

"Well, I want to see it," a sugary voice from behind them said.

Cheryl and Randy both swung around to see Sexy slyly grinning at them; one hand on her hip, the other holding an umbrella-topped cocktail.

Little sneaky bitch. I didn't even see her coming. "Oh, well, perhaps we'll send your boyfriend, Yusef, a copy once they're printed," Cheryl said coolly.

Sexy was unfazed. "Yusef's not my boyfriend," she said with a one-shoulder shrug.

Cheryl raised an eyebrow. "That's funny—does he know that? I mean, he did introduce you as his girlfriend."

Sexy gave another one-shoulder shrug. "Yusef can say what he wants, but as far as I'm concerned, I'm a free agent," she gave Randy a wink, "as they say in sports lingo."

Cheryl rolled her eyes. "Fine, give your contact information to the valet on your way out. I'll try to remember to get it."

"Oh, why take that chance?" Sexy said sweetly. "Why don't I give it to you now?" She turned toward Randy. "Give me your phone, and I'll put my info in. That way I'll be at your beck and call." She brazenly grabbed the cell phone Randy had been holding in his hand and began pressing buttons.

"Well, well," Cheryl said, smiling as she lightly pushed Randy aside and stepped in front of him, "why, aren't you a cute, little lollipop, triple-dipped in psycho-slut?" She snatched the phone away from Sexy, and carefully deleted the few letters the girl had managed to type before handing it to her husband.

"What the fuck is wrong with you?" Sexy snapped. "All I did was—"

"All you did is throw your skanky little ass at my husband," Cheryl hissed.

"Uh, Cheryl," Randy stammered, "why don't we—"

Sexy gave a wicked grin. "What's got you worked up...the fact that I'm throwing or the fact that he's so eager to catch?"

Cheryl's eyes narrowed. "You know I would slap you, but I don't want to get slut on my hands."

Not waiting for a response, Cheryl grabbed Randy's arm and pulled him away, immediately joining another group of people laughing at some drunken joke. From her peripheral vision, Cheryl could see Sexy standing there, not angry, but with what appeared to be an amused look on her face. It took a few seconds before the girl walked away with an enticing switch of her hips.

Cheryl continued to watch her, and when Sexy looked over her shoulder, their eyes met; it was like steel hitting steel. The mutual stare lasted only a moment before Sexy smiled and gave a wink, then finished her sashay across the room.

I was right, Cheryl thought as she turned back to the group's drunken banter, *this one's going to be trouble*. With the live performances over, the DJ had taken over, and if by cue, he suddenly started playing "Here I Stand" by Usher. It was the song that played the first night they met, and the song they had played at their wedding. Cheryl and Randy looked at each other at the same time and smiled. Randy gently took her hand and led her to the dance floor.

"I love you so much, babe."

"I love you, too, baby. I'm glad you enjoyed your party," Cheryl said, reaching over and turning off the lamp on the night table in their massive bedroom.

"Hey, you know I enjoy everything you do," Randy said as Cheryl snuggled up next to him in the bed.

"Everything?" Cheryl's hand slowly slid down Randy's body.

"Yeah, everything." Randy kissed Cheryl's forehead. "But, babe, I'm bushed tonight. I had a little too much to drink, and—"

"Oh, well, let's see what I can do to rejuvenate my man," Cheryl said with a wicked grin, sliding down in the bed.

A half-hour later Cheryl watched as her husband slept, a satisfied smile on his face. She had laid it on him, every which way possible, and had tears streaming down his face before finally letting him come to his final climax. One of her better blow jobs, if she would say so herself. After all, it was his birthday. And, though she hated to admit it, she wanted to make sure he didn't have reason to think about the skank from earlier in the evening.

The little minx was slick; she didn't make another play for Randy at the party, but Cheryl highly doubted that she'd completely given up. Anxious to get the four-one-one on the girl, she'd made it a point to ask the other wives at the party what they knew about her. While girlfriends of team members tend to be competitive and even backbiting, the wives banded together, if only to fend off groupies.

It turned out that while Sexy had only been around a short time, she'd already made quite a name for herself. She was twenty-one, from Philadelphia, and Yusef Rawls' wifey, a wifey who acted like an out-of-control jump off, that is. When Yusef reported to Tampa for spring training in mid-March, he'd come alone, but two weeks later, Sexy had come for a three-day weekend that stretched to almost a week. And the chick was scandalous. She looked like a ho, dressed like a ho, and acted like a ho, was the word from the wives. Cheryl wasn't above giving her husband an occasional hand job under the table at a restaurant, but never with another couple at the table. And especially not one she'd never met before, at that. Another time, she was told, they were at the VIP section of a popular night club when Sexy announced she wasn't wearing panties, then made a big production of sitting on Yusef's lap. The grinding that followed and the groans he emitted a few minutes later made it clear that a special part of his anatomy had also become clothing free.

It was a coincidence that Randy had been home in Alabama the week that Sexy visited, otherwise, they would have run into each other before. The one thing that Cheryl found out, which surprised her, was that while Sexy openly flirted with the single team members, she hadn't approached any of the married men. So why Randy? Cheryl wondered. Just my fucking luck.

There had been other girls who'd targeted Randy, but he paid most of them little attention. Why mess around with hamburger when he had steak at home, he'd told one of his friends. If Cheryl noticed a girl who did pique his interest, she made quick work of them. Sometimes she was antagonistic, occasionally aggressive, but most often, she simply let the true bitch in her come out. And then there were the couple of times when some chick appealed to Randy so much Cheryl invited her into the bedroom for a threesome. The next morning, the random chick would be out of their bed, out of Randy's senses, and out of their lives.

But this Sexy girl...Cheryl could sense she was really going to be hard to dismiss as easily as the rest. Thank goodness Randy hadn't mentioned her once they left the party. Maybe her aggressiveness had turned him off. She certainly hoped so.

During the ride back to the hotel, it was obvious that something had ticked Yusef off. Normally, he'd talk nonstop about the connections he'd made regarding endorsements and other money-making ventures. Or he'd brag about the close friendship he and Randy were developing. But tonight he was quiet and brooding.

If he thought Sexy was going to feed into his childish behavior by asking what was wrong with him, he had better think again. She wasn't into coddling grown-ass men. Turning away from Yusef, she gazed out the window. From the reflection of the glass, she could see him looking down at his phone, reading and responding to texts. He broke into a smile every now then, as if he'd read a suggestive comment from a female admirer.

If he thought he could make Sexy jealous, he was sadly mistaken. He was doing her a favor by keeping his mouth shut for a change. Little did he know, she had grown completely bored with him and had already moved on emotionally to bigger and better things. After hearing the salary that Randy Alston earned, Sexy realized that Yusef was only small potatoes compared to a star player like Randy Alston.

Silently informing Yusef that two could play the same game, she retrieved her phone from her purse and texted a few of her friends and updated her Instagram page with pics from the swanky party. She made a mental note that the next time she was in Randy's company, she'd be certain to get a pic of the two of them together.

The thought of Randy brought a smile to her lips. Sure, he had a shitload of money that she wanted a large portion of, but there was also something else going on that she couldn't quite pinpoint. Perhaps it was his quiet charm and Southern bashfulness.

From her peripheral vision, she could see that Yusef had put his phone away. Watching him cutting his eye at her, Sexy got the impression that he was ready to break the ice and talk about whatever was on his mind. Well, she wasn't going to make it easy for him. Keeping her eyes focused on the screen of her phone, she inputted a very important number—Randy's number—which she'd stealthily lifted from his phone and memorized during that brief moment she'd had possession of his phone.

When the limo pulled in front of their hotel, Sexy leapt out without waiting for the driver to open her door. As Yusef tipped the driver and said a few parting words, Sexy darted inside the hotel and sped toward the elevator without so much as a glance over her shoulder to check to see if Yusef was behind her.

Yusef managed to jump inside the elevator seconds before the doors closed. "What's your problem? Why'd you jump out of the limo like that?" he asked with his brows knitted together in agitation.

"You're my problem."

"Don't put this on me. You're the one who made me look like a chump tonight while you were flitting around the party, flirting and carrying on as if you're single."

"Excuse me," she said, holding up her left hand as a reminder that her ring finger was bare.

Yusef's facial features softened. "Is that what's wrong, baby? Are you upset because I haven't popped the question, yet?"

She rolled her eyes toward the ceiling. "Don't flatter yourself, Yusef."

He nodded his head knowingly. "You don't have to admit it, but I know women, and now I realize why you were deliberately trying to tick me off at the party. I get it. I realize that most of the other players have wives, and you feel out of the loop."

Yusef enveloped Sexy in his arms. "I love you, girl. It's not that marriage is out of the question, baby, but I need to marinate on the subject for a little while."

"How long is a little while?" she murmured, merely playing along.

"A major move like that isn't something I'm willing to consider until I get through the season. But as soon as the season ends, we'll start looking at rings—I promise."

"Okay." With her face buried in Yusef's chest, she was able to hide the smirk on her face.

Yusef has a history of being a womanizer, yet he's like putty in my hands. But it's not surprising that I'm able to manipulate men so easily. After all, I learned from the best—my mother! I watched that sophisticated ho pull the wool over my father's eyes my entire life, and now I'm going to put all those lessons learned to good use when I go after Randy Alston. Once I get him out of the clutches of that controlling wife of his, and use my powers of seduction, I'll be able to mold him any way I want.

Sexy turned toward Yusef with a frown. "I'm starving. It's a wonder I'm not sloppy drunk after drinking on an empty stomach."

"Why didn't you eat at the party? The food was banging."

"I wasn't hungry then, but I am now."

"It's too late for room service. Do you want to go back out and get dinner?"

Smiling devilishly, Sexy shook her head. "Nope, I'm not feeling any restaurants. What I have a taste for is right there," she said, caressing his crotch.

"Oh, shit." Yusef began undoing his fly while his eyes darted upward. "What about the cameras?"

Sexy hit the stop button, bringing the elevator to a standstill between floors. "Fuck those cameras. And fuck dinner. All I want is dessert," she said, moistening her lips as she dropped to her knees.

Only a few New York Yankees WAGs—Wives and Girlfriends— had been welcoming toward Sexy. Although it bothered Yusef that Sexy wasn't fitting in with the other WAGs, Sexy couldn't have cared less. In fact, she was relieved that no one had called and requested that she take on any tasks at today's 10K walk-a-thon, a charity event being held in Central Park to benefit some kind of endangered animal. It was much too hot for her to be burdened with tasks that required her to exert any amount of energy, and the only reason she was bothering to even show up was that she'd heard that Cheryl Alston would be in attendance, handing out T-shirts to walkers after they crossed the finish line.

Sexy had been irked by Cheryl's over-the-top reaction when Sexy had offered to input her number in Randy's phone. The guy obviously wanted Sexy, but his wife was too insecure to let him and Sexy indulge in a little playtime. Oh, well, if at first you don't succeed...

The best way to get to Randy was to figure out his wife's weaknesses. Showing up uninvited at the charity walk would be phase one of her plan to steal Cheryl's meal-ticket. She'd enjoyed many sexual conquests in the past, but to actually take Randy away from his snooty wife and claim him as her own would be the biggest coup of Sexy's life. The idea of succeeding in such a major scheme sent shivers up and down her spine.

When Sexy showed up at the charity walk, her intention was to merely observe Cheryl and get under her skin by prancing around in a string bikini and a pair of black and gold Chanel sneakers. It was an added bonus to overhear Cheryl and Mila Sawyer, another player's wife, gossiping about her as she stood outside a tent that was set up for charity staff.

"I can't believe that little hooker came to our event dressed like she's spending a day at the beach," Mila ranted. "I had hoped that Yusef Rawls was merely having a fling with the tramp, but apparently he plans to marry her when the season ends."

"I don't know Yusef personally, but he doesn't appear to be foolish enough to actually marry a raunchy hooker. Did he give her a ring, yet?" Cheryl asked.

"Not yet, but he's serious about her. He asked my husband, Brent, to recommend a good jeweler."

As she eavesdropped on the conversation between Cheryl and Mila, Sexy couldn't hold back a proud smile. How sweet of Yusef to want to let his teammates know that he intended to wife her. Unfortunately, she had no intention of being tied down with him. The only man she viewed as husband material was Randy Alston. And by hook or crook, she was going to take a walk down the aisle with Cheryl's soon-to-be ex-husband!

"Actually, a married Sexy Sanchez is good news. Maybe after Yusef has papers on her, he can get her under control, and stop her from hitting on my husband every chance she gets," Cheryl commented.

"But if he marries that slut, we'll be forced to accept her into our inner circle. And I can't imagine ever being in the company of the likes of her, ever again. I had the misfortune of having to sit through an elegant dinner at one of the most prestigious restaurants in the city with that little trollop. The way she grinded her ass on Yusef's lap in the midst of the meal was absolutely mortifying,"

Mila complained. "And throughout the raunchy dance, she was staring at Brent, flagrantly flirting and licking her lips."

With an ear pressed against the canvass fabric of the tent, Sexy covered her mouth, stifling a giggle as she reminisced about the lap dance she'd given Yusef during dinner. Sure, she'd thrown a few seductive smiles at the male onlookers, but she hadn't singled out Brent. Mila was delusional if she thought Sexy was interested in her buck-toothed husband.

"Don't worry, Mila. It's all going to work out," Cheryl said wisely. "Once she's captured her own baller and has a ring on her finger, she'll see things from our perspective and she'll calm the hell down. She'll have to focus her attention on keeping those cut-throat groupies away from Yusef instead of slithering up to our men and grinning in their faces. It's a good thing the boys are out on the road and didn't see her prancing around in that bikini. I hate to admit it, but her body is sick, and I may have to start hitting the gym twice a day."

"I don't know if revving up your exercise routine will be enough, Cheryl. I have a bad feeling about that girl. She's stirring up trouble in my bedroom workout without even trying."

"How'd she manage to do that?" Cheryl asked, sounding amused.

"Yusef has been bragging to the guys that his girl gives him head three and four times a day. He even claims that she drives to practice and sucks his dick in the car. Yusef attributes the extracurricular dick sucking to the improvement in his stats."

"Oh, God!" Cheryl groaned in disgust. "If she wants to suck a sweaty dick in a car during team practice, that's her problem, not ours."

"She comes equipped with baby wipes when she meets him at practice. And a jar of Marshmallow Fluff."

"Are you kidding me?" Cheryl screeched in irritation.

"I kid you not. You should have heard the yearning in Brent's voice when he relayed that information to me. I swear to God, if a jar of Marshmallow Fluff turns up in my kitchen cabinet, I'm filing for a divorce. Brent may not get three and four blow jobs a day like Yusef does, but he gets his fair share. I don't like the way Yusef is putting ideas into my husband's head, making him feel as if our love life is inadequate."

"Marshmallow Fluff, huh?" Cheryl said with a giggle. "I don't know about you, Mila, but after the walk-a-thon is over, I'm stopping at my favorite specialty shop to pick up a package of gourmet, Bavarian marshmallows. When Randy comes home, I'm gonna work some marshmallow magic by melting the exquisite marshmallows into a delectable spread, and slather it all over his dick, and then I'm gonna lick it all off with pleasure." Cheryl laughed and added, "Let me know if you hear about any of Sexy's other slut-stunts. That trick-bitch has no idea that she's gonna help me continue to keep my husband happy at home!"

"As usual, you're right, Cheryl," Mila conceded, and then ended the conversation by asking Cheryl what she planned on wearing to the next home game. "Being a former fashion model, I know you won't be wearing jeans and a Yankees shirt."

"No, I won't," Cheryl said with a chuckle. "I haven't decided yet, but whatever I wear will be couture-casual. I won't be sitting behind home plate with the other wives next week. Jeff Roberts invited me to sit in his sky box, and since this will be my first time having such choice seating, I plan to make a good impression."

"Mr. Roberts never invited me to join him and his hoity-toity friends in his skybox," Mila said in a pouty tone.

"What can I say? It's one of the perks of being married to Randy Alston. Maybe you'll get invited next time," Cheryl pacified.

Sexy was suddenly livid. Why hadn't she been invited to the owner's luxury box? She looked just as good, if not better than Cheryl Alston, and the owner should have been honored to have her gracing his stupid skybox.

Fuck this charity walk. I'm going back to the hotel to make an important phone call. If Yusef wants to marry me, he'd better figure out a way to get me in that damn skybox.

In Jeff Roberts' skybox at Yankee Stadium, Sexy exited the private restroom right in time to see Cheryl's arrival. Lingering near the restroom, she observed Cheryl with a scowl. Cheryl was overdressed in a whimsical white, embroidery and lace, calf-length dress, a wide-brim straw hat, and large sunglasses. The bitch was such a flamboyant diva. She was at a baseball game, for Christ's sake, not a semiformal event.

The scowl on Sexy's face deepened as she observed Jeff Roberts greeting Cheryl with a warm embrace and then introducing her to several surgically altered, cat-faced wives of team executives. The gratuitous way he was acting, one would have thought that Cheryl was the Queen of Sheba.

With one of the Botox-injected old crones at her side, Cheryl gave a big, fake smile as she accepted a mimosa and a lobster puff from the wait staff. Sexy could see right through Cheryl's façade. *The devious, gold-digging bitch is probably plotting on how she can trade up from Randy and get her greedy hooks into the owner of the team,* Sexy mused cynically.

Deciding it was time to make herself visible, Sexy emerged from the shadows with a sultry strut. Her slinky sauntering would put Naomi Campbell to shame. Her entrance was so spectacular, she turned every head in the skybox. Sexy got a kick out of observing Cheryl's smug smile vanish from her face when she spotted Sexy heading in her direction.

Wearing tiny, cut-off shorts, a tank, and stilettos, Sexy took long, runway-model strides while sensually swiveling her hips.

"I'd die for those toned legs," Sexy overheard the corporate wife say to Cheryl.

I bet you would, Sexy thought with a little laugh. *Unfortunately, your plastic surgeon can't manufacture these legs!*

With her lips screwed up, Cheryl was obviously too pissed to comment. She guzzled down her mimosa and beckoned the server to bring her another.

Adding insult to injury, Sexy sidled up to Cheryl. "So nice to see you," Sexy said with a smirk.

"Let's get something straight." Cheryl spoke through clenched teeth. "We are not and will never be friends, so please dispense with your twisted version of pleasant small talk."

"Excuse me, I had no idea you were such a mean drunk. Maybe you should water down your next drink and hopefully improve your mood. It's simply a suggestion," Sexy said with a one-shoulder shrug.

"I'm not drunk and I don't need your asinine suggestions." Giving a huge sigh, Cheryl excused herself and walked over to one of Jeff Roberts' other guests, a film producer who had expressed a desire to cover Randy, Yusef, and a few other Yankee players in a sports documentary.

"Hello, Mrs. Alston," the producer greeted.

Before Cheryl could return the greeting, Sexy made a beeline to Cheryl and the producer. "How are you, Mr. Producer," Sexy interjected, unknowing and uncaring of the man's name.

The producer's eyes immediately danced away from Cheryl and settled on Sexy.

Almost trampling Cheryl's feet in an effort to get to Sexy, he extended a hand as he introduced himself. "My name is Hal Stevenson. I don't believe we've met," he said, blushing boyishly.

"Sexy Sanchez. Nice to meet you." Sexy poured on the slut factor, batting her eyes and practically writhing, as if in heat.

"Can I get you a drink, Sexy?" Hal asked with a dopey expression that prompted Cheryl to roll her eyes.

"Sure. But I don't want that mimosa-shit they're serving. I want something stronger—like a Bone Crusher."

"Okay, whatever that is." Hal assumed his dopey expression once again, and Sexy wasn't surprised. She'd always had a strong effect on men.

"The bartender should know how to make it," Sexy said, giving Hal a playful wink. The poor sap seemed so eager to please, Sexy wouldn't have been surprised if he went behind the bar and tried to whip up the drink himself.

Sexy graced Cheryl with a glowing smile, but Cheryl turned her mouth down in disgust. "You interrupted an important conversation. There's nothing cute about your crude behavior, *little girl*," Cheryl said scornfully. "You need to learn some manners before you try to hang with a distinguished crowd like this."

"I didn't hear that producer dude voicing any complaints about my lack of etiquette. In fact, he broke his neck to cater to my desires...exactly the way your husband does whenever he's in my presence."

Cheryl let out a gasp and her face flushed. "My husband has never been in your presence except when you rudely inserted yourself into our conversation at his surprise birthday party."

"Is that what he told you?" Sexy shook her head pityingly. "Oh, you poor, naïve woman. Randy and I have been together a bunch of times, and if you can get past Randy's country-bumpkin ways, he's really sexy and a lot of fun."

"Keep my husband's name out of your trampy mouth," Cheryl hissed, carefully monitoring the pitch of her voice.

"What you need to be worrying about is how you're gonna keep your husband's face from between my legs."

Cheryl's mouth fell open, and then she quickly recovered. "Believe me, if my husband went after another woman, it wouldn't be the likes of you." She looked Sexy up and down sneeringly, her disapproving eyes lingering on the young woman's cut-off shorts.

Sexy laughed tauntingly and ran her hands over her curvaceous body. "Yo, ma, I don't blame you for being upset about the way your man has been trying to get up on this—begging me to let him smash." Sexy's words and the defiant way she planted a hand on her hip, sent Cheryl into a blind rage. Somehow the mimosa she'd been sipping, ended up in Sexy's face.

Incensed, Sexy charged at Cheryl with clawed fists. "You try to act all high and mighty, but you're nothing more than a ghetto-trash bitch," Sexy snarled.

Defending herself, Cheryl threw up her fists. And before the stunned group of esteemed guests, Cheryl and Sexy commenced to brawling.

Holding Sexy's drink in his hand, Hal Stevenson watched in stunned silence as the two women viciously scratched, slapped, and windmilled each other until security escorted them both off the premises.

That fucking ho!

Cheryl fumed as she drove up Amsterdam Avenue toward Washington Heights. She always prided herself on being a lady— at least in public—and to have gotten into a physical brawl with Sexy in the owner's skybox the previous night was not only out of character, it was completely out-of-line. If it wasn't for the fact that Randy was one of the Yankees' superstars whom the team couldn't afford to piss off, and also that she'd already made a good name for herself, she probably would have been banned from the skybox for life. She knew for sure, though, that Sexy wouldn't be so lucky. It would be a cold day in Hell before she was up there with the VIPs again.

After passing 195th Street, she started looking for a parking space. Amazingly, there was one right in front of the apartment building where she was headed. Of course the elevator wasn't working, and of course the stairway smelled like urine. Luckily, there weren't too many stairs to climb; Jocko lived on the third floor.

"*Hola, mami! Que pasa?*" he said when he answered the door.

Cheryl rolled her eyes. "When did you start speaking Spanish?"

The man grinned, revealing gold caps on his two front teeth. "Since moving up here with the Dominicans, babe. When in Rome..." He laughed, exhaling a revolting gust of rum and tobacco breath. "Come on and get your pretty little ass in here."

Cheryl walked past him into the living room and sat down on a raggedy and dingy-looking blue armchair without waiting to be asked. Her face and her actions both displayed the disgust she felt about being there, but she didn't care. He needed to know how she felt. "If your ass didn't get picked up on a parole violation, we could have had this meeting two months ago like we were supposed to."

"Hey, I'm lucky they only held me for sixty days. Wanna drink?" he asked, holding up a red plastic cup while pointing to a nearly empty bottle of Bacardi sitting on the coffee table next to her.

"No," she answered sullenly. "I merely came to take care of this business, and then I want to get the hell out of here."

"Yeah," he said, pouring a healthy dose of rum into the plastic cup and taking a sip. "I was *real* lucky. They could have violated me and sent my ass back up the river for seven years, all for dirty urine. Ain't that some crap?"

Cheryl rolled her eyes. "Well, thanks for the information. I'll file that under 'shit I don't care about.'"

"Damn, girl," Jocko sat down on the couch, spreading his legs open and his arms across the backrest, "No need for you to be sporting an attitude."

"It's not an attitude; it's the way I am," Cheryl snapped. "Now can we get down to business?"

A look of annoyance finally crossed Jocko's face. "Fine. Did you bring the—"

"I've got the seventy-five thousand handy," Cheryl said, cutting him off, "but first we have to get some things straight."

"Handy? Exactly what does that mean?" Jocko's lips twisted into a snarl. "You got the dough with you or what?

"It means," Cheryl said, leaning forward in the chair and putting her hands on her knees, "like I said...first we have to get some things straight."

"Like what?" Jocko growled.

"Like the fact that I think that it's real fucked-up that you charged me five thousand dollars for a social security card, passport and birth certificate, and I paid it without trying to chisel you down or anything; and now, eight years later, you contact me talking about you want another seventy-five thousand dollars."

"And?" Jocko didn't bother to try and hide his smirk.

Cheryl's eyes narrowed. "So is that how you usually do business?"

Jocko chuckled. "Occasionally. Like anytime I find that a person who was only probably worth a couple of ten thousand dollars when I did them a favor—"

"A favor?" Cheryl said incredulously. "People don't have to pay for favors!"

"Is now worth a couple of ten million dollars," Jocko continued, ignoring the interruption. "I'm a craftsman, top guy in my trade. I coulda charged you a lot more than a measly five stacks for those papers, you know. I cut you some slack because I knew you didn't have a lot of money. But now you do." He took a leisurely swig from the plastic cup, then got up and poured himself another large shot and sat back down. "The way I see it, you've been dancing to the rhythm for eight years, and now it's time for you to pay the piper."

"You're full of shit."

"And you're full of money, and I want some," Jocko said simply.

"And if I don't give it to you?"

Jocko chuckled, then took another swig before answering: "You figure it out."

Cheryl leaned back in the chair, and chewed her bottom lip while contemplating him. "So, if I give it to you, how do I know you won't come back at me for another shot?"

Jocko shrugged. "You'll have to take my word for it, I guess."

"Or," Cheryl reached inside her Versace bag and pulled out a neatly typed piece of paper, "you can sign this contract."

"This what?" Jocko started laughing. "Get the fuck outta here. You want me to sign a contract saying that I provided you with forged documents?"

"Not exactly," Cheryl replied. "The contract says that in return for seventy-five thousand dollars, you agree to not contact me, or anyone in my family regarding any financial situation, and that you also agree not to leak any confidential information about me or my family to the media or to the public."

"You're crazy." Jocko shook his head.

"I'm serious," Cheryl insisted.

"If you're serious, then you're not only crazy, but you're also stupid," Jocko said. "Even if I did sign it and then renege, what are you going to do? Take me to court? You'd be outing yourself, sweetheart."

"Maybe what I'm saying is that I'd rather out myself than keep paying you forever for something that's already been paid in full," Cheryl retorted. "I'm not going to lie down and play victim to blackmail."

Jocko let go a full laugh. "Bullshit. If you felt like that, you wouldn't be ready to give up the seventy-five thou."

"You're not getting it unless you sign," Cheryl insisted.

Jocko made a face, then waved his hand dismissively. "Fine, fuck it. I'll sign. Give me the money."

Cheryl pulled a white bank envelope from her bag and placed it on her lap, then handed Jocko the paper. "Sign first."

An hour later, Cheryl was on the third floor of Bloomingdale's. She and Randy were scheduled to attend a black-tie charity ball the following week, and while she had already bought a fabulous navy blue, floor-length Vera Wang formal gown for herself, Randy still needed something to wear. She looked over the tuxedos, vacillating between the Burberry London Milbury, and the Ralph Lauren Black Label Anthony. She finally chose the $3,000 Ralph Lauren, and then picked out a Ralph Lauren Black Label tuxedo shirt for $450 and arranged a time for Randy to come in the next day for custom fitting. She then purchased a pair of David Yurman Chevron cufflinks with black diamonds. Only $1,500.

Riding down the escalator to leave the store and passing the second floor, she couldn't help but remember the trip she had made there seventeen years earlier, when she was only fifteen and a wannabe shoplifter, trying to support herself. Now here she was dropping almost $5,000 on a single outfit without batting an eye.

She made it to the first floor and was walking toward the exit when a display with men's watches caught her eye. Randy needed two, she decided. One for special occasions and another for every-day wear. He needed to stop depending on his cell phone to know the time. It took her almost ten minutes, but she finally decided on a Movado and a Michael Kors. She looked up to catch the clerk's attention when she saw a teenage boy looking at her intently. Staring at her, actually. He was tall, a few shades lighter than her own bronze complexion, but with the same reddish tones. Under the baseball cap that he was wearing backward, she could see that his hair was a mass of curly ringlets. He looked almost identical to a picture she'd seen of her father playing baseball in high school. Cheryl gasped, her hand flying to her mouth as she did. It simply couldn't be. Or could it? She hoped the young man hadn't noticed, but all of a sudden, he started walking toward her.

She lowered her eyes, and started edging toward the exit, but he caught up to her before she reached it.

"Excuse me, is your name Cheryl Blanton?"

Cheryl was shaking inside, but she tried to keep her face composed. Was it him? It had to be him. He looked to be about fifteen or sixteen. It had to be him. This was the baby she'd given up all those years now. The doctor must have told him her real name after all. And now he was here confronting her. Had he been following her? For how long? What would he want? Should she lie?

"I'm sorry, ma'am. Are you all right?" the teenager said, a concerned look on his face. "Do you need to sit down or anything?"

"Why, why, why would you ask that?" Cheryl said, trying to control her breathing.

"Well, you suddenly look kind of pale," the boy answered. "And your hands are shaking."

Cheryl tried to broaden her smile as she leaned back onto a wall to ensure her knees didn't buckle. "No, I'm fine, but I need to get something to eat."

"Oh, do you suffer from hypoglycemia?"

"What?"

"Low blood sugar. My friend's mother has it. She gets dizzy whenever she misses a meal," the young man answered.

Cheryl shook her head. "No, I don't."

"Oh, good." The boy grinned and patted her arm. "You are Cheryl Blanton, though, aren't you?"

"Why?" Cheryl's heart raced. "Do I know you? Exactly who are you?"

"Oh, I didn't mean to be rude, ma'am. My name is Ronald Davidson," the boy said quickly, reaching out and shaking her hand. "No, we haven't met, but I'm a big fan of your husband, Randy Alston. I play third base, too. I was hoping he might be here with you."

Relief washed over her, and she felt she could breathe again. His last name was Davidson. The doctor who had adopted her baby was named Nehru. It wasn't her son. Her smile suddenly became genuine. "No, I'm sorry he's not. But I tell you what, since you're such a nice young man, if you give me your name and address, I'll have him send you some tickets to one of next weekend's games."

"Oh, man! Would you?!"

Why am I tripping like this? Why would I, all of a sudden, imagine a kid was my child simply because he looked a little like me? Probably because of Randy talking about wanting a baby. Wanting a son. Cheryl walked out of the store, completely forgetting about the watches she had planned to purchase for her husband. *I wonder what he does look like, though. Maybe he looks like me. Maybe he looks like his father, whoever the hell he is.*

Her face clouded as her thoughts drifted back to seventeen years ago, when her mother's former boyfriend had convinced her to give up her virginity in exchange for $15,000. She'd gone through with it, only to find out that the man had paid Jackson the money upfront. And of course, by the time she found out, Jackson had already disappeared.

Leaving her even more depressed and just as hard up for money.

A few weeks later, while on a school trip to Washington, D.C., she ran into a good-looking older man whom she at first thought was a friend of her late father. She went over and talked to him, then realized she'd made a mistake. Embarrassed, she excused herself, but the man was very gracious, and they continued to talk. When he asked her age, she lied and said she was seventeen. One thing led to another, and he propositioned her. She ditched her schoolmates and spent the evening with him in D.C., returning to New York City the next day in a limousine and with $500 in her purse.

Inspired, Cheryl began traveling out of town on a regular basis, and pretending to innocently bump into well-to-do men, whom she seduced—for pay. She was adamant about never going back to the same man twice. She rationalized that if she didn't see a man more than once, he wouldn't recognize her if they crossed paths later in life. She didn't need any skeletons in her closet that would come back to haunt her. In her young mind, Cheryl believed she had it all figured out.

Until she started feeling nauseous and her small young breasts became so tender it hurt when they were touched.

Pregnant? How could it have happened? Cheryl had looked at the urine strip in shock. She'd made every man she slept with use a condom, even when they offered to pay extra to ride bareback. Now what was she going to do?

Three days later, she was sitting in Planned Parenthood's Margaret Sanger Clinic on Bleeker Street, waiting for her name to be called so she could go in the back and get her abortion when she noticed one of the doctors kept walking through the waiting room, and staring at her. Finally, he quietly beckoned her to follow him, and led her into a private office. He spent a half hour explaining that she bore an uncanny resemblance to his wife, and that they'd been trying unsuccessfully for years to have a child. Seven months later, they had a child and Cheryl had $30,000 in the bank.

Cheryl shook her head, trying to clear her mind of the memories, as she climbed into her Maybach.

"Girl, you'd better stop worrying about the past and start concentrating on the present to ensure your damn future," she said to the image reflected in the rearview mirror she was adjusting after starting the ignition. "You had a baby once, dammit; you'd better hurry up and pop another one out, soon."

Yusef had successfully cultivated a public image of a macho athlete, but he was the complete opposite behind closed doors. It was sickening the way he was always upset about one thing or another. Most of the time, he acted like a little bitch on his period. After discovering Sexy had gotten thrown out of the owner's skybox, Yusef had become livid and stopped speaking to her.

Sexy didn't give a damn that they weren't communicating; what irked her was the way he had stomped around the hotel, slamming doors, cabinets, and drawers while packing for his game in Baltimore.

If they were sharing a roomy apartment, she could have retreated to another area and ignored his childish tantrum, but being holed up in the hotel together had been torturously confining for a couple at odds. She breathed a sigh of relief when Yusef finally vacated the hotel, taking his bad energy with him.

Yusef and his dramatic-self had behaved as if her getting thrown out the skybox was the ultimate embarrassment and the end of the world. Sexy, on the other hand, wasn't sweating it. She'd been thrown out of more places than she could count, and would probably get thrown out of many more if that bitch, Cheryl, continued to come out of her mouth with insults and slurs.

Her mouth twisted into a smirk as she recalled the turbulent path that had brought her to this point in her life. Before assuming the identity of Sexy Sanchez, she'd been Amanda, an honor student and captain of the girl's lacrosse team at the prestigious prep school she'd attended since elementary school. Unfortunately, along the way, she'd developed a festering anger toward her parents, whom she had begun to view as pretentious, dishonest, and totally obnoxious. Especially her mother. Bringing shame upon the distinguished family name became one of Amanda's favorite pastimes.

A devilish smile played at the corners of her mouth as she reminisced about all the hell she'd raised in her affluent community back when she was still living at home with her parents. To say that she'd been a wild child was putting it mildly.

Labeled a thief, a liar, and a ho, Amanda's reputation was so badly tarnished, she was no longer welcome in most of her classmate's homes. Wanting to give her daughter an opportunity to enjoy life with a clean slate, Clarissa encouraged her husband to introduce Amanda to the refined offspring of a few of his esteemed colleagues who lived in bordering Philadelphia Main Line communities— people who had no knowledge of Amanda's troubled past.

During a sleepover hosted by Abigail Whitaker, the daughter of Dr. Henry Whitaker, a professor in the department of Modern Literature at the University of Pennsylvania where Amanda's father was the dean of the medical school, Amanda found her new acquaintances to be terribly boring and immature for fourteen-year-old girls. While the silly girls made up fake profiles on Facebook, using porn-star images to entice boys from their school, Amanda thought of something much more exciting to indulge in.

Under the pretext of wanting something from the kitchen, she slipped out of Abigail's bedroom and found her way into Dr. Whitaker's study, where he sat at his desk, smoking a cigar and drinking a glass of sherry as he pored over a leather-bound volume of some boring-looking tome.

"May I help you, young lady?" he asked, looking over his glasses in bewilderment.

"Whatcha doing, Doc?" she inquired with a coquettish lilt to her voice as she stood in the doorway.

"I'm—uh—catching up on some reading. Can I help you with something, Amanda?"

Dr. Whitaker was a youthful forty-something. Not particularly handsome, but his toned body attested to many hours spent playing racquetball and tennis. Additionally, there was a sparkle in his eyes that was appealing in a sexy-nerd sort of way. But most importantly, his wife was right upstairs and Amanda loved living on the edge.

At five-feet-nine with super long, athletic legs and a curvaceous figure, Amanda had the body of a full-grown woman, and she loved flaunting her femininity. The short, frilly PJs she wore revealed her never-ending legs, and even gave a peek at her firm ass cheeks.

"You look stressed, Dr. Whitaker," she said, quietly closing the door behind her. "I know a great stress reliever." Mischief danced in her eyes as she moistened her lips.

Dr. Whitaker stood up, and said in a stern voice: "Now, listen, young lady—"

"Shh. No one has to know," she purred. "I won't tell if you don't," she whispered as she kneeled in front of him and ran a hand over his crotch.

"This isn't right," he said in weak protest while lowering his pants to his thighs and releasing his erection.

Men were so stupid and weak. Amanda couldn't suppress a smile as she skillfully pulled his hardened length inside her mouth. She took her time, leisurely licking him from the base to the head, and then lapping at the glistening pre-cum that bubbled out.

Suddenly out of his mind with lust, Dr. Whitaker began stroking inside Amanda's mouth with reckless abandon. "It's been so long," he growled. "Oh, God this feels so good." He pressed down on the top of her head as he aggressively drove himself in and out of her mouth.

Too bad Dr. Whitaker hadn't reached the finish line before the door to his study suddenly sprang open. Stunned, Mrs. Whitaker stood with her mouth agape, yet no sound emerged. She watched in horror as her husband yanked up his pants and blamed Amanda for seducing him.

Amanda burst into tears, wiping the side of her mouth and muttering, "He made me do it!"

"Oh, my God, Henry. What have you done? What kind of perverted monster am I married to?"

"I can explain," Dr. Whitaker cried, wearing a pained expression that begged for understanding.

"There's nothing to explain. A fourteen-year-old girl can't force the will of a grown man."

Alerted by the noise, Abigail and her friends began tramping down the stairs. A look of alarm flashed in Mrs. Whitaker's eyes, and she glanced at Amanda. Amanda interpreted the look in Mrs. Whitaker's eyes as the promise of untold material gain if Amanda helped with damage control.

On cue, Amanda hurried out of the study, closing the door behind her.

"What's all the yelling about?" Abigail inquired.

Amanda lifted a shoulder. "I don't know. I was in the kitchen looking through the fridge when your parents started arguing. I tried to find out what was going on, but I think we should give them their space." Amanda shooed the girls away from the study and herded them back upstairs.

A week later, Amanda requested that Mrs. Whitaker get her tickets to the Rihanna concert. The next week she demanded a new phone and an iTunes gift card. She'd been working her way toward requesting $600 to pay for a fake ID when she found out that Dr. Whitaker had resigned from the literature department and had moved his family to Europe where he'd accepted a position at a university in London.

Some months after that, bored in church one Sunday morning, Amanda decided to have some fun by luring pimply-faced, seventeen-year-old Nick Baldwin out of Sunday service and downstairs to the basement of the church. The awkward, bashful boy was a virgin, and although their sexual connection was completely unsatisfying, Amanda derived excitement from the idea of fornicating in the church while the pastor was in the midst of preaching a sermon.

There was an added bonus when Ms. Ramsey—the church secretary—came downstairs, snooping around for some unknown reason. The woman's response to catching Amanda's legs open and Nick with his pants down was priceless. She let out a shriek and then began rapidly patting her chest in an attempt to regulate her heartbeat. Moving as if Satan were on her heels, she raced out of the basement, fanning her face and muttering, "Oh, Jesus. Oh, Lord."

Eyes widened and sparkling with mischief, Amanda stared at Nick and fell out laughing. But Nick had a totally different reaction. Red-faced and gasping for breath, he rifled through his pockets and pulled out his asthma inhaler. Before Amanda's and Nick's parents as well as other members of the congregation had trekked down to the basement, Nick was in the midst of a full-blown asthma attack.

Nick was taken out on a stretcher, and Amanda's mortified parents hustled her out of the church through an obscure, rear door. Amanda and Nick were forbidden from attending future church services, and their return to the flock was contingent upon the completion of a psychotherapy treatment program.

For months, Amanda and Nick were the hot topic of the quiet community. Clarissa attempted to place full responsibility on Nick, who she claimed had coerced and manipulated her innocent, young daughter. The Baldwins countered by accusing Amanda of stealing Nick's class ring during the scandalous sex act, a claim that Clarissa found laughable. Amanda had no reason to steal anything. Amanda's parents indulged their daughter with the best of everything, including heaps of pricey, elegant jewelry, so why on earth would she need to pilfer a cheesy class ring?

But Clarissa had a rude awakening when she discovered a boy's silver class ring at the bottom of Amanda's jewelry box.

"Is this Nick's ring?" Clarissa had questioned.

Amanda flipped her hair nonchalantly. "Yeah, that's Nick's ring, but I don't know why he's claiming I stole it when he knows full well that he gave it to me. He said it was mine as long as I kept my mouth shut about what...uh...you know, what he talked me into doing at church."

Clarissa scowled at the ring, holding it between her fingernails as if it were something too vile and loathsome to touch her bare skin. "Amanda, we have to return this ring to that despicable Baldwin boy."

"Why should I?"

"For one thing, I don't want it in this house, and furthermore, the Baldwins should be made aware that their son is a pathological liar as well as a degenerate pervert. I want you to tell them exactly what you told me. How he tried to bribe you after forcing himself on you."

Amanda rolled her eyes heavenward. "What's the point, Mom? I told you that he took advantage of me. To force me to talk about it and to relive that horrible experience will feel like I'm being raped all over again."

A pained expression covered Clarissa's face. "You're right, Mandy. We should have taken you directly to the hospital, and we should have had that boy arrested, but your father didn't want to bring unwelcome attention to the family."

"Way to go, Mom. Your parenting skills are on point. Thanks so much for protecting me," Amanda said with biting sarcasm.

"Oh, sweetheart, I know I let you down, and I'm so sorry." Clarissa reached for her daughter, but Amanda recoiled, glaring at her mother through eyes filled with accusation.

Amanda's father, an esteemed scholar, could not be as easily manipulated as her mother could—at least not by Amanda. From Amanda's point of view, he'd always seemed mistrustful of her, as if he could see right through her lies. She got the impression that her father expected her to behave badly.

It was a shame that he wasn't as insightful when it came to his wife. He adored and doted on Clarissa and seemed clueless that she was having an affair with Mr. Narducci, a swarthy man who lived in a huge, ostentatious house that was considered a blemish in their prestigious neighborhood. Mr. Narducci wore flashy clothes, drove a Maserati, and was rumored to have mob ties.

One day, back when Amanda was eleven years old, she had come home early from summer day camp and found her mother and Mr. Narducci naked in her parents' bedroom. She'd never forget the utter shock of seeing Mr. Narducci's pale ass pumping as he pounded into her mother. In complete contrast to his white ass, the rest of his body was tanned to a golden bronze.

Startled by Amanda's unexpected appearance in her bedroom, Clarissa yelped and Mr. Narducci jerked around and gawked at Amanda, his bristly eyebrows rising in surprise.

"You can't tell your father what you saw. It would shatter him," Clarissa disclosed after Mr. Narducci hurried out of the house.

Buying her silence, Clarissa took Amanda on a shopping spree later that day. When Amanda's father returned from an out-of-town medical conference, Clarissa prepared his favorite meal, and afterward, the family convened in the living room and Clarissa entertained them by playing something by Mozart on the piano, smiling at her husband all the while with what appeared to be love and complete adoration.

Amanda often associated that day, when she was only eleven, as the time that she learned the art of deception. And over time, she became an expert at trickery.

Yusef's briefs had been in such a bunch when he left for Baltimore, Sexy was surprised he hadn't confiscated her credit card. But since he hadn't, it was as good a time as any to do some shopping. Although she hadn't adjusted to New York quite yet, she had to admit that the shopping experience was unlike anything that Philadelphia had to offer.

Sexy picked up items from several high-end shops, but fell completely in love with the Prada store. Every item she charged to Yusef's card was purchased with Randy Alston in mind. She couldn't wait to put on her new, black lingerie for Randy. One look at her prancing around in the sheer, beaded negligee and Randy would immediately want to serve that annoying wife of his with divorce papers.

She made a mental note to figure out a way to set up a situation where she could hang out with Randy Alston privately—somewhere away from the rest of the team. And most importantly, in a place where her every move wouldn't be scrutinized by Cheryl or any of her friends.

"You don't love me, you never did love me." Stephen sniffed, before taking a long sip of his Chablis.

"Aw, sweetie—"

"No!" Stephen put his hand up. "Don't even try it, Cheryl. We used to be BFFs. We counted on each other for everything. We talked all the time." He wiped the beginning of a tear from the corner of his left eye, then pulled a tissue from the pastel box on the sofa end table, and nosily blew his nose. "But since you've married young country boy—"

"His name is Randy," Cheryl said dryly.

"I know his name!" Stephen shot her a dirty look, then jutted his chin out and pursed his lips while crossing and uncrossing his legs. "I simply choose not to use it."

Cheryl sighed loudly.

"Anyway," Stephen blew his nose again before continuing, "as I was saying, since you married...him...I never see you. You don't care about me anymore."

Cheryl arose from her chair and walked over to the sofa to sit next to Stephen. "Sweetie, that's not true. We saw each other a few weeks ago at the party—"

"Where you had no time for me," Stephen snapped.

"Well, you saw that girl who was gunning for Randy," Cheryl protested. "I had to keep my eyes on him...and her."

"No, I didn't see it!" Stephen rolled his eyes. "I didn't even know there was a problem until I arrived at the game a few days later, right in time to see you get kicked out of the skybox. It's a good thing I was able to keep the press from finding out what happened. Can you imagine the scandal?" He sniffed, and gave her a cold stare. "Although they probably already know more than me."

"Well, if you want to know about that skank, Sexy—"

"I DON'T WANT TO KNOW ABOUT THAT SKANK AND I DON'T WANT TO TALK ABOUT THAT SKANK! I WANT TO TALK ABOUT ME!!!!"

"Of course, sweetie, of course," Cheryl said hurriedly, rubbing Stephen's back. "Please calm down."

"I'm going through a crisis," Stephen said, shaking his head, and dabbing at his eyes with the damp tissue.

"Well, I'm here for you, Stephen. Tell me what's going on," Cheryl said soothingly. She gently guided Stephen's head onto her shoulder, and tenderly smoothed his hair. "I'm sure we can work whatever it is out."

Stephen started sobbing. "Thank you, Cheryl," he was finally able to say. "I hate to bother you because I do know you're going through so much right now."

"Shhh, it's okay," Cheryl said calmly. "Don't worry about me. Let's talk about you. What's going on, sweetie?"

"Well," Stephen sniffed a few times before continuing, "I can't go on like this, Cheryl. I've had to make a major decision, and I'm going through with it. But it's going to be so hard." He shook his head dismally.

Cheryl rolled her eyes, knowing what was coming next. She'd been through it a few times in her tenure as Stephen's best friend. Usually after he'd been dumped by a lover, or after he'd come from visiting his parents in Connecticut. Dutifully, she asked: "What decision, sweetie?"

"I'm going to be celibate." Stephen sat up straight and looked Cheryl in the eyes. "I know I've said it before, but I mean it this time."

"Oh, sweetie, why?" Cheryl knew her lines well.

"Because what I'm doing is wrong. Men are not supposed to love men—at least not in a physical way. It's against nature." Stephen burrowed his head into Cheryl's arm and softly sobbed. "But the thing is, I can't help it."

Okay, it's the parents' thing. Damn!

"I went to see my parents this weekend," Stephen said, tears in his voice and rolling down his cheeks, "I was thinking, well, you know about how you're always telling me—"

Cheryl nodded.

"—that I should go ahead and let my parents know that I...that I—" Stephen paused to wipe his tears, but as soon as he did, more started pouring down. Still, he continued, obviously trying to keep his voice steady. "—that I should go ahead and tell them that I have a...an alternative lifestyle. I'm thirty-five years old, Cheryl. And I don't want to live my entire life as a lie, or feeling guilty because of who I am."

"Right," Cheryl said, in an encouraging voice.

"Well," Stephen cleared his throat, "we sat down to a nice Sunday dinner, and everyone was in such a good mood, everyone was so pleasant, that I thought it would have been the ideal time."

"Sure," Cheryl said, nodding her head again.

"Well, as soon as I began gathering up my courage, the doorbell rings." Stephen paused, and then started chewing his lips. "It was my brother. And his wife. His pregnant wife."

"Priscilla's pregnant?"

Stephen nodded. "They found out last week. That's why they had come over. To tell my parents the good news. That they were finally going to be grandparents."

"Oh," Cheryl said slowly.

"So, yeah," Stephen's voice started breaking again, "Mama and Papa were so excited, they were bouncing off the walls. Rubbing Priscilla's stomach, congratulating Jonathan, and then Mama looked over at me, and she must have thought that I was feeling bad or something." He paused again. "I wasn't. I might have had a disappointed look on my face, but it was only because I was kinda disappointed that I wasn't going to get the chance to talk to Mama and Papa about...you know."

"Right."

"So Mama comes over to me, and says, 'Don't feel bad, Stephen. Your turn will be coming soon. I know you'll find the right girl, won't he Papa?' So then Papa comes over and starts hitting me on the back like some kind of good ole boy. So then he says, 'Mama's right. You know your Uncle Richard was here a couple of weeks ago saying that the reason you don't have a girl is because you like boys. Well, I got up and told him to get the hell out of my house. Didn't I, Mama? And when he didn't get out fast enough, I got off my chair and threatened to throw him out. Didn't I, Mama? Can you believe he was trying to tell me that one of my sons is a faggot?'"

Cheryl's eyes widened. "Oh, no."

"Oh, yeah." Stephen shook his head. "So then Mama says, 'You don't need to use that word, Papa. Say homosexual...or homo. There's no need to insult those people. God will deal with them when it comes time to face their judgment.'"

"Oh, no," Cheryl said again.

Stephen nodded. "And of course that got an Amen from everyone in the house." He looked at Cheryl and tears once again welled up in his eyes. "Including me."

"Oh, Stephen." Cheryl started rubbing his shoulders, then pulled him into her bosom and began rubbing his back. "You poor baby."

Stephen sobbed loudly for a good five minutes before he could speak again. "My parents think that all gays...all homosexuals... will burn in Hell. How can I tell them I'm one?" He sat back up, though he was still sobbing, and looked Cheryl directly in the eyes. "Really? How can I tell them?"

"I understand, Stephen," Cheryl said soothingly.

"I can't do it, Cheryl. I simply can't," Stephen continued, "they've done so much for me and Jonathan. They sacrificed for us. Taking out second and third mortgages to put us through private schools and college. And they've never asked anything from us in return." He took a deep breath. "They live by the Bible, and they expect their children to do the same. I can't hurt them by letting them know I've been sinning since I was a teenager."

"Stephen, you can't be serious," Cheryl said. "You're one of the kindest and generous people I know. Being gay doesn't mean—"

"Yes, it does," Stephen said, cutting her off. He sat up and started wiping his eyes, then blew his nose. Cheryl could see that he was trying to compose himself. "Well," he said finally. "I can't force myself to sleep with women, but the least I can do for my parents is to stop sleeping with men." He chewed his lips again. "They're going to Heaven, and maybe if I become celibate now, God will forgive me and allow me to be with them when my time comes." He stopped and seemed to be in deep thought, then took Cheryl's hands in his own and said: "Do you think so, Cheryl? Do you think God will forgive me?"

"Oh come on." Cheryl tugged at Stephen's arm. "You love Lady Gaga. How about one dance? Please?"

"I don't feel like dancing," Stephen answered, pulling away and heading toward the bar. "And I don't feel like being around a lot of people tonight. I shouldn't have let you talk me into coming with you."

Cheryl sighed as she squeezed into the small space at the bar next to him. She hadn't really felt like going out either, but she couldn't think of any other way to cheer Stephen up. He'd gone through "I hate being gay" moods before, but this one seemed so much more severe than any of the other times. Usually he'd throw a four- or five-hour pity-party, get tipsy, and then insist they go out. Sometimes he would dress extra conservatively and try to act so straight it was obvious that it was an act; other times he'd dress so flamboyant he'd be downright gaudy. There seemed to be no rhyme or reason as to which way he'd go, but after they went out and had a few more drinks, he'd always declare, "To hell with it. I'm gay, and I don't care who cares." But this time was very different. He boo-hooed until he was almost hoarse, and wanted Cheryl to go home so he could stay in the house and boo-hoo some more. But Cheryl refused to leave. He was so depressed she was concerned he might try something stupid. Like maybe suicide.

"Okay," Cheryl said after she flagged down the bartender and ordered drinks for herself and Stephen, "I'll let you get away with sitting out Lady Gaga, but I swear if they play that new Pharrell joint, you'd better get out on the floor with me."

"Would you leave me alone?" Stephen grumbled.

"Nope," Cheryl said cheerfully, taking a sip of the martini the bartender had placed in front of her. "I'll have you know I was supposed to be driving to Baltimore this afternoon to see Randy play the Orioles this evening, but I called and told him I wanted to hang out with my best friend instead." She placed her head on Stephen's shoulder. "'Cause Cheryl loves her best friend, Stephen."

"You shouldn't have bothered," Stephen said sullenly. "I'm fine."

"No you're not." Cheryl sighed, straightening back up.

"Yes, I am."

Cheryl sucked her teeth. "There's no way you would have left the house to go to a club wearing loafers if you were really all right."

Stephen shrugged, but said nothing.

Cheryl turned around and leaned against the bar as she watched the couples on the dance floor. Shaman's had opened only a few weeks ago, but word had already spread around the city that it was the hot spot for out-of-town celebrities. Out-of-town celebrities because the native New Yorkers still preferred to get their party on in Manhattan rather than traveling all the way out to Queens.

Her mind started wandering, and she wondered if she'd done the right thing—making that telephone call after Jocko contacted her for even more money. *He left me no choice. I had to do something, or else he would have tried to bleed me dry.* She felt Stephen turn around next to her. "Ready to throw down yet?" she asked nonchalantly, while still staring in the direction of the dance floor.

"I thought you said Randy was in Baltimore playing ball."

"He is. I was supposed to be with him; instead I'm here with you not dancing," Cheryl answered with a smirk.

"So how come those two drink waitresses are arguing over who is going to bring up his drinks? He must be a damn good tipper."

Cheryl swung around to face him. "What?"

Stephen pointed to the end of the bar. Sure enough two waitresses were holding their trays with one hand, while playing tug-of-war with a magnum of Dom Perignon. Champagne was the only alcohol

Randy drank during the season, and he wouldn't even do that until Cheryl finally convinced him that an occasional drink of the bubbly wouldn't hurt his game. For him to be ordering a magnum, though, meant he was there with some of his teammates. Time to give him a pleasant surprise.

"I'll be right back," Cheryl told Stephen as she walked toward the women.

"Excuse me," she said when she reached them. "Is that bottle for Randy Alston?"

Both women looked at her, daggers flying from their eyes.

"I only asked because I'm his wife, and if you don't mind, I'd like to surprise him and bring up the bottle myself," Cheryl explained. "Of course I'll make it worth your while," she added quickly.

"His wife?" one of the women asked, surprise evident in her voice.

Cheryl noticed one of the waitresses nudge the other. *Oh, they were probably banking on getting with him tonight.* Cheryl smiled to herself. *That shit ain't gonna happen.*

"Yes, you don't mind, do you?" She reached into her handbag and pulled out her wallet. "Here, let me pay for that," she said, handing one of the women her American Express card, "and go ahead and give yourselves a two-hundred-dollar tip."

"Each?" one of them asked.

"Of course," Cheryl said, taking the waitress' tray.

"So? You're his wife?" one of them asked as Cheryl walked away.

"Uh-huh," Cheryl said over her shoulder. "But I hope you girls have luck finding another mark tonight. Ladies, Randy is already taken."

She heard one of them say something, but she couldn't make out the words, and she didn't care. *Boy, is Randy going to be surprised.* She made her way upstairs to the VIP section. She glanced at her watch. 1:00 a.m. *He must have caught a ride on the owner's private jet from Baltimore. And since I told him I had to stay with Stephen tonight, he decided to have a night out.*

It wasn't quite as dark upstairs as it was on the lower level, but as she looked around, she didn't spot Randy. And curiously, she didn't see any of his teammates. It wasn't like him to party by himself. She turned to head back downstairs to ask one of the drink waitresses exactly where Randy was, and that's when she noticed that both women had followed her up to VIP.

"Hey, I thought Randy was up here."

"He is," one of the women said, a huge grin on her face.

"Really?" Cheryl frowned. "Where? I didn't see him."

"Right there."

Cheryl looked over to where the waitress pointed, but all she saw was the back of a half-nude woman sliding up and down against the wall. Suddenly suspicious, Cheryl moved closer. She was about two feet away when she realized that the woman wasn't grinding against the wall, she was actually sitting astride a chair and standing up and then sitting down. Then, to her horror, she saw that it wasn't a chair that the woman was working on; it was a lap. Randy's lap!

Call it reflex, call it fury, but Cheryl let the tray and glasses drop to the floor but caught the magnum of champagne by the neck before it hit the ground, and in that same motion threw it at the girl's head. By some strange chance, Cheryl missed and hit the wall instead of the girl, but the commotion caused the girl to turn around. Cheryl was already seeing red, but her vision almost turned purple when she saw that it was Sexy Sanchez giving her husband a super-sonic lap dance.

"You bitch," Cheryl shrieked, moments before grabbing a handful of Sexy's hair. "I'ma fucking kill you, you fucking slut!"

Sexy screamed as she was pulled backward onto the floor, but before she could do anything else, Cheryl was on top of her pummeling her over and over.

"Cheryl, stop. You're hurting her." Randy grabbed his wife by her shoulders and tried to pull her off of Sexy. Though he wasn't fully successful, he lifted Cheryl up far enough for Sexy to wiggle from beneath her. Now it was Sexy's turn to get her licks in, and she went for it. She barreled into Cheryl, knocking both her and Randy onto the floor. Tables, bottles, glasses and even people were toppled as the two women bit, scratched, kicked, and punched each other; though truth be told—Randy—who was trying to break them up was receiving much of the beat down.

It took a good twenty minutes for security to be able to get the three of them outside. And once they did, Cheryl and Sexy went right back at it.

"You're a slut, you've always been a slut, and you'll never be anything but a fucking slut," Cheryl shouted at Sexy. She kept trying to get at the girl, but Randy was holding her back, while one of the security guards held Sexy.

"And you're nothing but a bitch," Sexy yelled back. Though one of the security guards had snatched up Sexy's blouse and given it to her once they were outside, Sexy hadn't bothered to put it on, and was standing outside bare-chested. Though her breasts weren't quite as big Cheryl's, they were big enough. And fabulous. Which only served to make Cheryl even more furious.

"Not a bitch. THE bitch," Cheryl said with a sneer. "And you're going to rue the day you crossed me."

"Sorry," Sexy retorted. "You might have to repeat that. I can't hear you over all the fuck I don't give."

"Oh, you're gonna hear my fist knocking out your teeth, you little whore."

"Hah! Please. Ain't nobody scared of you. You're mad because your hubby is looking for some new pussy."

"My baby don't want none of that stank pussy you got." Cheryl struggled to get away from Randy.

"Well, he must not think it's too stank; if you hadn't interrupted us, he woulda been licking it in a minute," Sexy said with a smirk.

"Like hell he would have, you fucking whore!"

"Oh, first I'm a slut, and now I'm a whore." Sexy laughed.

"That's right," Cheryl sneered. "And if dicks were airplanes, your mouth would be an airport."

Sexy opened her mouth as if to shout another insult, but suddenly seemed to change her mind as a smile slowly crossed her face. "You're pretty fucking witty, Cheryl. Too bad your husband is ready to trade up for a real woman. And the hell of it is the fact that you *know* it's a fact." Sexy chuckled, then started laughing. "You know beyond a shadow of a doubt that your husband wants this. And the fact that you're out here trying to weave and bob and throwing insults indicates that you're fully aware that if I want Randy, he's mine."

Her words stunned Cheryl into momentary silence. Not merely the spiteful content, but the way in which the words were delivered. Little Miss Hootchie-Girl-Slut was suddenly speaking and enunciating as if she had more than merely a fourth-grade education. *There's more to this chick than meets the eye.*

"Randy," Cheryl said calmly. "You can let me go."

"Cheryl—"

"I'm serious," Cheryl said quietly. "You can let me go."

Randy released her, but warily watched as she straightened her clothes. "Baby—"

Cheryl held up her hand. "Hold on one moment, please." She turned to look at Sexy. "Okay, let's get this straight once and for all." She took a deep breath. "Now, Randy," she said, still staring at the girl, "do you intend to—or want to—leave me for little Miss Sanchez?"

"Of course not, Cheryl," Randy said, moving even closer to his wife. He tried to pull her into an embrace, but she deftly side-stepped it.

Sexy rolled her eyes, though a big grin was plastered on her face.

"Are you sure, Randy?" Cheryl continued, still keeping her gaze on Sexy. "I believe you, of course, because you've never lied to me. However, little Miss Sanchez, here, might think you're only saying that to appease me. And," she paused, "it would be hard to blame her, since the two of you were all but fucking right out in public, when everyone knows you have a wife."

"Babe, I can explain—"

Cheryl held her hand up. "No, sweetie, I'm not asking for an explanation. I know she probably slipped something in your drink for you to act like such an idiot." The look on Sexy's face let Cheryl know that she had probably hit on the truth. "All I want is for you to inform little Miss Sanchez, right now, that's she's playing out of her league, because there's no way you'd let a slut like her break up our happy home. Would you mind doing that, sweetie?"

Cheryl crossed her arms, and waited. She breathed a sigh of relief when Randy immediately faced Sexy and without hesitation, grimly stated: "I love my wife and I have no intention of leaving her for you or anyone else. What happened tonight was crazy, should never have happened, and will never happen again." He then turned back to Cheryl and put his arm around her waist. "Baby, let's go home so I can get some of your good loving."

Cheryl smiled at Sexy, then put her arms around Randy and gave him a big kiss. She then winked at Sexy as she linked arms with her husband and walked toward Randy's Maybach. Though she was smiling, Cheryl was still seething inside. *If Randy thinks everything's going to be all lovey-dovey when we get home, boy, is he in for a fucking surprise. I'm going to—*

"Goodnight, Randy. Give me a call tomorrow and let me know when you want to get together again," Sexy called out in a sing-song voice.

Cheryl wanted so much to turn around and charge the girl, but instead she kept telling herself, *Remember, Cheryl, prison orange is not your color. Prison orange is not your color—*

"What were you thinking?" Yusef glowered at Sexy, swiping at his nose and stalking toward her in an aggressive manner.

But Sexy didn't cower. She looked him in the eyes and stated simply, "How many times do I have to tell you, I had too much to drink."

"Having too much to drink shouldn't make you come out of character and act like a slut unless that's what you are." Frustrated and angry, Yusef ran a hand down the side of his face. "Didn't it dawn on you that I'd find out that you got the hots for my boy and that you gave him a lap dance...in public?" Yusef shook his head. "What were you thinking? Did you even care about how I'd feel?"

"Look, I don't have any answers for you. How can I defend my actions if I was fuckin' drunk?" Sexy said in a shrill voice. "I refuse to be interrogated for hours, so..." She sighed in exasperation and then gazed at him challengingly. "If you want to break up, all you have to do is say so, and I'll pack my shit and leave."

Yusef gawked at her. "Breaking up is not an option. I've been bragging to the boys about how great our sex life is and now my teammates are looking at me crazy—like I can't control my woman. I have to prove them wrong. Now, this is the plan. We're gonna go look at rings, pick out something, and announce that we're officially engaged and planning a wedding."

She shot an icy look at him. "I'm not ready for marriage."

"Why not? Are you in love with Randy?" he asked disdainfully.

"No, I'm not in love with Randy, but I'm also not willing to get married merely to salvage your public image and to soothe your bruised ego. That's fake and hypocritical. I grew up with fake-ass parents and I'm not following in their footsteps."

"Ever since word got out about you throwing the pussy at Randy, I've become the laughingstock in the locker room—do you realize that?"

An idea popped into Sexy's mind and a glint appeared in her eyes.

"What's that look for?" he asked suspiciously.

Flirtatiously, she slid the thin strap of her top over her shoulder. "How about we make a sex tape for you to share with the boys? Let them see the steamy love we make." She unsnapped the front of her short skirt. "When they see the way I put it on you—the way I suck your dick three and four times a day, they'll be patting you on the back instead of throwing slurs."

"A sex tape? I don't know about that. I have to worry about my image. I could lose some big endorsement deals that my agent is working on if—"

"I want to make a sex tape, and you're worrying about your stupid image." She shook her head. "I had no idea you were such a pussy." Sexy gave Yusef a look of loathing as she pulled her strap up and readjusted her skirt.

"Babe, it's not like that." He reached for her hand. "We're talking about my future. I'd be a fool to allow myself to get caught on tape."

"I'll be sleeping on the pullout bed in the other room," she informed Yusef and closed the door that separated the bedroom and living area.

Hearing Yusef pacing around the bedroom gave Sexy wicked pleasure. She knew that having to sleep alone made him miserable, but she had no pity for him; it was exactly what he deserved for turning down her offer.

Eating Garrett's popcorn from a tin container and drinking white wine, she stretched out on the pullout bed and watched *Catfish* on MTV, and at some point, she drifted off to sleep.

In the midst of a steamy dream about Randy, warm, wet heat enveloped her as Randy ran large, callous-roughened hands all over her shoulders and back while his velvet tongue licked a damp trail around her tightened nipple. Fingers tugged gently on her other nipple, and then squeezed hard, almost to the point of pain. Sexy inhaled sharply as pleasure spiked through her. Her body thrummed with anticipation and she grew instantly wet. Yearning for him to go lower—to place his skilled mouth on her heated center, she arched upward, moaning as she widened her legs, inviting him to lick inside her creamy center.

His mouth grew more urgent, sucking greedily, biting at the tips of her nipples until they were aching and swollen.

"My body is yours," she murmured as she writhed with yearning. "Do you forgive me for acting like a jerk, baby?"

At the sound of Yusef's voice, Sexy's eyes popped open in disappointment and alarm. How dare Yusef crawl into bed and trick her into thinking Randy was making love to her. Her first instinct was to bat his hands away and kick him out of the sofa bed, but when he lowered his head and his tongue began stroking down her belly, stopping short of her mound, she began slowly gyrating. Teasingly, his fingers played in the curly hair at the juncture between her thighs. His playfulness was torture, causing her sensitive bud to ache with need.

"Suck it for me," she pleaded as she squirmed and pressed her hips upward.

But Yusef continued teasing her, caressing her inner thighs with a feathery touch that gave Sexy shivers of pleasure, but also gave her a tremendous amount of frustration.

Allowing her legs to fall wide open, Sexy's tone went from pleading to sounding pissed off. She propped herself up on an elbow. "It's time for you to stop playing and eat this pussy, Yusef. If you're gonna keep teasing me, then get the hell out of here and leave me alone."

Yusef looked confused and wounded. "I thought you liked it when I played with your pussy until it's soaking wet."

She sat upright and stared at him. "We're not even speaking to each other, so don't be trying to get back on my good side by touching all over me. Fuck the foreplay; eat it!"

Yusef complied, spreading Sexy's pussy open and exposing her rose-colored clit. "You don't have to tell me twice," he uttered. His satin soft tongue ran between her inner lips and then settled on her throbbing nub, licking and alternately sucking with hot, urgent lips. Tiny bursts of flames sparked through her body, inciting her to cry out and beg him to delve deeper—to assault her with his tongue.

While Yusef vigorously thrust his tongue in and out of her wetness, Sexy reached for his dick, stroking it and telling him how hard she wanted him to fuck her and how deeply she wanted to be filled with his cum.

Unable to endure another second of her dirty talk, Yusef bit down gently on her clit, bringing Sexy to a shuddering climax. She shrieked as her orgasm tore through her, and while in the midst of riding wave after wave of pleasure, Yusef straddled her and inserted his thickness inside her clenching pussy.

"Is Randy's dick bigger than mine?" Yusef asked in a gruff voice.

"I didn't fuck—"

"Did you like the way his big dick split you in two?" he interrupted.

Huh? What the fuck? Yusef was a bigger freak than Sexy had realized, but she instantly decided to go along with the sexual fantasy he was leading her into. "Randy's big Alabama dick had me so sore I could barely walk when he finished with me."

"Oh, baby, I know he loved getting his dick wet inside my pretty baby." Yusef groaned in ecstasy as he drove himself in deeper, winding his hips and moaning. "Did you make him strap up?" he asked breathlessly.

"There wasn't any time for that."

Yusef's body went still momentarily. "You let that nigga raw-dog the pussy that belongs to me?" he asked incredulously.

"Uh-huh. He came hard and splashed a load of hot cum inside me."

"Oh, God," Yusef responded, sounding blissfully tortured, as if he were caught between ecstasy and emotional anguish.

"I bet Randy wants some more of your sweet pussy, doesn't he?" Yusef quickened his stroke, his breathing choppy as he grew close to climaxing.

"You know it," she bragged.

"Are you gonna give it to him?" Yusef sounded like a tortured soul.

"Randy Alston can get all the pussy he wants—anytime and anyplace."

"Argghhh." Yusef exploded as lightning bolts of torturous pleasure shot through him. In a weakened state, he collapsed on top of Sexy. He rolled off her and lay flat on his back. "You have no idea how much I love you," he murmured.

I don't know about love, but your dumb ass is thoroughly whipped, she thought as she watched his chest rise and fall.

"I got a new card, and it's all yours. You can get whatever you want," Yusef had said with a broad smile when he handed her the shiny card before he left for practice.

Sexy was pleasantly surprised. Who knew that talking dirty—especially dirty talk that detailed getting it in with another man—would earn her a new credit card?

After treating herself to a day at the spa where she had her fingernails and toenails embellished with Swarovski crystals, it was time to go back to the hotel and prepare to play wifey to Yusef. She checked the time on her phone and was surprised that the hours had flown by. Practice had ended several hours ago, and Yusef was no doubt, back at the hotel, pacing around the suite, anxious to get his dick sucked. Oh, well, he'd have to wait until after she indulged herself with a little retail therapy.

With a fresh credit card in her purse, she could shop anywhere, but having recently developed an intense love affair with Prada, Sexy made a beeline for the upscale store. After selecting two pairs of pricey sunglasses, she traipsed over to the handbags and her heart skipped several beats as she ogled a pink tote with metal studs and stones. At $3,150 the bag cost more than any bag she owned, but she had to have it. Hopefully, Yusef wouldn't complain about the price. After all, he did say that she could get anything she wanted, didn't he?

The shoe department was calling her name, and as she headed in that direction, she skidded to a sudden stop. Were her eyes deceiving her or was that Randy Alston browsing and looking terribly awkward as he checked out women's scarves?

That's Randy, all right. And out of all the places he could be in New York City, he's in here with me. If that's not a sign that we're meant to be together, then I don't know what is. Her face alight with a bright smile, Sexy sashayed over to Randy.

"Hello, stranger," she greeted in a melodic tone.

Randy did a double-take, stunned to find Sexy standing next to him. "What, uh, what the heck are you doing here?"

"Shopping," she said, twirling her hair.

He backed up a little, putting a safe distance between him and Sexy, but she advanced toward him. "I owe you an apology for my conduct the other night at the club. That's not how I usually act, but I had too much to drink, and sometimes liquor causes me to behave in an unladylike manner." She sighed and shook her head regretfully. "I'm really sorry that I got you in trouble with your wife."

"Apology accepted," he replied, nodding earnestly, and then walking away.

"I wish there were something I could do to make up for my actions; I don't think a mere apology is enough," Sexy said, following him.

"No, really. It's okay."

"But I feel so bad for your wife. She didn't deserve to be humiliated in that way. The last thing I wanted to do was to cause problems in your marriage. Maybe I should give Cheryl a call and tell her personally how very sorry I am." Sexy gazed at Randy through eyes clouded with remorse. She sniffled and dabbed at the lone tear that trickled down her cheek.

"Aw, don't cry. It's all right," Randy assured her while giving her several pats on the shoulder. "Cheryl and I will be fine. We have a strong bond and whenever life throws a monkey wrench in our path, we step over it, and somehow we become stronger."

A monkey wrench in their path? Sexy had never heard that expression. Randy sure had a country-bumpkin way of expressing himself, but it was all good; a little bit of country talk wouldn't dissuade her. She plastered on a smile and nudged her head back toward the scarves. "Are you looking for a gift for Cheryl? After all the trouble I caused, the least I can do is to help you pick out something awesome for her."

"Thanks. I'm out of my element in the women's department, and I could use some help. Cheryl's a model, you know, and she's so classy, she only wears the latest fashion." Randy paused a beat and then continued, "I should rephrase that. Cheryl *used* to be a model, but now she's concentrating on starting our family."

"Is she pregnant?" Sexy asked, worriedly gnawing on her bottom lip.

"Not yet, but we're working on it." Randy smiled broadly, like he was already a proud father. "It's all I can think about."

Sexy gave a sigh of relief. *Over my dead body will that haughty bitch bear your child. I'm gonna have to work fast to get Randy out of Cheryl's tight clutches and into bed. Once I whip it on him, he won't give a damn about that bitch on wheels whom he had the misfortune of marrying. My pussy is so good, he may be tempted to miss practice so he can lay up in bed with me.*

"If you want to get back in Cheryl's good graces, you should forget about these corny scarves and get her a new bag. I saw one that cost a small fortune, but it was the exquisite sort of accessory that someone like Cheryl would carry. You know, if you're willing to spend that kind of dough."

"Money's not a problem, and nothing's too expensive for my baby. Show me the purse."

Sexy led the way to the handbags and led Randy to the exact pink tote that she'd purchased for herself. She pointed to it. "Doesn't this sparkly tote scream Cheryl's name?"

"It sure does," Randy agreed, and whipped out his credit card.

After Randy completed the purchase, and had the tote bag beautifully gift-wrapped, he and Sexy exited the store together.

Sexy frantically racked her brain, trying to think of a way to prolong her time with Randy.

Outside the store, the laughter of a young couple riding in a horse-drawn carriage rang out.

Sexy sighed. "Even though I've been living in the city for three months, I still feel like a visitor."

"That's exactly how I feel," Randy exclaimed. "New York is so huge, I still don't know my way around."

"I've yet to see any of the tourist attractions, and my family has been bugging me for T-shirts and other souvenirs," she lied. Her parents had no idea she'd moved to New York.

Randy clunked himself upside the head as if struck by a sudden idea. "That reminds me. My cousin Nettie and my Aunt Pearl are gonna pitch a fit if I don't hurry up and send them a couple of those *I Love New York* T-shirts."

"If you have some time, we could go to Times Square and pick up some souvenirs for our families."

"I don't know if that's a good idea."

"Making our families happy is a great idea."

Randy hesitated momentarily, then bit his lip and said, "Well, I don't think Cheryl would mind if I'm a little late getting home."

"I'm sure she won't mind at all when she sees the awesome present you bought her."

Randy escorted Sexy to the parking lot and retrieved his Maybach. As they drew close to Forty-Second Street with all the flashy billboards and neon signs, Sexy detected a glimmer in his eyes.

"I love seeing this area at night. It's always lit up like the Fourth of July," he said happily. "I done drove past Times Square mo' times than I can shake a stick at, ya know..." Flushing in embarrassment, Randy paused. "Uh, I meant to say, I've driven past

Times Square quite a few times, but I've never taken the time to walk around and explore."

"I haven't either, and it'll be fun sharing the experience with a friend." Sexy smiled warmly at Randy. "By the way, Randy, you don't have to be self-conscious about your Southern accent or the way you speak when you're around me."

"Well, Cheryl put a lot of effort into getting me diction lessons—"

"She's a smart and savvy woman, and I have to give her props for making sure that you speak articulately when dealing with the media." She gave him a sympathetic look. "But it has to be a burden trying to speak the King's English all the time. I think you should be able to relax and be yourself when you're away from the cameras and chilling with family and friends." She gazed at him and cracked a smile. "Besides, I like the way you talk. You sound a lot like the rapper, T.I."

"You think I talk like T.I.?" Randy laughed heartily. "That's a new one—I never heard that before."

After Randy parked, they walked along Broadway. Sexy suddenly tugged at his hand. "Ooo, let's go in here," she urged, pulling him into a three-level video arcade.

Randy didn't require much persuasion. "Wow, this is the bomb," he enthused, clearly impressed as he peered around the environment of the high-tech gaming center. Amidst swirling lights and techno music, Sexy and Randy were like two kids, racing from one activity to the next. They put on headsets for Virtual Pac-Man, cocked shotguns as they played Total Recoil, and tested their skills in the laser maze, laughing uproariously as they wove their way through a complex web of laser light beams.

Worn-out and ravenous, they peeled themselves off the Virtual Hang Glider and went upstairs to the venue's eatery. Entering the cybercafe where patrons were hunched over computers, munching on cheesecake, crepes, and some were guzzling beer, Sexy was suddenly famished.

"I smell burgers—yum!" Filled with youthful exuberance, Sexy rushed ahead to the food counter.

"You're like a little kid," Randy remarked when he caught up with Sexy. They both ordered cheeseburgers with mushrooms and fried onions. At their table, when Sexy bit into her burger, ketchup oozed out the corner of her mouth. Reflexively, Randy reached over and dabbed at the ketchup with his thumb. Sexy stopped chewing. Momentarily suspended in time, they both stared into each other's eyes.

Randy broke their gaze, and self-consciously picked up a napkin and wiped away the ketchup on his thumb.

"It's getting late. We'd better get those T-shirts and head home," Sexy commented in a sad tone of voice.

"Are you okay?"

"Yeah, sort of."

"What's wrong?" Randy leaned forward, his brow creased in concern.

Sexy frowned. "Nothing's wrong."

"Why do you look so sad all of a sudden?"

"Well, I had so much fun today, and it reminded me of times when life was simpler. When I didn't have to be around so many fake people. A time when I didn't have to worry about fitting in with the Yankees wives, or using the correct utensils when dining at elegant places...you know what I mean?"

Randy nodded. "I do. I wish I could simply play ball and not be concerned about the cut of my suit or letting my country grammar slip out."

Sexy reached out and caressed the top of Randy's hand. "We're more alike than I realized. Two small-town, ordinary people tossed into a world of pretentious New Yorkers."

Randy nodded and then slid his hand from beneath Sexy's stroking fingertips.

They left the arcade and instead of buying souvenirs, they went straight to Randy's car. Randy was pensive during the drive to Sexy's hotel.

"Hey, Randy, I have an idea," she piped in, sounding upbeat and bubbly.

"What's on your mind?"

"Have you been to the Empire State Building?"

"Nah."

"Me either. Wanna check it out tomorrow?"

"Uh, no. Cheryl wouldn't like that."

"Why not? We're only friends...it's not like we'll be doing anything wrong."

Randy thought for a while and then said, "You're right. And you're a lot of fun, Sexy. Yeah, let's go for it."

He glided to a stop in front of the Ritz-Carlton hotel. "Sounds like a plan," he said, smiling at her.

Sexy leaned over to give Randy a quick peck on the cheek. But somehow, their lips met, and what was intended as a friendly gesture, turned into an actual kiss. Although there was no tongue involved, Randy's lips lingered upon hers and the tenderness of the kiss caused her heartbeat to quicken.

"I didn't mean that. I'm sorry," Randy muttered after abruptly pulling away. Looking troubled, he dropped his head and let out a groan.

"Don't worry about that kiss, Randy. We're only friends...it didn't mean anything," she said nonchalantly. Randy popped the trunk and they both exited the car. Standing near the open trunk, Sexy retrieved her shopping bags and then gave a fluttery hand wave. "See you tomorrow, Randy."

"Leave me alone," Cheryl shouted at the top of her lungs. "I hate you."

"Babe, I'm sorry. I really am," Randy said, continuing to knock on the bathroom door. "Aw, please come on out."

Cheryl slammed the toilet seat down and sat down, butt-naked, as tears rolled down her face. *This can't be happening. Not to me. How could he?*

"Cheryl, come on now," Randy pleaded on the other side of the door. "Give me a chance to explain!"

Explain? How could he possibly explain? How could he have done this to her? And here she was the perfect wife. Well, maybe not the perfect wife, but as perfect as she could possibly be. Yes, she spent a lot of money, but then he had a lot of money, and he never complained. And hadn't she polished him up? Given him a makeover—got rid of the horrid Jheri curl, sent him to one of the best dermatologists in the city to get rid of the acne, bought him a whole new wardrobe, and sent him for diction lessons? Sure, it was his money that paid for it all, but it was all at her urging.

And she'd never denied him sex. She'd given him loads of sex. Incredible sex. Mind-blowing sex. Sex that had him crying with gratitude afterward.

She'd even forgiven him for that ridiculous night in the club with that tramp a few weeks earlier. Well, okay, not forgiven him, but at least she had stopped holding it over his head after she blasted him when they got home that night.

And this is how he repaid her?

"Cheryl, I swear, if you don't unlock this bathroom door, I'm going to call a locksmith."

"Oh? Is it really a locksmith you want to call? Not your girl-friend?" Cheryl shouted.

"Oh, come on," Randy whined.

"It's not like you have some aversion to calling her!" Cheryl jumped up and stomped her bare foot on the cold marble floor. "You called me her name while I was down on my knees sucking your dick!"

"Baby, please! I said I'm sorry, and I so mean it."

Cheryl could hear the tears in Randy's voice. Yes, he was sorry. He hadn't meant to call her Sexy. But that didn't make it okay. Nothing could make it okay. She sank back down onto the toilet seat and buried her face in her hands, sobbing loud and uncontrollably.

"Cheryl, baby, I love you. Please don't cry," Randy said, through his own sobs. "I've never wanted to hurt you, and I'm so sorry I have. You've got to forgive me, baby. You have got to. Don't you know you're my whole world? I'd die without you, Cheryl, baby."

That damn slut! How did she manage to get into Randy's head? Cheryl had to admit that the girl was pretty. No, truth be told, she was downright beautiful. But Randy had been around plenty of beautiful girls since becoming one of the Yankees' most valuable members. What was it about Sexy? She was crass, crude, and well... a slut. Randy had never been attracted to women like that before. Why now? And why Sexy?

She could hear Randy slump to the floor outside the bathroom.

"I don't know what else to say, Cheryl," he said dismally. "I messed up. And I don't know what to do about it." He took a deep breath before continuing. "I don't deserve for you to forgive me," his voice started breaking again, "but I'm hoping you will. I'm hoping you know how much I love you and—"

Cheryl wrapped a towel around herself and then quietly opened the door. "And I love you, too." She sat down on the floor next to her husband. "I don't forgive you, but I love you."

Randy pulled her into his arms, squeezing her so hard she had to pull away in order to breathe. "So what's going on, Randy?" she asked wearily.

"What do you mean, babe?"

"With that girl." She let out a loud sigh. "What's going on between you and Sexy? You say you love me, and I do believe you...but what's up? Do you love her, too?"

"Aw, hell nah, Cheryl," Randy said in a whiny voice. "I don't believe you could even ask me something like that."

"Like what? It's not like all the indications aren't there. You two have been texting—"

"She started texting me," Randy protested. "I texted her back and asked how she even got my number."

"So you're saying that you only texted her that once?"

Randy hung his head and said nothing.

Cheryl sighed, tears welling up in her eyes again. "Exactly. And then I call to tell you I have to miss one of your games to hang out with Stephen and damn if you don't go out to a club with Miss Thang—"

"I told you I didn't go there with her," Randy said. "The owner of the club was at our game a couple of days before that night, and we got to talking, and I promised I'd stop in one evening. Since you were with Stephen, and I didn't have anything to do after I got back from Baltimore, I thought I'd stop by. I didn't know she was going to be there. And I sure as hell didn't know she was going to slip me a mickey."

"That's right, she slipped you a mickey, she and I have physically fought twice, and yet with all that, you still can't get her off your mind," Cheryl said angrily. "What is it? Don't I satisfy you anymore, Randy?"

"No, babe, it's not like that at all," Randy said quickly.

"Then how is it?" Cheryl asked, standing up; the towel she'd wrapped around herself fell to the floor. "How is it that I'm giving you a blow job and you moan, 'Oh, Sexy, yeah.' Exactly how does that come about?"

She walked into the living room, not waiting for an answer. Picking up the remote, she clicked on the television, but immediately muted it, then snuggled into a corner of the plush white, crushed-velvet sofa, pulled her legs up into her chest, and arms folded around them. She stared at the television screen, but saw nothing as she rocked back and forth thinking about Randy, Sexy, herself, and her marriage. Everything had been going so well, she thought, and they had been so happy. But then, somehow, Sexy Sanchez entered the picture.

I guess the only thing to do is to get her out of his head. I guess I'm going to have to—Cheryl shook her head. She hated to even think of it...but the thing is, it had worked in the past. She closed her eyes, and struggled to come up with another idea. She didn't realize she'd fallen to sleep until she heard, "Babe, come to bed."

Cheryl woke to Randy's gentle caresses on her face. She stretched, and then said in a little-girl voice and a fake pout: "Don't wanna."

She smiled inwardly as Randy's face broke out in a huge grin.

He knew this was her indication to him that she was back to being his loving wife, and was ready to play games.

"Well, then, I'm going to have to carry you to bed." Randy scooped her up from the couch and gallantly carried her into the bedroom as she giggled, and put up a playful struggle.

"I'm getting ready to walk in my door now. How soon can you get here?" Cheryl unlocked the door, and placed the bags from her latest shopping spree on the floor in the foyer. "Fifteen minutes? Great!"

Cheryl quickly called Randy, after hanging up, and made sure practice wouldn't be over for an hour; she was on a mission, and she needed privacy.

"Come on in." Cheryl waited until the man walked in, then peered into the hallway before closing the apartment door behind him.

"I can't stay long. I have another appointment in another hour." The man sat down on the plush velvet sofa without waiting to be asked. He set a black leather satchel next to him, and then leaned back; spreading his arms out over the back of the sofa as if claiming it, forcing Cheryl to sit on the matching overstuffed armchair. Not that she would have it any other way. Dwayne Ligon was someone perfect for the business she needed done, but was not someone she wanted to be close to in any other way. He was tall, dark, and undeniably handsome, but the air of danger around him—accented by a long thin scar on his left cheek—was anything but appealing.

"You want something to drink, Ligon?"

"Naw, ma, I'm good." The toothpick in his mouth switched from one side to the other. "But you go ahead and do you."

They had met while she was a teenager, and a working girl. She was entering a Washington, D.C. restaurant with a "date" as he was casually strolling out. She noticed him because of the scar, but also because he wore a long black leather coat, though it was early spring. Minutes after she and her date were seated and there was a commotion, someone found a wealthy stockbroker in a stall in the men's room. Shot in the head.

The next time she saw him was a few months later when she was leaving her Harlem apartment building heading to the store. He was standing on the stoop with his arms crossed, as if waiting for someone. Her eyes widened, but she tried to keep them focused in front of her. Before she turned the corner, she turned to look at him and almost had a heart attack when she saw that he was staring intently at her as if trying to remember where he'd seen her. She decided not to go home that night.

When she did return to her building a few days later, she was relieved not to see him. She rang for the elevator, but when the doors opened, the man with the scar was inside, along with the body of a local small-time dealer. She ran outside, leaned over the stoop and started vomiting. As soon as she halfway recovered, she ran down the block—not sure where she was going but wanting to put distance between her and the gruesome sight she'd seen. Not looking where she was going, it was no wonder she ran into someone. Cheryl gasped when she saw who it was.

"Sorry," she said, trying to now move past him.

He grabbed her by the arm, slightly twisting it as he removed her pocketbook from her shoulder. With one hand, he reached inside and pulled out her school ID. He looked at it, and then slipped it into his pocket. "If I don't hear anything bad, I'll figure I owe you one, Cheryl Blanton. If I *do* hear anything bad, I'll figure I owe you one."

Cheryl didn't run into him until seven years later when she and Stephen were dining at The Cecil on 118th Street in Harlem. If she had seen him when they walked in, she would have turned right back around, but it wasn't until the waitress was placing their salads on the table that her eyes wandered to the corner of the restaurant. He was sitting there, as cool as could be, drinking a bourbon and nodding his head to the tune the saxophone player was blowing while looking at her.

She was about to signal Stephen that they needed to leave, but before she could, he jumped up to go say "hi" to a cute guy he recognized. Before she was aware, the man was sitting in Stephen's vacant chair.

"I saw you in *Essence* magazine, Cheryl Blanton."

She didn't know if she were more surprised that he remembered her name, or that he actually read *Essence*. She wasn't inclined to ask about either, but he responded as if she had.

"Naw," he said with a dry chuckle, "I don't normally read *Essence*. I was taking my lady to the doctor's office, and there was nothing else to read. And when I saw your picture, I recognized you and later dug up that card I took. Then I looked you up on the Internet."

"Oh, that's nice," Cheryl said, trying to keep her voice level and a smile on her face.

"Do you have a card?"

"A card?" Cheryl looked at him quizzically.

"A business card." The man reached into his pocket and pulled out a gold business card holder, removed a card, and handed it to her.

"Dwayne Ligon," Cheryl read out loud. "But it doesn't say what you do."

"I do whatever needs to be done," Ligon said carefully. "Do you understand, ma?"

Cheryl nodded.

"Good. Now give me your card."

Cheryl handed him one, and for the first time, she saw Dwayne Ligon smile.

"I'm glad you've done well for yourself, Cheryl Blanton. Get in touch with me if you need me," Ligon said, getting up from the table. "But only if you need me." He winked at her, then added before walking away: "After all, I owe you one."

The first time Cheryl called on Ligon (she always referred to him by his last name) was when a client she booked on her own, rather than through an agency, refused to pay her. Two days later, she had her pay, minus the ten percent commission Ligon charged for his services. Over the years, she had used him a few more times, but she had never been to his home, and this was the first time he was in hers.

"You got a lotta flowers."

Cheryl tried to hide her surprise. It was true there were vases of flowers of all sorts around the room—and around the entire house—but most people who visited the apartment for the first time mentioned how fabulous and spacious the place was. And Ligon certainly didn't seem to be the type to be in interested in flora. But then again, who knew? Maybe he studied botany while he was in prison. After all, if there could be a Birdman of Alcatraz, why couldn't there be a Flowerman of Leavenworth?

"Shall we get down to business?" Ligon asked, pulling out three folders from the satchel.

Cheryl eagerly leaned forward.

"Okay, I've shadowed your man and I have his schedule down." He handed her one of the folders. "All I need is your word and I'll take care of it."

Cheryl nodded, and placed the folder on her lap without looking at it. "And you're sure that you won't get caught or anything? Will you be doing it yourself?"

Ligon answered her with a cold stare.

"Sorry," Cheryl said, biting her lip. "I say let's go forward as soon as possible. But please make sure that he knows that if he ever contacts me again, it'll be worse the next time."

"Not a problem," Ligon said, with a nod. "I'll let you know as soon as it's done." He tapped his finger on the second folder. "Now, the first matter is already paid in full, but as we discussed on the telephone—"

Cheryl pulled an envelope from her pocket and handed it to Ligon who placed it in his satchel without looking inside.

Ligon tapped the folder on his knee before handing it to her. "There's a full report on your second matter—from her birth to present. I don't know how much you know about the young lady, but this one here is a trip. And," he stood up and picked up his satchel, tucking it under his arm, "if you want a job done on her, it's going to cost a little more."

"Why? Because she's female?" Cheryl took the folder, and had to call on an enormous amount of willpower not to immediately flip it open.

"No." Ligon was already halfway to the door. "Because there will be a lot more people asking questions. That family of hers will be all over it."

Cheryl locked the door behind Ligon, then leaned against it, breathing heavily as she gazed at the folder still lying on the chair. *Okay, Miss Sexy Sanchez, let's find out what dirty secrets you have that I can use to hang your little stank ass.*

She tried to calm her breathing as she poured herself a glass of Chablis. If there was one thing she knew about the Yankees organization, it was that they hated even the possibility of a scandal. If there was something really dirty in Sexy's past and they found out about it, they would be quick to call Yusef in and give him an ultimatum, get rid of the skank or get put on the chopping block. And that would automatically cool Randy's ardor for the slut. He might have the hots for her, but he wouldn't put his playing career on the line for her. Of course the Yankees wouldn't get rid of Randy—under any circumstances—but he still didn't really realize his worth to the team. No, he wouldn't want to take the chance.

Cheryl sat down and slowly opened the folder, surprised at the neatly typed report Ligon had prepared. She wondered if he had a secretary or if had typed it himself. She ran her fingers over the papers, her mouth actually watering as she anticipated the salacious information she would soon be reading. She took a sip of wine, and settled to read.

Amanda Nehru, huh? She knew, of course, that Sexy wasn't her real first name, but she had assumed that Sanchez was authentic. However, her exotic features and wavy hair could very well be attributed to an Asian heritage rather than Latino.

Birth date, April 15, 1997. Figures she would be born on tax day— if there was ever a taxing bitch, she was certainly it. Whoa! Cheryl reread the birth date. *Nineteen ninety-seven? That means Sexy, or whatever the hell her name is, is barely seventeen! Oh, shit!* Cheryl jumped up, not caring that the folder fell to the floor, and pumped her arm in the air. *Oh, I got that little bitch now!*

She picked up her glass and gulped down the rest of her wine, then poured herself another. This was too good to be true. She'd only recently turned seventeen in April. The wives said Sexy had flown down to spring training to play freaky-deaky with Yusef, and spring training had ended in March. That meant Yusef had actually been fucking an underage girl back in March! *Ooh, wait until the Yankees' brass hears about this!* Cheryl took another gulp of wine. True, the news would end Yusef's playing career, but, oh, well, she thought. Collateral damage. And perhaps Sexy would do the right thing, and simply back out of the picture if told what would happen if she didn't. Then no one would have to find out. But somehow, Cheryl doubted it. That skank didn't care about anyone but herself.

Cheryl reached for the telephone, eager to tell Stephen the dirt she'd dug up, but then changed her mind. She bent down and retrieved the folder and papers from the floor, intent on seeing the other scandalous information that was available. May as well hit Stephen with everything at the same time. One of the papers, however, was a photocopy of a photograph—a headshot of a man who looked vaguely familiar. She hurriedly put the papers in order, and eagerly sat down again to resume her investigation.

Born in New York City, but raised in Bryn Mawr, Pennsylvania. Father: Dr. Patag Nehru, dean of the University of Pennsylvania Medical School. Mother: Clarissa Nehru, a socialite.

Patag Nehru? Cheryl flipped through the papers until she found the photograph again. Could it really be? The same Dr. Nehru who'd adopted her son? But the report showed that Amanda was the couple's only child. She flipped through the papers until she finally found the birth certificate. There it was. Patag Nehru was listed as father, and Clarissa the mother. Child born... Cheryl gasped. Child born at New York Hospital at 6:17 a.m. The same year, the same day, the same time, and the same hospital—could this all be a series of coincidences? But no, her child was a boy. Dr. Nehru had told her so. Cheryl closed her eyes, remembering that day. Yes, that's what he told her, but she'd never seen her baby. Had he lied?

Cheryl stood up and slowly walked toward the window in a

daze. She held the folder loosely in her hands, and the papers fell out, one by one, with each step she took, but she didn't notice. She stared out at the beautiful view, but saw nothing. Her last thought before she lost consciousness and fell to the floor: *That little bitch is my child.*

S exy and Randy didn't have to wait in the ridiculously long
line at the Empire State Building. Putting his celebrity status
to good use, Randy was given the VIP treatment, and management whisked them past the throng of tourists waiting to visit the
world's tallest structure.

The view from the eighty-sixth-floor observation deck was
breathtaking. "I'm not super religious," Sexy commented, "but
being so high up in the sky makes me feel closer to God."

"I know what you mean," Randy said, nodding.

Sexy glanced at the ESB brochure and grinned at him. "Are you
ready to go higher and visit the Top Deck on the one hundred-
second floor?"

"I thought we were at the top."

"Nope. There're sixteen floors above the observation deck."

"Okay, let's do it."

They boarded an elevator and when they exited and looked out
the window, Randy muttered, "Whoa, this is a little too high up
for me."

"Don't tell me you're afraid of heights," Sexy teased while snap-
ping pictures of the spectacular view of the city and beyond, and
with several clicks, she posted the images on Instagram.

"Can't say I've ever been up this high—except in an airplane."

"It feels incredible being up here," she said excitedly, continuing to take pictures from different angles. "Don't you want to get some pictures of the view?"

"No, thanks; I'm good," Randy said, looking somewhat nauseous. Sexy gazed at him with her head tilted to the side. She noticed that his complexion had taken on a grayish tint. "Aw, you're not kidding around—you're really feeling a little woozy, aren't you?"

Randy nodded, and Sexy returned her camera phone inside her purse. "Let's go to one of the restaurants and see if we can find something to settle your stomach," Sexy said, sounding mature and nurturing. In reality, she didn't know the first thing about caring for a sick person. She was merely repeating something her mother often said when Sexy was a child and complained of a tummy ache.

"Yeah, let's go," Randy agreed, eager for a decrease in altitude. As the elevator descended, Randy's complexion returned to normal.

"Feeling better?" Sexy inquired.

"Much," he replied, looking embarrassed.

"Lots of people are afraid of heights. That's nothing to be ashamed of."

Randy peered at Sexy curiously. "How is it that you read me so well?"

She shrugged. "I feel like I've known you for a long time. Like maybe in another lifetime, you were my big brother." She glanced down at the brochure. "Hey, you wanna get something to eat? Inside the building, there's a Chipotle and also Europa Café."

"I'm not crazy about Mexican food, so let's try that Europa place."

They found their way to Europa Café, and Sexy ordered a quiche and lemonade and Randy ordered a hearty turkey breast sandwich and a cup of coffee.

Sexy wrinkled her nose. "Never could understand why people

drink coffee. It tastes bitter and it gives you the jitters, so what's the point of it?"

Randy laughed good-naturedly. "It tastes good to me, and I don't know anything about getting any jitters. It gives me an energy boost. Besides, I'm grateful to get a regular cup of Joe. It's nice to have regular coffee instead of always drinking that African kind that Cheryl brews at home."

Sexy tilted her head curiously. "African kind?"

"Cheryl is into this imported, African coffee. She says the high-quality beans are grown a certain way and it's the only coffee she allows in the house. She drinks two and three cups a day, but I don't touch the stuff. It's too strong for me. I love me some Dunkin' Donuts coffee, and usually get a large cup every day. My wife is a class act, and you wouldn't catch her stepping a foot inside no Dunkin' Donuts—she's a Starbucks kind of girl. Yeah, Cheryl is something else; she really enjoys the finer things in life," he said fondly and with a trace of pride.

Argh! It was a struggle for Sexy to keep her mouth shut and not speak her mind about Cheryl's pretentiousness, but she managed to smile sweetly, as if she thought that haughty, self-absorbed tramp was absolutely adorable.

At the table, Randy fussed with his sandwich, painstakingly, pulling out slivers of onion and slices of tomato. "I have a confession," he said, looking up at Sexy.

"Oh, yeah? What do you want to confess?" she asked with eyes widened, inquisitively.

"I really enjoy gazing at your face. Aside from my wife, you have to be one of the most beautiful women I've ever set eyes on. Those Hollywood celebrities ain't got a thing on you, girl."

Sexy pretended to blush, but hearing that she was beautiful was not a news flash; it was something she'd heard her entire life. "Thank you for the compliment," she replied with a demure smile.

"Another thing... I think you're a really sweet girl. You're nothing like the way people try to make you out to be."

"People shouldn't judge another person until they know them," she said with a weary sigh, and then suddenly brightened. "I'm glad we're becoming friends, Randy. I don't know anyone in New York and the players' wives have a clique..." Her words trailed off and she briefly dropped her gaze. She looked up and said, "I've tried to make friends with the ladies, but I guess I'm not sophisticated enough to be in their inner circle."

Randy scowled. "You've got plenty of sophistication as far as I'm concerned. You're smart and pretty...well-dressed. I think some of the wives might view you as a threat."

"Why? Yusef and I are getting engaged soon, and after the season ends, we're getting married. So, if anyone thinks that I'm trying to steal their husband, they're mistaken."

"You and Yusef are getting married?"

"Mm-hmm."

"Wow. Congratulations...I suppose."

"You suppose?"

Randy shifted in his seat uncomfortably. "Wanna hear the rest of my confession?"

"There's more?" she asked with laughter.

He nodded. "I wish my feelings for you were like a big brother's, but to be honest, I'm attracted to you. And it's not only about your looks. You're beyond attractive and desirable and everything, but there's something else about you. Something that makes my heart beat fast when I'm near you. I don't want to feel this way, but I can't help the fact that I want you."

"But what about Cheryl? Aren't you in love with your wife?"

"Of course. I love her to death. That's why these feelings are so confusing." Frowning, Randy pushed away the plate containing his partially eaten sandwich and interlocked his fingers.

Sexy ran a gentle hand over Randy's tightly entwined hands. "I have feelings for you, too. Deep feelings. But I respect the sanctity of marriage so much that I'm willing to accept that we can only be friends."

"But, the thing is, I'm in an open marriage."

"Really?"

"Well, maybe not quite an open marriage, but my wife is pretty open. We have threesomes all the time, and Cheryl usually picks the girls that she knows I'm attracted to. But for some strange reason, she has a problem with you."

Hit with enlightenment, Sexy nodded her head knowingly. *That bitch, Cheryl is scared of me because she knows she can't puppeteer me and pull my strings. When I fuck her husband, it's not gonna be for fun and games or for her entertainment. Hell, no! When I fuck Randy Alston, I'll be playing for keeps!*

"Do you think I'm a bad guy for admitting that I want to get with you, even though I know that my wife won't approve?"

"I don't think you're a bad guy. I want you, too, but we have to agree on something."

Randy gave her his full attention.

"We can't be involved in any type of ongoing affair. That would be wrong as hell and unfair to Cheryl and Yusef."

"I agree."

"Okay, so as long as you're one hundred percent certain that Cheryl is the one you love, I don't think a one-time fling with me will affect your marriage or my relationship with Yusef."

"You're so wise and understanding. How did I luck up like this?"

"We have to get what we feel for each other out of our systems, and then move on with our lives."

"You don't have to say another word; let's get out of here."

Their room at the W hotel was all kinds of luxurious, but neither Sexy nor Randy had time to check out the features of the beautifully appointed room, when they were busy shedding their clothes.

Standing in the middle of the room, Randy pulled Sexy into his arms. His calloused palms stroked her hips and thighs, and squeezed her ass. "You are so beautiful," he declared, tilting her chin up and then kissing Sexy with all the passion he possessed.

He guided her to the bed, and gently nudged her onto her back. She was right about his big 'Bama dick. It was much bigger than Yusef's and it swung like a heavy pendulum between his muscled thighs. He climbed on top of her, his mouth seeking out her breasts, and Sexy reached for his dick, yearning to feel its warmth and smooth texture.

She clutched his manhood, enjoying the feeling as it pulsed inside her fist. Randy released a deep, guttural moan. "I gotta get inside you," he mumbled as he repositioned himself, holding his dick at the base and aiming it at her moist opening.

Normally, Sexy would expect lots of foreplay from her partner: pussy eating, ass licking, and titty sucking. But she felt the same sense of urgency as Randy. The sexual tension between them was so strong, Sexy shuddered beneath Randy and cried out, "Fuck me, baby, please. I want you so bad."

He plunged into her pussy with long, deep strokes. Sexy tightened her muscles, possessively holding him captive inside her velvety walls.

"Oh, baby, what you doing to me?" Randy groaned. "It feels like you're trying to milk the cum out of me. I'm not gonna last long if you keep this up."

Reluctantly, she released him from her grip, and offered him a wet pussy that was relaxed and wide open, and willing to accommodate him. Randy's dick seemed big enough to rip her in two, but she didn't care. She wanted him to take her—to beat up her pussy with a savage pounding.

"Harder," she demanded as Randy delved deeply, and she could feel his dick inside her, throbbing and pulsing, and growing impossibly harder.

"Goddamn, Sexy. Your pussy is so good. Sexy! Baby! Oh, Sexy, baby!" He power-fucked her, yelling her name with each deep stroke. The pressure of his dick embedded inside her like a hunk of steel, increased the throbbing sensation in her clit, bringing her passion to a feverish pitch.

An orgasm was building, but she fought against it. She wasn't ready, and so she struggled to keep it at bay. The pebbled tips of her nipples were so sensitive, she could feel the breeze from the air conditioner caressing her nipples like a feather-soft tickle.

Their sweat-slick bodies rubbed together, and they both emitted guttural noises that sounded barely human. On fire, Sexy's inner muscles involuntarily clenched and unclenched convulsively against the onslaught of Randy's thick, ramming appendage.

"I'm gonna bust if you don't stop squeezing my dick like that," Randy warned.

"Pinch my nipples," she instructed. And the moment he did, she was consumed by a powerful orgasm that rocketed through her system. Unable to control herself, she screamed out in pleasure— a primal sound that was loud and long.

Following suit, Randy howled as he flooded her with semen. The warm, sticky fluid spurted into her, filling her, and marking her as his woman.

Held in Randy's strong arms, she snuggled into his body. "That was so good," Sexy whispered.

"Yeah, it was." Randy's words sounded hollow, like they held no real meaning.

Sexy sat up and peered at Randy. "What's wrong, baby?"

He pressed the heels of his palms against his forehead and groaned in anguish. "I never cheated on my wife before and I feel sick to my stomach with guilt."

Sexy's first impulse was to slap the shit out of Randy for acting like a pussy, but having long-term plans for the two of them, she had to control her temper and think rationally. "I feel bad, too," she disclosed. "But since Cheryl knows you've been with other women, and since you love Cheryl with all your heart, it's not as if you did anything to hurt her."

"I know, but Cheryl has always been there when I was with other women, and..." He shook his head. "I already messed up by calling her your name."

"You did?" Sexy asked delightedly.

"I don't know what came over me, but I had you on my mind while she was giving me head."

"Wow." Sexy couldn't think of anything else to say. This was exciting news and she was struggling to contain her sheer glee.

"Cheryl is an open-minded person, and she doesn't consider it cheating as long as she's involved and can see exactly what I'm doing. But she would never be okay with me having sex with another woman unless she was able to watch me like a hawk."

Sexy rubbed Randy's arm to console him. "You're a standup guy,

Randy. And under the circumstances, I think you should be true to yourself and get it off your conscience."

"What are you saying?"

"I'm saying that I think you should go home and confess."

Randy scowled at Sexy as if she were crazy. "You think I should tell my wife that I was creeping?" He laughed and shook his head. "Are you trying to get me killed or something?"

Sexy shrugged. "I'm merely saying, if your marriage is based on honesty, I think you'll feel better if you man-up and tell Cheryl that you slipped up. She loves you, Randy, so it's not as if she's gonna kick you out of the apartment and file for a divorce. From a woman's perspective, I think she's not only going to forgive you, but she's also going to have a newfound respect for you for coming to her like a man."

Randy pondered Sexy's words for a few moments, and then looked at her. "I think you're right." He got out of bed and went into the bathroom and began running the shower. Sexy thought about joining him, but decided against it.

If my plan works the way I think it will, I'll have the rest of my life to take showers with my husband, Randy. Giggling softly, she rose from the bed and went through Randy's pockets. Purely for the hell of it, she lifted several hundred-dollar bills from his wallet. Bored while waiting for him to emerge from the shower, she looked around the room, taking in the décor and ambiance. When her eyes settled on Randy's gold and platinum link bracelet that he'd placed on a tabletop, she took in a sharp breath. Powerless to control her klepto tendencies, she immediately stalked across the room and stuffed the costly piece of jewelry inside her handbag.

Before exiting the hotel, Sexy pocketed all the Bliss products from the basket in the bathroom. It wasn't that she needed extra toiletries, but oh, how she loved accumulating mementoes, particularly those acquired with a five-finger discount. And this momentous evening that she'd spent with Randy Alston—this night that would alter not only the course of her life, but also Randy's and Cheryl's—was truly a night to remember.

Cheryl

"Honey, you've been acting strange all day." Cheryl put down the *Vogue* magazine she was reading, and patted the bed next to her. "Come tell wifey what's bothering you."

Randy gave a sheepish smile, but shook his head, sitting down on the divan near the bedroom window. "I'm okay, babe."

Cheryl propped herself up on her arm. "No, you're not. But... well, if you're ready to talk about it, I'm here, okay?"

When Randy didn't answer, Cheryl shrugged and grabbed her magazine and started flipping through the pages again, making a mental note to give the agency that represented her a call soon. She had cut down on her modeling gigs since getting married, but was considering getting back into the swing of things. She figured she'd stop once she got pregnant, but she might as well do a couple of jobs in the meantime—especially since it didn't appear that she was going to get pregnant anytime soon. She'd gotten off the pill as soon as they married—but so far no good. But, in a way, maybe that was a good thing. With her luck, she figured, she might have another demon child like that damn Sexy Sanchez. Merely thinking about it gave her the shivers. But she had to chance it. Though she acknowledged she probably didn't have a maternal bone in her body, she knew how badly Randy wanted to start a family. *And let's face it*, she'd said to herself, *it wouldn't hurt to have a little marital insurance.*

"Cheryl?"

She looked up, and to her surprise Randy was looking at her with tears in his eyes. She quickly got up and walked over to sit next to him. "What's wrong, Randy?" she said, softly caressing his cheek.

He wiped at the corners of his eyes, and then paused a few seconds before speaking. "Baby, I messed up."

"What do you mean," she said soothingly. *Oh, please don't tell me. Please, no!*

"Cheryl," Randy said urgently, grabbing her hands in his. "You know I love you, don't you?"

Oh, God no. Please, no! "Of course I do, Randy. Tell me what's got you so upset."

"Well, I—" He dropped her hands and looked away. "I—"

"Randy, you know you can tell me anything. Whatever it is, we can work it out." *But it better not be what I think it is.*

"I really hope so," Randy said, wiping his eyes.

"Of course, we can," Cheryl said, putting her arms around Randy. "Unless, of course, you're going to tell me that you fucked Sexy Sanchez."

"Huh?" was all Randy could say.

"Because that's the one thing I'm sure you know would hurt me to the core." Cheryl kissed Randy's neck. "And you promised you would never, ever hurt me."

She stood up and walked over to her vanity, knowing without looking, that Randy was watching her. She sat down on the cushioned seat and began brushing her hair in the mirror. The silence in the room was deafening. After she counted a hundred strokes, she put the brush down. Reaching for her mascara, she began putting on makeup. First she did her eyes, then applied blush, and a deep shade of burgundy lipstick. She then picked up her two-hundred-dollar-an-ounce French perfume, and sprayed her neck and her wrists. Finished, she smiled at her image in the mirror, then stood up, turned, and hurled the large bottle of perfume at Randy with all her might.

"Cheryl!" Randy shouted, ducking just in time. The bottle missed him, but smashed into the window. "Baby," he said, looking at the shattered glass pane, then Cheryl, and then the window. "What are you—" The heavy metal jewelry box hit him smack in the middle of his forehead. The lock on the box opened and dozens of diamond, pearl, and ruby earrings spilled onto the carpeted floor. Randy tried, unsuccessfully, to dodge the picture frame containing their wedding picture. The corner cut into his right temple, and blood immediately started oozing from the large gash. Cheryl picked up another perfume bottle and was taking aim when Randy yelled, "For God's sake, Cheryl, stop!"

Cheryl stopped suddenly, her throwing arm frozen in air, and she looked as if she suddenly realized what she'd been doing. She slowly sank back down into her seat, but only for a second. She jumped up, and screamed, "You bastard!" The bottle smashed into the wall, barely missing Randy who darted into the bathroom.

This time it was Randy locked inside and Cheryl urging him to come out. But while Randy had used pleas and apologies, Cheryl hurled threats and curses. While Randy had repeatedly knocked and begged, Cheryl did her best to kick the door in.

"Cheryl, calm down."

"Don't you dare tell me to calm down," Cheryl screamed at the top of her lungs. "Out of all the women in the world you had to fuck her? You had to fuck my..." Her unfinished sentence served to bring her to her senses. She gave the door one more kick, then stomped back into the bedroom, and threw herself on the bed and collapsed into tears. *Out of all the women in the world you had to fuck my daughter!*

"Thanks, Stephen, but I have to go home sometime."

"Hmph, I don't see why." Stephen rolled his eyes. "If I were you, I'd be pulling out that pre-nup and be on my way to a lawyer to see how to break it so you can take young country boy to the cleaners."

"I never signed a pre-nup."

"What?" Stephen jumped up from the couch. "You're kidding."

"Nope. Don't you think I would have told you if I had?"

"Wow." Stephen sank back down. "I thought you had but didn't want to tell me the details."

"Please, you know I tell you everything." Cheryl gave a tingly laugh, though she felt a little guilty for the lie. She had told him that Randy had slept with Sexy, but she hadn't told him that Sexy was her daughter. And she didn't intend to. In fact, she'd never told Stephen that she'd ever had a child. And she also didn't plan to ever tell him.

"So, if you don't have a pre-nup, why aren't you at the lawyer's office? Damn, I'll drive you there myself. New York might not be a community property state, but honey, the courts tend to be very generous to the wives of cheating millionaire athletes."

"Because," Cheryl said, opening up her makeup compact to check her lipstick, "I don't plan on divorcing Randy."

"Why not?"

"Because I love him." Cheryl snapped the compact shut and slipped it into her pocketbook.

"No, I'm serious. Why not?"

"I love him, Stephen."

Stephen's eyebrows shot up. "And when did that happen?"

"And what is that supposed to mean?"

"Oh, come on, Cheryl." Stephen sucked his teeth. "You and I both know you fell in love with young country boy's money."

"Maybe." Cheryl sighed. "Okay, yeah. But, I don't know, Stephen, I really do love him. How can you help but love someone who loves you as much as he loves me."

"If he loves you so much, why did he sleep with Sexy?"

"Because he's a man, and men are dogs." Cheryl picked up her Versace shoulder bag, kissed Stephen on the cheek, and walked toward the door. "If he calls—"

"It's been a good fifteen minutes; he'll be calling any second now."

Cheryl chuckled. "Well, when he calls—"

Ringgggggggg.

They both broke out in laughter.

"If that's him, don't tell him anything. Let him sweat it out a little more. It'll be a surprise when he gets home and finds me there," Cheryl said, walking out the door.

Fifteen minutes later, Cheryl handed her car keys to the valet and marched into the lobby of the Ritz-Carlton. It was ridiculous that Yusef had been in town three months and was still staying at one of the most expensive hotels in the city, but Cheryl had no doubt that is was at Sexy's instigation. She could imagine that the girl would rather have room service and hotel housekeeping rather than actually taking care of herself and Yusef at an apartment. Never mind that it had to be costing Yusef a fortune.

Bypassing the hotel desk, Cheryl walked over to the elevators, and rode up to the nineteenth floor. She stood in front of suite 1901 for a few minutes, trying to steel her nerves, before determinately knocking on the door. To her surprise, the door opened immediately, and there stood Sexy Sanchez, clad only in a towel. The girl slowly looked Cheryl up and down before speaking.

"Oh, I thought it was room service. I ordered the fresh catch of the day, but instead I find old, funky fish," Sexy said in a disinterested voice.

Keep your cool. Keep your cool. "May I come in?"

Sexy smirked. "Must you?"

"I must," Cheryl said, walking past the girl without further invitation. "I think we need to talk."

Sexy shrugged, and closed the door. "Okay. Hope you don't mind if I slip into something more comfortable." She strode to the middle of the room, then undid the towel, letting it drop to the floor. She then emitted an obvious fake, but very long yawn, accompanied by an expansive and exaggerated stretch.

Cheryl smirked as she gave Sexy a slow up-and-down look to let the girl know that her brazenness didn't bother her, but the truth was she was impressed to the point of jealousy. Sexy's body was as ill as the singer Rihanna's; firm, sleek, muscular and curvy at the same time. Cheryl hadn't been obsessed with looking at herself in the mirror when she herself had been sixteen, but now she wished she had. She had to hope that at least, at one point, her body was as hot as Sexy's. Mentally she shook her head to rid it of the thought. *Hell, my body is rocking now. Maybe not quite as firm or as sleek, but...*

"You have to excuse me, I didn't get much sleep last night. Yusef had to go to Philly on some family business, so I was, uh, entertaining." She flashed Cheryl a wicked grin. "Randy didn't mention you were stopping by. He's such a naughty boy."

Cheryl gave the girl a cold stare. "If you're trying to imply Randy was the man you were—"

"Oh, I wasn't trying to imply anything," Sexy said in an innocent voice, bringing her hand to her bare breasts. "Why would you think that?" She walked into the bedroom and returned, still naked, with a bottle of scented lotion. She lifted one of her long shapely legs onto the back of the chair in which Cheryl was sitting and began applying the lotion.

Keep cool. Keep cool.

"So, what did you want to talk about?" Sexy asked, switching legs.

Cheryl moved from the chair to the sofa. "Us."

"What about us?"

"Well, I think we got off on the wrong foot, Sexy. You've said some horrid things, and I've said some horrid things. And then, of course, there's the fact that you slept with my husband—"

"I would hardly call what we did sleep," Sexy said with a chuckle.

Keep cool. Keep cool. "If you're trying to get under my skin, give it up. I've already gotten over it. I've decided to forgive my husband his little indiscretion—"

"Well, you and I both know there's nothing little about Randy's indiscretion. Whew, and boy does he know how to use it, huh?" Sexy now sat down on the chair, crossed her legs and started massaging her breasts with the lotion. "But you know what? I taught him a few new tricks. Believe me, you're gonna thank me for it." She giggled. "Let's call it an early birthday gift, from me to you."

"I came here trying to have a civilized conversation with you, Sexy, but you're really making it hard."

"Girl," Sexy leaned forward and waved her hand in a friendly manner. "Talk about hard, that Randy—"

Cheryl stared at the girl for a moment, then rolled her eyes and sighed.

Sexy laughed. "Yeah, I know, I'm a smart-ass—"

"Oh, girl, please." Now it was Cheryl's turn to wave her hand. "In order to be a smart-ass you have to be smart. You? You're simply an ass."

Sexy's eyebrow shot up. "Well, aren't you a bitch."

"I thought I told you before, I'm not a bitch, I'm *the* bitch." Cheryl stood up and walked over, and leaned on the back of Sexy's chair, and glared down at the girl. "And I don't play kiddy games with little kiddies."

"Oh, am I supposed to be all scared and shit now?" Sexy said with a sneer.

"I don't give a shit if you're scared or not, but I will tell you what you *are* going to be."

"Yeah? And what's that?" Sexy said defiantly.

"Off my husband's dick, slut."

"Hey, it's not my fault he can't get enough of this good pussy, here," Sexy said, cocking her legs and patting her crotch. "If your shit was as good as this, you wouldn't have to worry about me taking your man."

"Taking my man?" Cheryl threw her head back and laughed. "Skank, don't get it twisted. You borrowed him for a night."

"Borrowed him, huh? Bitch, I put my fucking stamp on him. You thought you had him all pussy-whipped, but I got that mother-fucker ready to jump through hoops to get back in this saddle."

"Not likely since you're gonna be trotting your pony ass back to Bryn Mawr, little girl."

Sexy's face turned red, and she began breathing hard, though she seemed to be struggling to hide her surprise. Cheryl grinned at Sexy's reaction. It was the first time she'd ever seen the girl actually taken aback. "Oh, yes, I know all about you, you little juvenile-delinquent slut. Does Yusef know he's been fucking jailbait?"

"I don't think my age or background is any of your business, bitch."

"Ooh, is that the snappiest comeback you've got?" Cheryl laughed and walked back over to the couch, though she didn't sit down. "So, here's the thing. I'm not worried about Randy coming back and sniffing around for your little twat; he's had you, and he's forgotten you. But, still I think you need to carry your ass home so you don't start trouble in other people's marriage. So, if you don't want me to—"

"To tell? Are you sure you want to do that?"

Cheryl noticed that the smirk Sexy always seemed to wear had returned. "Oh, yes, I'm quite sure."

"Really? Because if you do, a lot of people can get hurt." Sexy's smirk turned into an evil smile. "Me, least of all, though."

The little bitch is calling my bluff. "How so?" Cheryl asked coolly.

"Because, maybe if you tell, then I tell."

Damn. "Tell what? I've done nothing wrong. And since Randy didn't know your age, he didn't do anything wrong, either. And while you might have been underage when you started fucking Yusef, by the time you seduced my husband, you had already turned seventeen—which is the legal age of consent in New York."

Sexy shrugged. "Sure, Randy didn't do anything wrong in the eyes of the law. But in the eyes of public opinion, well, that might be a whole other matter."

Cheryl stood up and smiled. "Well, I'm sure Stephen—"

"Your little gay friend?"

"—will be able to handle public opinion." She pulled the chain strap of her Versace bag high on her shoulder and headed toward the door. "Oh, by the way," she said before closing the door behind her, "you need a lot more lotion. You're still quite trashy. I mean ashy."

Yusef was at a meeting with his agent, and Sexy was relaxing in the hotel suite. Butt-naked, she reclined in bed, eating gummy bears and Doritos while watching the ratchetness of *Bad Girls Club*. She glanced at her orange-tinted fingernails and frowned. Two crystals were missing. For all the money she'd spent at that high-end spa, the crystals that the manicurist had applied should have remained intact for at least a few weeks.

Disgusted, she yanked back the bed linen, searching for the small crystals. But no luck. She glanced at her nails again and concluded that they looked absolutely dreadful with the missing jewels. But she didn't feel like being bothered leaving her luxurious suite to get them repaired at a nail salon.

Hmm. The Ritz-Carlton had a salon on the premises, and maybe she could convince one of the manicurists to drop by her room to fix her nails. Celebrities got the royal treatment all the time, and why shouldn't she? Sexy called the salon, but was sorely disappointed when she was told by a woman with a snooty voice that the manicurists didn't provide room service.

Hmph! I bet they'd rush to my room with an entire glam squad if I were Mrs. Randall Alston.

Heaving a sigh, she resigned herself to gluing those suckers back on if only she could find them. She dropped to her knees and searched the carpeted floor. With her naked ass tooted upward, she looked beneath the bed.

"Is that the position you were in when you let Randy run his dick up in you?"

She hadn't heard Yusef enter the suite and she was startled by his gruff voice and malicious accusation. "What are you talking about?" she asked innocently, looking up and meeting eyes with Yusef as he towered above her, staring daggers at her. His shirt was rumpled and his eyes were bloodshot, and she could smell alcohol on his breath.

"You know exactly what I'm talking about, so don't fuckin' play dumb, you slut."

"But...but...um, I thought you wanted me to go to bed with Randy. That's what you said the other night."

"That was sex talk. Nothing more than a harmless fantasy...and you know it."

"I didn't know; I thought you were serious." Sexy rose from the floor and sashayed over to Yusef. "Listen, I'm really sorry about our misunderstanding, baby. Let me make it up to you," she said seductively, placing her arms around Yusef's neck.

She kissed him, but he didn't kiss back. He stood stock-still like a statue.

"Don't be mad, Yusef," she cajoled. "I said I'm sorry." She licked her lips. "I bet I know how to get you out of your bad mood."

He disengaged her arms that were looped around his neck. "You're nothing but a dirty tramp," Yusef spat.

"How can you say that when you know how much I love you?" she said with a little giggle.

Yusef shook his head. "You can't even say those words convincingly. I want you to pack your shit and get the fuck out."

"And go where?" Sexy asked in a loud, screechy voice. "You sold the condo in Philly, so where the fuck am I supposed to go?"

"Bitch, I don't know and I don't give a fuck. All I know is the lush lifestyle you've been enjoying with my hard-earned money is over. You're Randy Alston's side chick, so let that nigga foot the bill and take care of you."

The steely look in Yusef's eyes and the way his nostrils flared, informed Sexy that there was no reasoning with him. And so, with a nonchalant shoulder shrug, she whirled around and began filling her luggage with her belongings.

"Oh, yeah. You can hand over that credit card," Yusef said with his hand stuck out.

Sexy dug into her Prada bag and reluctantly retrieved the card from her wallet. She started to place it on the top of the dresser, but in a moment of sudden rage, she flung it across the room.

"Fuck you, Yusef, with your little-dick, no-fucking self," Sexy snarled. "You're doing me a favor by kicking me out because it's been torture having to sleep with a pussy-bitch like you. Fucking another woman would be more fulfilling than putting up with more bad sex from you."

Yusef exhaled in a long stream, his shoulders sagging forward as if Sexy's attack on his manhood had knocked the wind out of him.

Sexy smiled, pleased that she'd struck a nerve.

While Yusef sat slumped in a chair, Sexy put in earphones, and finished packing while singing along with "Wrecking Ball" by Miley Cyrus. By all appearances, she seemed unfazed, but she was livid. Sure, it was only a matter of time before she left Yusef for Randy, but that big-mouth Cheryl had no business running to Yusef and being a tattletale. Cheryl's interference had caused Sexy to get thrown out on the streets with nowhere to go.

In Sexy's eyes, Cheryl, the so-called model, appeared to be somewhere in her late twenties—too old to be relevant in the world of modeling. Modeling was a young girl's game, and that washed-up, over-the-hill, old-ass bitch was going to deeply regret fucking with Sexy Sanchez.

Sexy had had access to Randy's phone number since the night of his surprise birthday party when she'd slyly found it on his phone and quickly memorized it before his bitch of a wife had snatched his phone from Sexy's hand. Although she and Randy had texted back and forth, she'd never called him in distress.

With a sneaky smile on her lips, she tapped the screen of her phone. "Hello, Randy?" she said, sniffling, and with a question mark in her voice. "It's Sexy. I hate to bother you, but I didn't know who else to call."

"What's wrong, Sexy? You sound like you're crying. Is something wrong?"

She turned on the waterworks. "I don't know how Yusef found out, but somebody told him about you and me. He stormed into our hotel suite, calling me names, shaking me, and pushing me around."

"He put his hands on you?" Randy yelled so loud, Sexy had to pull the phone away from her ear.

"Yes, but he didn't slap or punch me or anything. He mainly roughed me up and scared me with threats of violence before he kicked me out like I was a piece of trash," she said shrilly.

"Where are you?"

"I'm standing outside Penn Station, and that's why I'm calling you. Randy, would you loan me some money to buy a train ticket? Yusef was acting like a madman. He dumped out the contents of my purse and took all my cash and credit cards."

Randy groaned in dismay. "Don't worry. I got you, Sexy. Stay right where you are. I'm heading for my car now, and I'll be there as fast as I can."

"Okay, Randy, but please hurry," she said in a tiny, broken voice. "I'm so upset, I can hardly breathe. Feels like I'm having a panic attack."

"Maybe you should go inside and have a seat. I don't want you fainting or anything."

"I can't go inside," she wailed.

"Why can't you?"

"It's hard to explain, but whenever I get upset and have a panic attack, it's like I can't catch my breath," she said, making gasping sounds. "I can't breathe and I can't move. All I can do is stand here. Oh, Randy, I'm so scared," she sobbed.

"All right, all right. Try to calm down." Randy's voice took on a frantic tone. "I'm in the car, now, and I'm breaking speed limits, baby. Don't you worry about anything...I'm coming to get you."

"Okay," she murmured pitifully, and then hung up the phone and broke into laughter.

In less than ten minutes, she saw Randy's Maybach coming to a screeching halt behind the row of taxis that were waiting at the curb. On cue, Sexy slumped against a pole. Head hanging low, her chest heaved as if gasping for breath. The sound of Randy's pounding footsteps racing toward her, put a huge smile on her face. It was a good thing her hair was hanging in her face, concealing the smirk on her lips and the glint of triumph in her eyes. *Cheryl can kiss her husband goodbye. I'm through with fun and games; this mutha-fucka is mine!* It took every ounce of willpower for Sexy not to pump her fist in victory.

"Sexy! Sexy!" Randy approached, calling her name.

Pretending to be woozy, Sexy teetered on her feet, and didn't respond.

"I'm so sorry this is happening to you. But don't worry; I'm here, now, and I'm gonna make sure you're all right," Randy said, lifting her in his arms, and then reaching down and grabbing her over-stuffed, designer duffle bag. "Excuse me, coming through. Excuse me," he called out, weaving through pedestrians and parting crowds as he made his way to his car, carrying Sexy and her heavy luggage effortlessly.

Gingerly, he placed her in the front seat, and adjusted it to a reclining position. "Comfortable?" he asked.

"Yeah, I'm starting to feel a little better."

"I don't know anything about panic attacks. Uh, do you need to see a doctor?" Randy asked as he pulled away from the curb and merged into the flow of traffic.

"No. It's not a physical condition. It's psychological, and only happens when I'm extremely afraid. The way Yusef was acting, I feared for my life."

Angry, Randy clenched his teeth and gripped the steering wheel tightly. "If Yusef so much as looks at you the wrong way, I'll break his jaw and bust a couple of ribs. I swear if he thinks about hurting you, I will fuck him up."

Sexy had never heard Randy use profanity, and she glanced at him in surprise. He was obviously feeling some kind of way over the thought of Yusef manhandling her.

Sexy managed to work more tears into her eyes. "I couldn't imagine how he found out about our little fling, and to be honest, I initially thought you had bragged about it in the locker room."

Randy shot Sexy a look of horror. "I would never do anything like that. I don't know how he found out, but he didn't get it from me."

"Somebody told him. Did you have that talk with your wife, yet? You know, uh, did you confess about what we did?"

As Randy drove aimlessly through the streets of Manhattan, he suddenly slapped a hand on his forehead. "Cheryl! Oh, my God, she went to Yusef and told him. But why would she do that? That information should have stayed between me and her. I explained to her that I was sorry that I messed up, and I promised it wouldn't happen again. I can't believe she ran her mouth to Yusef and put your life in danger." Scowling, Randy shook his head in disbelief.

"You're driving in circles, Randy. Where are you taking me?"

"I don't know. I thought I'd drive around until you calmed down, and then buy you the train ticket." Eyes filled with remorse, he gazed at Sexy. "But this is all my fault and I have to man-up and take care of you."

"It's not your fault. We were both to blame. Listen, I care about you, Randy, but I couldn't live with myself if your marriage fell apart because of me."

"You're the sweetest little angel I've ever met. You know that, Sexy? You always put the happiness of others before yourself, and that's one of the things that I dig about you."

Sexy gave him a weak smile. "I try my best to be a good person."

"And you are." With a determined look in his eyes, he steered the car along Lexington Avenue. "I'm gonna get you a room at the W hotel, but as soon as I have some free time, we're gonna look at apartments and find you a nice place to live. And if anyone even thinks of trying to kick you out of your new home, they're gonna have to answer to me."

After settling into a plush suite at the W, Sexy complained of aching joints from being manhandled by Yusef. Randy offered to give her a relaxing massage and with the sexual chemistry sparking between them, one thing quickly led to another. Taking charge, Sexy sucked Randy's dick like her life depended on it, and he responded to her skillful blow job by calling for Jesus. Next, she rode him like he was a stallion, and then, stretched her body like a contortionist, putting to use the gymnastic training she'd had as a child. Sexy worked Randy over, fucking him until he conked out, and was sprawled on the bed, and snoring like a bear.

She thought he'd be sleeping contentedly through the night, and she was surprised when he jumped up a few hours later, rushing into the bathroom to wash up, and then hurrying to put on his clothes.

"What are you doing?" Sexy asked, doing a superb job of keeping the annoyance out of her voice.

"Look at the time!" Randy gawked at the bedside clock. "I gotta get home. Cheryl is probably worried sick."

That bitch ought to be worried; her marriage is hanging by a thread, Sexy thought contemptuously, and then looked at Randy with a patient smile. "Your thoughtfulness is one of the things that I love about you." She picked up a hairbrush and pointed to his hair. "I don't want you going home looking like you just rolled out of bed," she said, handing him the brush.

"Thanks." He quickly brushed the wayward strands of hair, checked out his reflection in the mirror, and brushed his hair once more before heading for the door. He stopped suddenly and turned around. "Don't worry about where you're gonna live. I'm a man of my word, and I'll be back tomorrow so we can find you a nice place to live."

"You're so sweet, Randy. I don't know what I would have done without you."

"Aw, it's nothing," he said, blushing.

"It's everything to me. I want you to know that you're my hero, Randy Alston." Sexy plastered on a smile that was so angelic, the only thing missing was a halo and a set of wings.

Cheryl

"Stephen? You heard anything yet?"

"No, girl, and believe me, I've been keeping my ear to the ground. All I know is what you know: Yusef kicked her little skank ass out, but I can't find out what happened to her. She probably dragged her little slutty ass back home."

"Yeah, maybe so," Cheryl said into the telephone. "I wish we knew for sure. But I have to give it to the little ho, she's smart. And sneaky, too." Cheryl paused, and then added, "Sneaky as all hell."

Cheryl couldn't get over the feeling that there was something terribly wrong. The uneasy emotion had overwhelmed her ever since she'd talked to Yusef, the day after meeting Sexy at the hotel. She hadn't planned on actually telling him that Sexy had slept with Randy; she only wanted to warn him that his little girlfriend was acting up, and he needed to keep a better eye on her. That, she thought, would be enough for him to go home and read her the riot act, and make Sexy think it was better to keep the bird she had in hand rather than lose it chasing after another she might not get. But Yusef dismissed Cheryl's suspicions, saying he knew all about the outrageous lap dance Sexy had given Randy at the club, but that she was drunk, and anything else—like her slipping Randy a mickey—were merely rumors. She then had no choice but to pull out the big guns. She told him that Randy had confessed having smashed Sexy, and in the hotel bed she shared with Yusef, no less. She actually had no idea where Randy and Sexy had fucked, but it couldn't hurt to rile Yusef as much as possible.

Yusef's face turned crimson while she talked, though he maintained an obviously fake grin. By the time she finished talking, his face was purple, and the grin had turned into a crooked grimace.

"Well, look at the time," he said, getting up from the table and throwing down a hundred-dollar bill to cover what couldn't have been more than a thirty-dollar tab. "I really have to be going." And with that, he was gone.

On the drive home, she couldn't help but wonder if she had pushed Yusef too hard. For a moment she questioned if it was some kind of maternal instinct kicking in—her worrying about what Yusef might do—but then convinced herself that couldn't be it. She simply didn't want Yusef to kill Sexy; then there would be a scandal, and Randy might get pulled into it.

She hung up, and sat at the kitchen table, perusing the newspaper and drinking her coffee, an expensive, special blend called Ethiopian Fancy, imported from Africa and which she had become addicted to since marrying Randy and being able to afford it. What if Yusef threw Sexy out, but then later went after her and really hurt the girl?

"Hey, babe, whatya doing?"

Cheryl had been so absorbed in her thoughts that she hadn't heard Randy come in the door. She hurriedly jumped up, and then scurried to close the newspaper before realizing that there was nothing she had to hide—except the guilty look on her face.

"Nothing," Cheryl said with a light laugh. She walked over and put her arms around his neck. "I talked to Mila this morning."

"Oh? And, uh, what did you two girls talk about?"

"Nothing much." Cheryl nuzzled her husband's neck. "How gallant you were for coming to the rescue when their car broke down in Jersey yesterday." She kissed him lightly on the neck. "I told her that she and Brent need to spend some of the millions the Yankees pay them on a car that can make it a hundred miles without breaking down."

"Aw, honey, you know Brent woulda did the same for me."

"Would have done the same for you."

"Huh?"

Cheryl lightly tapped her finger against Randy's cheek. "A little reminder about your grammar, babe."

"Um, yeah. Sorry." Randy gently disengaged himself, and walked over to the window. "I don't know why it's so important to you that I talk like a northerner, though. I don't mind people knowing I'm a hick from Eufala, Alabama."

"Baby, I love your Southern accent, you know that," Cheryl said, going over and hugging him from the back. "But being from the South doesn't mean you shouldn't use good English. We talked about it, remember? After all, when you give statements to the press—"

"Isn't that what your friend, Stephen, is for?" Randy said, a growl in his voice. "To make sure my statements come out right?"

"Yes, and no," Cheryl said slowly. "He can't always correct statements you've already made. He's not equipped with a time machine."

"Well, what's he good for then?" Randy snapped.

Cheryl let go of him and backed up. "Randy, what's wrong with you today? Why are you acting so crabby?"

Randy shook his head, then turned around, a weak smile on his face. "Aw, I'm sorry, babe. I guess I didn't get enough sleep."

Cheryl nodded. "I guess not. You didn't get in until almost three in the morning."

"But I called and let you know—"

"I know, I know! Randy, calm down!" Cheryl was trying not to get irritated, but now Randy was getting on her nerves. "I'm not upset, babe. I was merely saying I understand you not getting enough sleep is why you're crabby. But don't take it out on me. What did I do?"

For a moment, it looked like Randy was going to go at her again, but he suddenly stopped and let out a sigh. "Yeah, I'm tired, and I got a lot on my mind, I guess. Sorry, babe."

"What's got you worried, babe?" Cheryl asked softly. Damn, had the Yusef/Sexy situation absorbed her so much that she'd been missing cues about her own husband? "Tell me about it."

"It's really nothing. Coca-Cola is offering me five hundred thousand dollars for a one-year endorsement, but Pepsi is offering a hundred thousand more."

"And this is a problem, why?"

"Well, Danny wants me to take the Pepsi deal, of course—"

"Of course."

"The thing is, I don't drink Pepsi; I drink Coke. Everyone in Eufala does." Randy's face broke into the sheepish grin that Cheryl loved so much. "I'd feel like a hypocrite taking Pepsi's money and then sneaking Cokes behind their backs."

Cheryl giggled in relief. "Is that all?" She started caressing his chest. "Well, you tell your big-time agent, Mr. Danny Archer, that my baby has morals and would never do anything dishonest."

"I love you, Cheryl," Randy said, kissing her.

"I know you do, baby. I love you, too." Cheryl kissed his neck, as she began unbuckling his belt. When he'd come home so very late last night, she had been too tired to welcome him home properly when he finally got into bed. But stimulated by all this talk about endorsements and money, her juices were now flowing like a faucet. And there was no time like the present...but to her surprise, Randy gently held her hands, stopping her from unzipping him.

"I'm sorry, Cheryl. I'm really tired."

His words were apologetic, but there was something else in his eyes she couldn't read. And he had never, ever, turned her down. *What the hell's up?* "That tired?" she asked with a lightness in her voice that she didn't really feel.

"Yeah. And actually, I gotta go right back out. I promised Brent I'd go back to Jersey with him to take a look at his car and see what's wrong with it. I'll probably be gone all day."

Cheryl's eyebrow shot up. "Really? You're going to Jersey, again? Why didn't Brent get the car towed when it broke down last night?"

Randy shrugged as he refastened his pants.

"It's odd that Mila didn't mention that you and Brent were going to work on the car. I wonder why she didn't say anything."

"Maybe Brent didn't tell her. I don't know."

Cheryl frowned. "I'm only saying—"

Randy let loose a loud sigh. "Cheryl, if you don't believe me, why don't you call Brent? Or call Mila; I don't care."

Cheryl backed toward the table and picked up her cell phone, never taking her eyes off Randy. She'd been too tired to fuck Randy when he came in, and she'd also been too tired to check his cell phone, either. *Had Sexy gotten in touch with him? Was he planning on spending the rest of the day with that little hooker?*

"Hey, Mila. What's up?" she said when her friend picked up the phone.

"Girl, not a damn thing. What's up with you?"

"Nothing. I wanted to see if you and Brent wanted to go over to

Stefano's this evening for some Italian with Randy and me. An early dinner, and maybe a show? We haven't done the couples' thing in a minute."

"Oh, Randy didn't tell you?" The surprise in Mila's voice was genuine. "He and Brent are supposed to go back to Jersey this afternoon to look at the car. You know how men are. As much money as they've got, they want to tinker with the damn thing themselves instead of letting the professionals handle it. Serves us right for both marrying country boys, huh? But, yeah, if they get back in time, I think it's a great idea."

"Satisfied now?" Randy asked when Cheryl hung up.

Cheryl bit her lip, feeling stupid, but saying nothing.

"Well," Randy shrugged, "I'm glad you didn't come right out and accuse me of lying. Thanks for that, at least."

"Sorry," Cheryl said in a low voice. "I guess, well, I've been under a bit of a strain, too. It's not easy forgetting...you know."

Randy lowered his eyes. "I know."

"Forgive me, Randy?" Cheryl's voice broke as she talked. "I really don't want you to think I don't trust you."

"Yeah, baby, of course." Randy rubbed her back for a moment, then pulled her tightly into this arms. "Look, we've been a little crazy lately, and it's my fault. I apologize, Cheryl. I really do. You're the best thing that has ever happened to me, and I'm sorry if I don't always show it."

"You're the best thing that's ever happened to me, too, babe." *You really are. You really are.* "And I love you, Randy, like I've never loved anyone else."

"I'm going to make it up to you, babe, okay?"

Cheryl smiled and nodded. *God, I'm so stupid! He messed up once, yeah, but who hasn't? I'm going to lose him if I hold too tight. Damn that*

Sexy! God, I hope she's okay. Cheryl grimaced, angry at herself for her conflicting emotions. Then it occurred to her, maybe Randy wasn't acting strange because of Sexy, but because of Yusef. Had he told Randy about their conversation? She'd asked him not to... but you never know.

"Cheryl?"

"Yes, babe," she answered, her face nuzzled in his chest.

"I really want you to know that you shouldn't hold what happened against Sexy. It was my fault, not hers, babe."

Cheryl strained to control herself. "If you say so."

"I'm serious, Cheryl. I'm not suggesting you guys should become friends or anything, but, well, I don't want you to think too bad of her. She's really not a bad girl."

"Yeah, she's the typical girl next door," Cheryl said, moving away from him. "That is, if you happen to live next door to a whorehouse."

Randy sighed. "Okay. Well, anyway. I'm going to change into some jeans and go get Brent so we can get to Jersey before we lose the sunlight."

"Cheryl!"

"Hey, what's up, Stephen?"

"Gurlllll... you'd better wake the hell up," Stephen said urgently into the telephone.

"Why? What's wrong?" Cheryl glanced at the clock. 11:35 p.m. She jumped and looked around. And Randy wasn't home. "What's wrong?" she said, more urgently this time.

"You're not gonna believe this! I just got off the telephone, and... girl, I'm telling you you're not going to believe this...but Jocko's dead."

"What?!" Cheryl sank back down on the bed. "When? How?"

"I just got off the phone with him—"

"I thought you said he was dead!"

Stephen snorted. "Not Jocko, Raphael."

"Oh."

"I got off the phone with him a couple of minutes ago, and he said he'd just found out, but that it happened around ten o'clock."

"What happened around ten o'clock?"

"My God, haven't you been listening? Jocko died!"

"I have been listening, Stephen. But how did he die?" Cheryl shouted into the telephone.

"Oh. Sorry." Stephen chuckled. "Hit-and-run right in front of his house."

"Oh my God," Cheryl said in a hoarse whisper. "I can't believe it." *I paid Ligon to rough him up, not kill him! What went wrong?*

"Are you okay, Cheryl? I thought you might be surprised; you sound downright upset."

"What do you mean?"

"Well, it's kinda too bad he was killed, but it's also kinda good, too. At least for you, if you know what I mean," Stephen explained. "You don't have to worry about him trying to hit you up anymore."

"Right, of course," Cheryl said, her mind racing. She hadn't told Stephen about Jocko's subsequent contact, or her hiring Dwayne Ligon, and now she was glad she hadn't. She didn't want anyone to know she was involved in a murder. "But he probably wouldn't have bothered me again, anyway. Poor guy. I hope he didn't suffer too much. Do you know if he died instantly?" Not that it mattered, really. The bottom line was he was dead, and it was her fault. How could she live with herself?

"I have no idea. I guess it'll be in the morning newspaper."

"Yeah, you're right. Well, look, I'm going to get to bed," Cheryl said, faking a yawn. "Talk to you in the morning."

"Okay, darling. Give young country boy a goodnight kiss for me and tell him I'm sorry for waking you up."

Cheryl hung up, and briefly wondered where "young country boy" was, but that was the least of her concerns at the moment. She reached over and turned on the radio, tuning into WINS-AM, the New York City all-news station. It only took fifteen minutes before the story she was both waiting for and dreading came over the airwaves.

Police report that a Washington Heights man was the victim of a fatal hit-and-run about 9:48 this evening. Forty-five-year-old Jack Fagin was rushed to the hospital after being hit on Amsterdam Avenue but was dead on arrival. Witnesses tell police that the car which hit Fagin was a Gray Ford Taurus. Police say they have the license plate of the car and are currently looking for the driver.

Cheryl's hand flew to her mouth, and she struggled to stop herself from hyperventilating. They have the license plate? How long would it be, then, for them to catch Ligon? And could she really trust that he wouldn't rat her out to help save his own skin?

Cheryl Blanton Alston had always considered herself a strong woman who could think her way out of any situation, but all the lies and secrets... it was becoming too much. The secret of the baby she'd sold. The lie about her age. The secret about Sexy being her child. Now this.

Cheryl looked over at Randy's side of the bed and began to sob. Now, if never before, she needed to be held—tightly—in her husband's arms.

T
he real estate agent walked Sexy and Randy through the attractive, one-bedroom apartment on the prestigious Upper East Side. As they moved through the rooms, the agent pointed out the amenities and services that the luxury property offered.

"I don't want to sound ungrateful, but although this building is awesome, I'm not feeling this particular apartment. It's too small," Sexy said quietly to Randy.

He patted Sexy on the shoulder soothingly and said to the agent, "She likes the building, but do you have something roomier?"

The real estate agent brightened. "I certainly do. All of our residences are distinctive, with their own unique charm, and there's an exquisite three-bedroom on the twenty-fourth floor with an expansive view, a large gourmet kitchen, floor-to-ceiling windows, and it even has a terrace."

"Let's take a look at that one," Sexy said, smiling. Randy may have thought they were shopping for an apartment exclusively for her, but Sexy was intent on finding a spectacular place for the two of them. A place where Randy would be proud to invite his friends. A place that he would soon call home.

The moment the real estate agent opened the front door of apartment 2417, revealing an expansive apartment with high ceilings and unique architecture, Sexy turned to Randy and said, "I want this one."

"You haven't even looked around," Randy said with a chuckle.

"It's beautiful. I love it!" Childlike, Sexy ran through the spacious apartment, squealing and twirling around in utter delight. Her happiness was infectious, creating bright smiles on both Randy's and the agent's faces.

After the lease was signed, the agent asked Sexy if she needed the assistance of an interior decorator.

"Yes, if Randy doesn't mind the added expense," Sexy said, looking up inquiringly at Randy.

"I don't mind at all."

"Yay!" Sexy exclaimed, her eyes twinkling as she clapped her hands. "But, I want to decorate the master bedroom, myself. I don't want to have to sleep on the floor, tonight."

Randy squeezed Sexy's hand. "You won't have to. I'm free for the rest of the day, so let's go pick out your bedroom furniture."

Our bedroom furniture, Sexy was tempted to correct, but she restrained herself. Sexy smiled as she told herself that the day was fast approaching when Randy would realize that Cheryl was a has-been who deserved to be left in the past, while she was the present and the future, the chick with that bomb-pussy that he couldn't get enough of.

In the furniture store, Randy stood back while Sexy examined mattresses and headboards. Wanting to include Randy in the selection process, Sexy continually asked his opinion and before long, Randy became a full participant, going so far as to stretch out on one of the beds that they both admired.

The manager of the store promised to deliver the selected furniture in two hours. After plunking down $11,000 without blinking an eye, Randy escorted Sexy out of the high-end store.

"What are your plans in life?" Randy asked, striking up a conversation during the drive back to the new apartment.

"I'm interested in a career in sports medicine," she said off the top of her head. "I injured my knee while at gymnastics practice when I was a kid, and I hated being out of commission for so long. But getting treatment for the injury was the catalyst for my interest in becoming a sports medicine physician." She exhaled, pleased with how convincing she sounded.

"I'm surprised that you want to become a doctor. I thought most girls as pretty as you want to be a model or an actress or be involved in some kind of glamorous field."

"No, that's not me at all. I'm not that shallow. Beauty eventually fades, so I prefer to rely on my brain instead of my looks," she said, making a sneaky dig at Cheryl. "I want to do something that makes a difference in someone's life. The idea of practicing a medical specialty concerned with the prevention, diagnosis, treatment, and rehabilitation of injuries due to athletic activity is thrilling to me. It's a booming business, and I plan to eventually own a state-of-the-art facility."

"There's a lot more to you than meets the eye," Randy remarked, sounding impressed.

"I don't usually admit to people that I'm actually a math and science geek, but that's the real me; a nerdy girl with a business plan and a desire to heal. I probably didn't mention that I'm going to start college at Columbia University next year," she said, continuing the big lie.

Randy looked worried. "Where's that? Is it far away?"

Sexy smiled indulgently. "No, Columbia is right here in New York." *Boy, Randy really is a hick. How do you live in America without knowing the whereabouts of one of the country's top universities?*

As they neared the apartment building, Sexy asked Randy to

make a stop at a liquor store. "I'd like a couple bottles of champagne to celebrate my new home."

Inside the store, Sexy picked up two plastic flutes and set them next to the chilled bottles of Moët on the counter. While Randy paid for the purchases, Sexy sneakily stuffed her handbag with mini bottles of vodka and gin and simply for the hell of it, she also stole a couple small bags of cashews and peanuts.

Randy had been a perfect gentleman all day, but after downing his first glass of champagne, he became extremely complimentary and somewhat touchy-feely. "You sure are a beautiful girl," he commented, staring in her eyes. "And your hair smells like green apples," he said, taking a deep sniff as he stroked her tresses.

"Thanks, Randy. More champagne?"

"I try not to drink too much during the season, but since we're celebrating, why not?"

As she refilled his glass, the doorman called to let her know that her furniture had arrived. Twenty minutes later, the deliverymen were assembling the furniture and Randy pitched in, speeding up the process and delighting the men with his down-to-earth attitude. They left with hefty tips and autographs from the Yankees' star player.

After the bed was made, Sexy asked Randy to get the other bottle of Moët out of the fridge, but the moment he turned around, she jumped on his back, insisting that he take her with him, piggyback style. Randy laughed uproariously as he carted Sexy off to the kitchen.

While riding his back, Sexy rested her head on Randy's shoulder.

He smelled faintly of cologne and clean male sweat, and the combined scents aroused her. She covered his neck with kisses, and smiled with satisfaction when Randy emitted a soft moan.

He positioned her on the island and embraced her. His strong arms felt hard and protective, and there wasn't a chance in hell that Sexy was going to let Randy get away. She stared up at him, willing him to kiss her. He hesitated briefly, and then leaned downward. His lips were soft and his searching tongue tasted like champagne. With her palms cupping his face, she pulled him closer as she kissed him slowly and gently.

The soft, throaty sounds he made let her know that she was getting to him, breaking his gentlemanly resolve.

"No, I can't," he whispered, pulling away.

"Why not? No one needs to know except us. It's our secret." She began working on his zipper.

"It's not right," he protested.

"I want to taste you, baby," she cajoled, slipping her hand inside his briefs. "Can I suck your dick, Randy? Please? One last time?" she asked, her hands running over the swell in his crotch, touching him intimately.

Randy released a groan that was a mixture of defeat and raw passion. Sexy hopped off the island and dropped down to her knees.

Randy stepped closer and lowered his jeans, the bulge in his cotton briefs creating a huge dick print, sending hot coils of need throughout Sexy's body. He made a guttural sound in the back of his throat as she guided the smooth head of his dick to her eager lips.

A pure wave of lust ran through her. "Mmm," she moaned as he pushed inside her moist mouth.

"Mmm," he responded, his dick smoothly gliding along her champagne-coated tongue, and then plunging deeply in the back of her throat. "Oh, God!" Randy trembled and moaned. Her hands moved to his firm ass, which she cupped, holding him securely in place.

With his dick imprisoned inside Sexy's hot mouth, Randy was a willing captive. She gripped his ass and he gripped her head while thrusting in and out of her mouth. Damp heat blossomed between her thighs, and Sexy was nearly hyperventilating, panting with need.

She pulled back, allowing his dick to slip away from her lips. Randy gave a small cry of protest, but she stroked and appeased his slippery dick for a few moments and then flung off her top and wriggled out of her skirt. Clad in only pink lace panties and bra, she began rubbing her breasts and stroking her moist crotch with her middle finger. Her long fingers unhooked the bra and let it fall to the floor. Next she stepped out of her panties, and kicked them on top of the mound of clothes on the kitchen floor.

Fingering herself, she kept her eyes on Randy, who watched through half-lidded eyes that were glazed over with lust. "You want to taste this pussy, Randy?" she asked softly.

Mesmerized by the wanton display, Randy bit his bottom lip, and then nodded his head helplessly. Sexy stuck out her middle finger, and Randy unreservedly slurped on her finger.

"My pussy needs some tongue, baby," she cooed. And now it was Randy's turn to lower himself down to his knees. Sexy gasped in shock as his hot fingers parted her sex while his tongue ran up and down the soft slit. Her head tilted backward when she felt his plump lips pulling on her swollen clit. He tongue-fucked her so thoroughly, she gapped her legs open and squatted over his face, urging him to probe even deeper. Randy dipped his tongue in to the hilt, slurping loudly as he drank her honeyed juices.

With Randy's head locked between her thighs, Sexy realized she'd never experienced anything as wonderful as the way Randy gave head. Suddenly, lightning bolts blasted through the core of her being, causing her to shudder violently. She didn't try to hold back; she wanted to fill his mouth with her passion. And when she felt his throat constricting as he swallowed her sweetness, she smiled with the knowledge that a part of her very essence had been released inside his body.

Randy licked every drop of dewy stickiness from her vaginal lips and her clit. He then carried her to the bedroom and tossed her on the bed.

Randy, the gentleman, had vacated the premises. On top of Sexy was a growling sex fiend, who was grunting as he rammed hard dick inside her. "Fuck me, Big Daddy," she urged. "Beat this pussy up; split my shit in two."

Spurred on by Sexy's raunchy dialogue, Randy drove himself inside her with a vengeance, drilling inside her body as if his dick were a power tool.

"After you finish tearing up this pussy, I'm gonna need you to fuck me in the ass. You want some ass, baby. Huh? Do you?"

In the midst of a down stroke, Randy's knees gave out. "Yeah, I want some ass," he admitted in a growl—and then he came with a roar.

The combination of champagne and wanton sex in the kitchen, bedroom, and more sex in the bathroom had Randy out for the count. Sprawled out and sleeping with his mouth open, the man was dead to the world. Triumphant in the knowledge that Randy wouldn't be leaving her bed until morning, Sexy smiled down at Randy and kissed him on the cheek.

Now, it was time for payback. Grinning devilishly, she slid Randy's phone out of his pants pocket and called his bitch of a wife.

"Randy! I've been so worried, baby. Where are you?" Cheryl asked frantically.

"Sorry to disappoint you, Cheryl. This isn't Randy; it's none other than your girl, Sexy," she said in a saccharine-sweet tone of voice.

"What are you doing calling me from Randy's phone? Where is he?"

"He's right here lying beside me. But he's knocked out and can't come to the phone right now. Yeah, I fucked your husband to sleep; do you wanna hear my man snore?"

While Cheryl hissed and hurled a string of profanities, Sexy held the phone up to Randy's mouth and the unmistakable sound of his snoring rumbled into the phone.

"I'm gonna beat your ass, you trifling little hooker," Cheryl raged.

"Whatever," Sexy said, sounding bored. "Anyway, I'm gonna let my baby sleep for another hour or so, and then I'm gonna wake him up so he can give me some more of that big, juicy dick. By the way, there's no point in waiting up for him because Randy won't be coming home tonight—he's staying right here in bed with me, fucking and sucking until the sun comes up and the birds start chirping."

Cheryl

"STEPHEN! STEPHEN," Cheryl shouted at the top of her lungs while banging on the apartment door. "STEPHEN!"

"Cheryl, what the hell is wrong?" Stephen said, after opening the door.

"Get dressed. We've got to go." Cheryl charged into the apartment, clad only in slippers, a flimsy nightgown, and an unbuttoned, ankle-length sable coat which flared out behind her as she flew into Stephen's bedroom.

"Where we gotta go? It's three o'clock in the morning," Stephen said, following behind her. "And why are you wearing a fur coat in this weather?"

Cheryl shrugged and said, "Here," as she flung a pair of pants that were hanging on the back of a chair at him. "Put these on. And this." She threw him a shirt, and then headed toward the door. "Come on."

"Where are we going?" Stephen was hopping on one foot, trying to put on his pants as he walked. "What's going on?"

"You're going to take me to that bitch so I can kill her!" Cheryl screamed, beckoning him to hurry and get dressed.

"What bitch?" Stephen said, slipping his shirt on and closing the apartment door.

"That skank, Sexy!" Cheryl shouted as she raced down the hall. At the elevator, she jabbed her finger against the button. Too impatient to wait for the elevator, she headed for the stairs with Stephen trying to keep up. "Can you believe that bitch is somewhere fucking my husband?" Cheryl broke into a trot when she reached the ground level.

"Cheryl, wait for me, honey!" Stephen cried out.

The midnight air hit Cheryl in the face as she flung the building door open and stomped out into the street, but she took no more notice of it than she did the tears and snot running down her face. Her nostrils flared as she approached her Maybach haphazardly parked in the middle of the street, holding up traffic. She jumped in the car, and pulled off before Stephen even had time to properly close his door.

"So, okay," he said, exhaling loudly, "where are we going?"

"You tell me," Cheryl answered as she peeled around the corner on two wheels.

"How the hell do I know?"

"You've got to know!" Cheryl pounded on the dashboard with one hand while steering with the other. "Someone's got to know. I've called everyone. Where the fuck is that bitch?"

"Wait, who did you call?"

"Everyone. All management. The players. Their wives—"

"You've got to be kidding!"

"And I went to Brent and Mila and kicked Mila's ass. Do you know that bitch, who's supposed to be MY friend, was covering for him?"

"You've got to be kidding!" Stephen repeated.

"DO I LOOK LIKE I'M KIDDING?" Cheryl hollered, fully turning in her seat to face Stephen.

"My God, Cheryl! Look out!" Stephen grabbed the steering wheel, swerving the car moments before it hit a fire hydrant. "Put your foot on the brakes."

Cheryl swiped a hand over her face, and then wiped it on her fur coat, before grabbing the wheel again. "We're gonna find that bitch, Stephen, and then we're going to kill her."

"Okay, honey, we'll do that." Stephen opened the glove compartment, and pulled out a tissue and started dabbing at Cheryl's face as she drove. Her eyes were red, and would likely be near swollen shut if she weren't so wide-eyed with fury. Stephen used his fingers to gently pull the strands of hair plastered onto Cheryl's face. "Sweetie, you do realize it's too hot for that fur coat, don't you?"

Cheryl glanced down at her coat. "It's fine," she said dismissively.

"If you say so," he said, turning up the air conditioning in the car. "So, where are we heading first?"

"Right here." Cheryl screeched to a stop in front of the Ritz-Carlton, and jumped out the car, leaving the car running.

Stephen pulled the keys out of the ignition and handed it to the valet. "I wouldn't bother to move it. We'll likely only be a moment."

He rushed into the lobby right in time to see Cheryl point her finger at the concierge and scream: "No, I don't need any damn help!"

Stephen held his hand up to the man in a reassuring manner. "Thanks, but we know where we're going." He then ran after Cheryl, barely making it inside the elevator before the doors closed. He stood straight, his hands folded in front of him as the elevator made its way to the nineteenth floor.

Cheryl didn't bother knocking when she reached room 1901; she immediately started kicking. "Bitch, get the fuck out here. Come on out so I can kick your ass!" she screamed. When the door didn't open immediately. she backed up as far as she could and did a couple of flying kicks.

"Cheryl, she's obviously not there, honey," Stephen said in a soft voice.

"And I guess her pussy-ass bitch boyfriend isn't there, either,"

Cheryl screamed, before aiming another flying kick at the door.

"Right," Stephen said calmly.

"Okay," Cheryl said, breathing heavily. "Okay. If she's not here, she's got to be somewhere. And we're gonna find her."

"Right," Stephen answered, taking her arm and leading her to the elevators.

They got on an elevator going down right as the doors for another elevator opened and three hotel security officers disembarked.

"You know—"

"I don't want to hear it," Cheryl snarled.

"Right," Stephen said, through pursed lips.

Cheryl stomped outside to the car, snatched her keys from the valet who rushed toward her and jumped in her car, which was still parked in front of the hotel.

"Sorry, it seems I didn't bring my wallet," Stephen shouted out the window to the valet as Cheryl once again peeled off. This time Cheryl drove stone-faced and silently, her eyes fixed on the road, concentrating hard. She didn't know where she was going, but somehow she wound up in front of the Four Seasons hotel. She turned the car off and turned to Stephen. "Okay, I'm calm."

Stephen gave a huge sigh, seemingly of relief. "Cheryl, I'm so glad, because—"

"HOW COULD HE DO THIS TO ME? WITH HER OF ALL PEOPLE?" Cheryl furiously pounded her fists against the dashboard. "WHY, STEPHEN, WHY?" she screamed over and over again until her voice was so hoarse barely a sound came out.

"Oh, honey! Please try and calm down."

Stephen tried to pull her into his arms, but she fought him off, and then jumped out the car. Somehow one arm had come out of her coat, and it dragged behind her, and the already flimsy nightgown was soaked with tears and perspiration, rendering it see-through. But appearance was the last thing on Cheryl's mind as she stomped over to the hotel lobby desk.

"What room is Sexy Sanchez and Randy Alston in?" she managed to croak out.

"I'm sorry, ma'am. Who are you looking for?" the astonished clerk asked, trying hard to look at her face and not at the nipples protruding from her nightgown.

"Sexy Sanchez and Randy Alston!" she repeated a good deal louder.

The clerk looked down and started tapping keys on a computer hidden by the counter. "I'm sorry, ma'am. We don't have anyone with those names registered with us this evening."

Cheryl's eyes narrowed. "You're lying."

"Come on, Cheryl. They're not here."

"No, Stephen. He's lying. He's lying. Everyone's lying!" Cheryl walked away from the lobby desk, and at first, it seemed she was going to simply stomp out the door. But immediately before reaching it, she grabbed a brass lamp and swung it with all her might against the lobby window.

"Look at that, Stephen. A home run!" She started laughing hysterically. She then swung again, shattering another window, and then another.

"Cheryl, please, they've called the police," Stephen said, running up to her, but then ducking as Cheryl swung the lamp against one of the oil paintings on the wall. She continued laughing, so hysterically she fell to her knees still holding the lamp. She was still laughing when the police carried her to their van. It was there that she finally blacked out, with a smile on her lips, and her eyes wide open.

Sexy

W hile Randy slept like a log, Sexy went into the kitchen and searched through the pockets of his jeans that were lying in a heap on the floor. She couldn't resist pocketing a few hundreds from his wad of cash, and then she took an additional fifty bucks to buy something to eat. The jangle of his keys gave her an idea. *I should take his Maybach and go for a spin. Maybe drive to Philly and show my old roomies, Emma and Arielle, how great my new life is. Randy will never know*, she thought with a giggle.

She glanced at the key ring and was suddenly struck by an even better idea. Her eyes twinkled with glee as she used her phone to check online and discovered there was a twenty-four-hour hardware store within walking distance. With Randy's key ring in hand, she quickly threw on her clothes and hurried out of the apartment.

"How many key copies do you want?" asked a pimply-faced young man whom she'd caught dozing when she'd entered the store.

"Um, how about two?" she replied, figuring she might need a back-up key to Randy's and Cheryl's apartment. She doubted she'd ever have the opportunity to use the key, but she couldn't resist the prospect of having access to Randy's marital abode.

On the way back to her apartment, she picked up a sausage pizza, an orange Gatorade and two bottles of water. She could hear Randy still snoring when she crossed the threshold of her apartment. With the kind of racket he was making, she doubted if she'd get very much sleep tonight. She wished she had bought a TV today, but since she hadn't, she had to resort to playing around online for amusement.

It was fun taking pictures of her new apartment and posting them on Instagram. She even took a picture of Randy, asleep in her bed with his mouth open. Thoughtfully, she cropped out his face before posting the photo that she captioned, "My Baller Boo" on her Instagram page.

She sat out on her terrace until she grew bored of the magnificent view. Sometime around three o'clock in the morning, Sexy finally returned to the bedroom and drifted off to sleep. An hour later, awakened by a full bladder, she drowsily wandered to the bathroom. Suddenly thirsty, she trekked to the kitchen to grab a bottle of water. As she reached for the handle of the fridge, she was startled by the blaring ring of a phone. Frowning, she retrieved the phone from Randy's pants where she had returned it after making her spiteful telephone call earlier. There was no doubt in her mind that it was Cheryl blowing up Randy's phone.

That desperate housewife needs to let her husband have some breathing room. Damn! Can't my man get a decent night's sleep without this trick always tracking him down? She sucked her teeth and with brows furrowed, she peered at the screen. She squinted at the caller ID, which read: *NY-Presbyterian Hospital.* Curious, Sexy brazenly answered Randy's phone.

"Hello?"

"May I speak to Randall Alston, please?"

"Uh, what's this in reference to?"

"I'm calling from New York-Presbyterian Hospital, Department of Psychiatry. There's an emergency concerning Mrs. Cheryl Alston."

"Really?"

"It's urgent that I speak to Mr. Alston," said the crisp voice on the other end.

Sexy heaved a sigh. Cheryl had probably faked a suicide attempt simply to lure Randy away from the woman he loved. *What a bitch!* Although it was against her better judgment, Sexy padded to the bedroom and shook Randy until he jolted awake.

"What is it? What's wrong?" he bellowed, wild-eyed, arms flailing. Geez, the way Randy woke up, looking and acting all crazy, wasn't attractive at all. Sexy blamed it on the champagne he had drunk earlier in the evening. Surely, this wasn't his typical way of greeting a new day.

"The psych hospital is on the phone, calling about Cheryl," Sexy said casually.

Randy bolted upright, and this time his eyes were wide with fright. "Did something happen to Cheryl?"

Momentarily forgetting her role as the loving and supportive side chick, Sexy grimaced in disgust and shrugged one shoulder as she handed Randy his phone.

"Hello?" he said in a desperate tone of voice. "Cheryl has been admitted? Why?" He listened for a moment and then said, "I'll be there right away." He jumped out of bed and turned in a complete circle, scratching his head as he attempted to orient himself.

"Is Cheryl all right?" Resuming her role, Sexy's words and facial expression were now tinged with concern.

Instead of answering Sexy's question, Randy said gruffly, "Where're my clothes?"

"I'll get them. They're in the kitchen." Sexy trotted to the kitchen and then returned to the bedroom with Randy's jeans, briefs, and shirt.

Randy snatched his belongings from Sexy's hands. He nearly toppled over, struggling to hastily get into his pants. In less than five minutes, Randy was dressed and racing toward the living room.

At the sound of the slamming front door, Sexy rolled her eyes. *Bastard! I hope that psycho-wife of his smells my pussy on his breath and tastes it on his tongue. If she's only faking being crazy, getting a taste of my pussy on her husband's tongue ought to really send that bitch over the deep end!*

Sexy cancelled her appointment with the interior decorator. She was much too stressed out to listen to a prissy-acting bitch talk about color schemes and displaying swatches of fabric. She'd been calling Randy for the past two hours to no avail, and at this point, she didn't give a damn about getting the apartment furnished. Whatever the interior decorator wanted to do with the place was fine with Sexy. All she really needed right now was a new TV and Randy.

Where's my baby? And why isn't he returning my calls? I hate Cheryl and her conniving ways.

Although she was frantically waiting for Randy's call, the ring of her phone startled her, causing her to nearly jump out of her skin. She glanced at the screen and gave a long sigh. It wasn't Randy, it was her mother calling.

"What?" she answered grumpily.

"That's not a proper way to greet a caller. You were raised better than that, Amanda, and you know it."

"Give it a break, Mom. I don't feel like listening to you bitch about my uncouth ways."

"Watch your language, young lady," Clarissa warned.

"Or what? What are you gonna do if I don't watch my language? Put me on punishment? Withhold my allowance?" Sexy emitted a burst of wicked laughter.

"Amanda!"

"Seriously, Mom. What are you gonna do? In case you haven't noticed, I haven't been following your militaristic rules about checking in with weekly phone calls. You don't have any power over me anymore because I don't care about that miserly pittance you were putting in my bank account. I have my own money now, and I don't need yours."

Clarissa went uncharacteristically silent.

"I hope you didn't call me so I could listen to you breathe over the phone," Sexy complained.

"What's with you, Amanda? Why're you being so ornery? I called to find out what's a good day for the two of us to go shopping for new school clothes," Clarissa said in a chipper tone. "Daddy said the sky is the limit. He wants his little girl to get a brand-new wardrobe for her new start in London."

"You've got to be kidding. I'm not going to school in London or anywhere else."

"Be reasonable, Mandy," her mother cajoled. "You have one more year of high school and if you live up to your academic potential while attending the prep school in Europe, Daddy can pull some strings and get you in the University of Pennsylvania or possibly Princeton. He has clout with numerous Ivy League schools across the country."

"I'm not going back to school."

Now Clarissa's voice turned to steel. "We had an agreement, Amanda, and I will not have a daughter of mine wandering this earth without a decent education."

Sexy laughed without mirth. In fact, the sound of her laughter held a ring of malice. "You're right. No daughter of yours will ever walk the earth, period. Wanna know why? Because you don't have a daughter!"

Clarissa gasped. "Why would you say something so cruel?"

"Get real, Mom. The charade is over. I'm adopted and you know it. The thing that puzzles me is why in the world you and Daddy tried to keep it a secret?"

"Oh, my God." Clarissa began to sob. "I wanted to tell you, but your father thought it best that you didn't know the truth. He didn't want you to grow up feeling inferior."

"Well, the plan didn't work."

"Oh, Mandy. I'm so sorry. How'd you find out, sweetheart? We tried to be so careful."

"I overheard you two discussing my aberrant traits. You said my propensity for stealing had to be a genetic trait—something I must have inherited from my biological parents."

"Amanda, listen to me, sweetheart. Daddy and I both love you. We chose you—"

"Cut the crap. That's the spiel you give to a four-year-old. What century are you living in? People don't hide the fact that a kid has been adopted. Why couldn't you have been honest with me?"

Clarissa sighed. "We were wrong to withhold that information. Can you forgive us, dear?"

"I don't know. You allowed me to live a lie, telling me I was half Pakistani and half African American. How could you and Daddy live with yourselves after feeding an innocent child so many lies? What am I mixed with, Mom? I mean...who exactly am I?"

"You're Amanda Nehru...our daughter."

"Can you at least give me my birth parents' names?"

"I'm sorry, dear. I truly don't have that information."

"Whatever."

"We made a big mistake, Mandy, but we had your best interest at heart. You've got to forgive us. We love you with all our hearts."

"Maybe I could forgive you if you'd give me a little information."

"What else do you want to know?" Clarissa asked, sounding somewhat panicked.

"I've been contacting adoption agencies since I was fourteen years old—"

"You have?"

"Yes, but I constantly hit brick walls. I deserve to know the names of my birth parents—if only to get info about my family medical history."

Clarissa sobbed as she spoke. "I wish I could give you that information. All I know is that your mother, uh, died in childbirth, and I have no idea who your biological father is. So, please, darling, let it go."

"I can't let it go, so please don't ask me to pretend that I'm your daughter any longer when clearly I'm not. Not with all my personality defects and character flaws that I've heard you and Daddy quietly complaining about numerous times."

"Oh, my God. We never actually complained. It's only...well, you had certain behaviors that were so foreign to us. The constant stealing and lying. We didn't understand it and we were afraid for your future."

"Yeah, I can imagine how much it sucked not knowing what to expect out of the stranger you were raising as your own. I bet it sucked about as much it sucks not knowing whose blood is flowing through my veins. Not knowing your true identity is a bitch," she said callously.

"But we can start all over. We can have more open dialogue—as a family."

"It's too late for that," Sexy said wearily. "Back off, Mom; stop interfering with my life. I'm doing quite well on my own, so consider me emancipated."

"You're barely seventeen; how can you possibly take care of yourself?"

"Easily. I use my looks and my feminine wiles—like you! Isn't that how you snagged Daddy? I learned a lot about duping men into taking care of me by watching you, Mommy," Sexy said callously, and then hung up on her mother.

Having the upper hand over her pretentious mother felt good. And her wimp of a father, who wasn't man enough to control his cheating wife, yet constantly complained that Sexy was genetically flawed, could kiss her flawed ass. Sexy walked over to the window and looked out. She didn't feel bad about hurting her mother's feelings; as far as she was concerned, the bitch deserved it. Still, she knew the only reason she lashed out the way she did at that moment was because she was so pissed at Cheryl. The bitch was fucking up all her plans. At least she thought she was. But there was no way Sexy was going to lose this fight.

S he didn't want to be ungrateful, but she needed Randy to get the hell out of the house. It was sweet of him to stay with her at the hospital for those two nights, but now that she was out, she had some serious business to take care of that he couldn't be privy to.

"Oh, snap, I've had this for a minute. I can't believe I forgot to give it to you," a grinning Randy said, coming into the living room with a gift-wrapped package. He placed it on the table next to the couch where Cheryl was lying.

Cheryl gave him a withering look, and then picked up a magazine that was also on the table, and started flipping through it.

"Um, aren't you going to open it?"

Instead of answering, Cheryl took a sip of her Ethiopian Fancy coffee, turned another page, and made believe she was suddenly engrossed by an article on Kendall Jenner. She had been super nice to Randy since coming to at the hospital, not wanting to push him back into the arms of Miss Skank, but now she had to try a different tactic. She simply had to get him out of the apartment.

"Cheryl, is there something wrong?"

Cheryl rolled her eyes and continued to ignore him.

"Babe?"

Cheryl finally put the magazine down and stared at Randy. "We really haven't talked about what happened—"

"Babe, I apologized." Randy lowered his eyes, and started wring-ing his hands together. "I felt sorry for her. She had nowhere to go after Yusef put her out, and it was really my fault that they fought in the first place."

"Why? You didn't rape her. She lay down like a woman, and you took it like a man." Cheryl put down the magazine and crossed her arms over her chest. "Yusef threw her out because of what she did, not what you did. I'm the one who was hurt over what *you* did."

"I know, Cheryl," Randy said, in a voice barely above whisper.

"And I can't believe you actually got Brent and Mila to lie for you." Cheryl shook her head. "Do you know how embarrassing all of this is for me?" She sighed and turned her head. "Thank God, Stephen somehow managed to keep all of this from the media. Bet you won't ask what good is he anymore."

Randy nodded dismally. "I'm sorry I hurt you, and I know I've said it before, but it's never going to happen again."

"Yes, you have said it before. And I believed you." Cheryl let out a big sigh. "And you actually have the nerve to expect me to believe, again, you're never going to see Sexy, huh? How big an idiot do you expect me to be?"

"I don't think you're an idiot at all, Cheryl. I think you're a woman who loves me, and knows, deep down, that while I messed up big time, I really love you, too."

"And I guess you love Sexy, too, huh?" Cheryl said sadly.

"Naw, babe." Randy shook his head. "I admit I had it bad for her, but I don't love her."

"Then how could you have done this to me?" Cheryl demanded.

"I don't know, I really don't know. I tried not to do it." Randy's shoulders slumped. "She, I don't know, she—"

"She what? She sucked your dick so good you had to go back

for more?" Cheryl's voice turned shrill. "The pussy was so good you had to go back and hit it again?"

"Cheryl, no!"

"Then what was it?" Cheryl said, jumping up from the couch.

"I don't know," Randy said, tears in his voice. "She was sweet. Very sweet."

"Sexy? Sweet? You've got to be kidding." Cheryl started laughing. "Boy, she's got you fooled."

"And, she kinda, well, she kinda reminds me of you," Randy continued, as if he hadn't heard Cheryl's sarcastic remarks.

Reminds him of me? Cheryl gasped. Once again she was face-to-face with the fact that her rival was her daughter. Covering her face with her hands, she sank back down on the couch and started crying.

"Oh, babe, I'm so sorry. I'm only saying that the close resemblance might have been part of the attraction, that's all," Randy said, trying unsuccessfully to pull her into his arms.

Instead of comforting her, the words made her cry even harder. He was going to leave her for her daughter; she absolutely knew it. Of course, she could prevent it by simply telling him the whole truth. Tell him that Sexy was only seventeen. Tell him that Sexy was her child. That's it!

"Randy, I'm so miserable," she said, falling into his arms.

"I know, babe, I know," he said, rubbing her back.

"No, you don't know." Cheryl sat up, then wiped her eyes. "Randy, there's something that I should have told you, but...but, I couldn't bring myself to."

"What, babe?"

No. She couldn't bring herself to tell him the truth. She couldn't take the chance that he might leave her. "Well, you know how we've been trying to have a baby?"

Randy gasped. "Cheryl, you're pregnant? Oh, honey!"

Cheryl shook her head frantically. "No, you don't understand." She took a deep breath before continuing her lie. "I thought I was. My period was three days late, and I was so thrilled. But then—" She started crying again. "But then it came down suddenly. The same night I was waiting for you to come home. I was so depressed I thought I would die. I needed you to comfort me, Randy, and I waited all night for you to come home. But instead I got that mean phone call from...from, you know who."

"Oh, Cheryl." Randy's eyes filled with tears. "Oh, Cheryl, I'm so sorry."

Cheryl sobbed. "I think that's why I went so crazy that night, not only because of you cheating on me, but because I was so depressed about not being pregnant with your child. There's nothing more that I want than to have your baby; you know that. And the two things simply pushed me over the edge."

"Oh, my God, oh my God." Randy grabbed her in his arms and started rocking back and forth. "Cheryl, can you ever forgive me?"

The only thing breaking the silence in the room for the next few minutes was the sound of sobs—genuine weeping from Randy, well-rehearsed crying from Cheryl.

"Wait a minute," Randy said, gently unfolding his arms from around Cheryl and reaching for his phone. He quickly scrolled through his contacts, tapped the send button, and then tapped another button to set the phone on speaker.

"Hey, Randy!" Sexy's voice came through loud and clear. "I've been texting, calling and leaving voice messages for you for the last two days. What's going on?"

"Sexy," Randy said in a solemn voice. "I'm calling you to tell you that I'm sorry, but I won't be able to see you again."

"What?" Sexy shouted. "What the hell are you talking about?

You—" Her voice suddenly lowered. "Wait a minute. Is Cheryl there? Are you saying all of this for her benefit? Don't worry. Go right on talking, and then when you get by yourself, call me back and tell me what's going on."

Randy let out a deep breath. "It's not like that, Sexy. Cheryl is here, but I'm not calling for her benefit; it was my idea to give you a call."

Cheryl grinned happily.

"Randy, is Cheryl listening? Is she coaching you on what to say?"

"I'm not going to lie; she is listening, but she's not coaching me," Randy said impatiently. "I was wrong to get involved with you, and it's not going to happen again. I love my wife, and I'm going to devote my time to her and the family we're starting. I think it's best you go on back home to Philadelphia and get on with your own life, because we're getting on with ours. You take care of yourself, and I wish you the best."

And with that, he hung up. "I love you, babe, and I'm never going to hurt you again," he said, kissing Cheryl.

"What say we get busy trying to get that family started again?" Cheryl said in a husky voice.

It was three o'clock before Randy had rested up from an hour of passionate lovemaking and headed to Madison Avenue to meet with his agent and executives from Coca-Cola. Against both Cheryl's and his agent's urging for him to take the Pepsi deal, Randy had remained true to his principles and had accepted the lesser sum of money offered by Coca-Cola—the beverage he actually preferred to drink.

"Stephen," she said as soon as she got her friend on the phone. "I'm back. What's been going on?"

"Girl, if you weren't my best friend, I'd hang up on you."

"Yeah, yeah, yeah, I love you, too," Cheryl said with a little chuckle. "I want to thank you for everything. I'm fine, now. And I'm sorry, etcetera, etcetera. Now, can we simply move on?"

Stephen sucked his teeth. "No, we can't. Do you know how much trouble I had covering all that shit up? Not to mention how much of the Yankees money I had to spread around to make sure nobody saw or heard what they actually saw and heard."

"Um, hundreds?" Cheryl couldn't suppress a giggle.

"Hmph! Try thousands."

"Oh, damn!"

"Oh, yeah. And the boys in the big offices sure don't find it as amusing as you seem to," Stephen said with a huff. "You'd better be glad that young country boy is such a hot commodity. He sure as hell better not go into a batting slump this season."

"Stephen, I'm sorry." The contriteness in Cheryl's voice was genuine. "I guess I was trying to pretend it was all funny because I'm so embarrassed. But you know all the shit I was going through."

"Well, no, I don't," Stephen snipped. "I know that somehow you found out that Randy and Sexy were together, but the Cheryl I know wouldn't have suffered a nervous breakdown over that. Care to expound?"

With a sigh, Cheryl told all. Well, not all. She omitted that she was responsible for Jocko being murdered. She left out that Sexy was her daughter. But she did tell him about the telephone call she'd received from the girl.

"She actually said that," Stephen said with a gasp. "She actually said, 'Yeah, I fucked your husband to sleep; do you wanna hear my man snore,'?"

"That's an exact quote," Cheryl said bitterly. It hurt recounting the episode, but she at least owed Stephen that. "See why I went the fuck off?"

"Oh, hell yeah," Stephen all but yelled. "I probably would have gone off worse if some bitch called and told me that about my man." He paused a moment, then added in a concerned tone: "Are you really okay now, honey? I wanted to visit you in the nut house—"

"It wasn't the nut house," Cheryl snapped. "It was New York-Presbyterian, the most prestigious hospital in the city."

"Uh huh, and how was the food in the nut ward?"

"Fuck you, Stephen," Cheryl said, laughing. "It was only two days, and I did need a break. So, anyway," she said, now serious. "What did I miss? What's been going on?"

"Nothing. Same as usual. Yankees on top, Mets at the bottom. All is right with the world," Stephen said in a bored voice.

"Well," Cheryl said slowly, "anything new on the Jocko front?"

"No, he's still dead."

"Very funny. Have they found out who did it?"

"I don't know. I haven't been following the papers."

Cheryl grimaced. She had actually gone through the two days' worth of newspapers piled in front of their apartment door when she and Randy had returned home, but there was no mention of anything. But the fact was that the apprehension of a hit-and-run driver of a non-descript Black man in Washington Heights might not make the paper, unless it was a slow news day. "But, you being a PR guy and having all kinds of sources in the media, you haven't been able to find out anything?"

"Can't say that I've tried. Why are you so interested, anyway?"

"I'm not really. Simply wondering, that's all." *Now what do I do?* "Listen, I gotta go. I'll give you a call later."

Normally, Cheryl was a bubble-bath person, but she was too

worried to even think about relaxing. All she could think about as the water from the shower cascaded over her body was whether Dwayne Ligon had been caught, and whether she was going to be arrested. She badly wanted to call him, but the many episodes of *Law & Order* she'd watched over the years cautioned her that to do so might give her away. They always found out who hired the contract killer by pulling his phone logs to find out what calls he received before and after the murder, and then traced the number.

The best thing to do, she decided as she dressed in a stylish blue pants suit, was to call him from a pay phone. And not one in her neighborhood. And to use gloves so that they couldn't pull finger-prints from the telephone or the coins.

Cheryl was heading out the door when she spied the gift-wrapped present that Randy had placed on the coffee table earlier; she'd forgotten all about it. Now her curiosity got the best of her. Besides, she could use a little pick-me-up. She sat down, placing her shoulder bag on the couch next to her, and eagerly tore open the wrapping.

She gasped when she saw it. A pink Prada Saffiano Lux tote! And she'd never seen one with metal studs and stones. She'd never seen one for less than $2,500, and this one had to be even more. Cheryl gently caressed the bag, then brought it to her face and inhaled the soft leather. She had bags, but none this beautiful, or this expensive. She dashed back into the bedroom and quickly changed her clothes, putting on an ivory dress with pink accents that perfectly matched her new acquisition. She topped it off with a wide-brimmed sun hat and a pair of Prada sunglasses and headed out the door; her mood greatly lightened, she was now sure of the success of her mission.

God, I love Randy, she thought as she drove up Lexington Ave-nue. And not only because of all his gifts, all his money, and all the luxuries he provided her; and not even because he loved her more than any man she'd ever known. She loved him for him. He had his faults and weaknesses, of course, but he was basically a good man. He was loving, considerate, sincere, a damn good husband— at least until that damn Sexy showed up in their lives.

Spotting a pay phone near a very rare parking space a few feet away, Cheryl pulled over. She adjusted her sunglasses, slipped on her lightweight gloves, and grabbed her new bag and hopped out the car. Taking a deep breath, she walked toward the phone. She was about to insert the necessary coins when she noticed a woman window-shopping sporting the same Prada bag she had on her arm. Same color, and same unusual metal studs and stones. Cheryl smiled to herself. Maybe someone else was lucky enough to have as generous a husband as her. The smile, however, suddenly contorted into a furious scowl when the woman turned and faced her. It was Sexy.

Slamming down the telephone receiver so hard she almost broke it, she stomped toward her. Sexy didn't see her until she was only a few steps away. Instead of backing away or cowering, Sexy looked at her with a wicked smile and said: "Nice bag."

Cheryl stopped in her tracks, speechless for perhaps the first time in her life. And as bad as she wanted to slap the girl, she was paralyzed. And she was uncertain as to why.

Sexy, for her part, seemed to be enjoying the situation. "Why, Cheryl, fancy seeing you in my new neighborhood. I was planning to give your friend, Stephen, a call to get a contact list for all the players' wives so I could invite them over for my housewarming. Wait until you see the apartment Randy rented for me. And the furniture is simply to die for. Are you available, say, next Sunday?"

Instead of answering, Cheryl smiled and reached into her now hated new tote bag, and pulled out her cell phone. "Hey, Randy, baby. How's it going?"

"Fine, babe, I'm on my way home to you now. Do you need me to pick something up for you?"

"No, sweetie, I'm out myself. In fact, would you believe I ran into Sexy? She wants to know if we're available next Sunday to attend a housewarming for the apartment you rented for her."

There was a pause, then: "Cheryl, I was going to tell you—"

"No, I didn't tell her. Should I? Oh, okay." Cheryl grinned and pulled the phone from her ear. "Sexy, Randy said to tell you that he's already called the landlord to find out how much he has to pay to break the lease, and he suggests that you start moving out by this weekend. I suppose there'll be no housewarming next weekend, huh?" Cheryl struggled hard to hide the grin that was battling to make itself known. Sexy's emotions, on the other hand, were evident on her face. She was furious.

"Do you want to talk to him?" Cheryl asked, holding the phone toward the girl.

"No, thanks, I'll be seeing him later this evening," Sexy said, in a voice that she was obviously trying to keep steady.

"Oh, okay." Cheryl brought the telephone back to her ear. "Randy, Sexy said she'll talk to you when she sees you this evening. Should I call and cancel the airline reservations we have for our Bahamas getaway?"

"Cheryl, I don't know what you're doing, but okay, handle this any way you want." He paused, and then added, "But please don't be too mean. She doesn't deserve it."

"Gotcha. Love you, babe. And don't worry, the bags are all packed so we can head to the airport as soon as you get home." She slipped the telephone back in her bag. "He asked me to tell you that he filed for a restraining order against you—"

"What!" Sexy's mouth dropped open.

"And that you'll probably be served later this afternoon, or maybe tomorrow." Cheryl looked at her watch. "Oh, look at the time. I still have to pick up a couple of bathing suits, so I've got to run." She turned, and slowly sashayed her way back to her car, letting the tote bag lazily sway back and forth on her arm. Right before getting in the car, she turned and looked at Sexy, smiled, and twirled her fingers goodbye, in the same way Sexy had done to her too many times.

But once inside the car, Cheryl was anything but calm and relaxed. *He fucking rented her an apartment? On the Upper East Side, one of the most expensive neighborhoods in New York. And he actually bought both of us the same exact bag? What is that? Some kind of male ego thing, branding his women? I hate him!* She started the car and pulled off, tears in her eyes. *Damn, I wish I didn't love him so much.*

Abandoning her plan to call Ligon, Cheryl got on the FDR Drive heading north, not caring where she'd end up. After twenty-five minutes she realized she was almost at the George Washington Bridge. Maybe a ride through New Jersey would help clear her mind. She was debating whether to go over the bridge or not, when her cell phone rang. She looked down at the screen. Ligon!

"So let me get this straight," Cheryl said, shaking her head in disbelief. "You mean you had nothing to do with his death?"

"Not a damn thing," Ligon said while nonchalantly chewing a wooden toothpick. "Our contract was for a thorough roughing up—"

"But not too rough," Cheryl hurriedly broke in.

Ligon smirked at her, before continuing: "Our contract was for a thorough roughing up, but nothing too drastic."

"Right. And?"

Ligon shrugged. "And so he was gifted a broken leg, a broken wrist, and a broken nose, along with a warning that if he ever contacted you, he'd be in for much worse. Nothing more, nothing less."

"So you did not run him down with a car?"

A look of annoyance crossed Ligon's face, but his voice remained cool. "No, like I said before, I didn't have a damn thing to do with it. It's a bad coincidence that it happened the same day."

Cheryl leaned back in her chair and breathed a large sigh of relief. "Oh, God, you don't know how relieved I am, Ligon. You can't even imagine how it was tugging on my conscience and—"

"On your conscience, huh?" Ligon chuckled. "Sure you weren't afraid I was going to get caught and maybe rat you out?"

"Not at—" Cheryl paused and smiled. "Okay, I'm not going to lie. That was my primary concern. But I always kinda knew that even if you were caught, you'd never implicate me."

"True." Ligon winked, and gave one of his rare smiles. "I wouldn't have. But I understand you worrying, since there isn't any way for you to know that."

Cheryl poured herself another cup of Ethiopian Fancy coffee after offering Ligon a cup, which he turned down. "Ligon, we've known each other for a few years now, and I've never had the nerve to ask before, but how did you, well, get started in your, uh, business?"

Ligon shrugged. "I was a Navy SEAL for five years, then a Marine for another four years, and so when I got out, it seemed like a natural fit." He gave Cheryl a meaningful look and added: "And let's leave it at that."

Cheryl nodded. "Well, so you know, I really appreciate you."

"Nice to know." Ligon stood up. "Okay, I've got to run. Nice seeing you again."

"It took you forever to return my calls," Sexy said anxiously when Randy finally called. "Are you really kicking me out of the apartment and getting a restraining order on me?"

"What? No!"

"I'm only repeating what Cheryl said."

"Oh, yeah, about Cheryl..." Randy paused for a beat. "Like I told you before, she usually doesn't mind if I have an occasional fling, but she's not happy with what's been going on between the two of us. She wants it to stop."

"What do you want?"

"I want whatever makes my wife happy. She already had a mental health crisis on account of me cheating with you, and I need to be the good husband that I vowed to be when I married her. She's been breaking her neck, tryna get pregnant, and the least I can do is be faithful."

It was insulting that Randy had allowed Cheryl to come between them, but Sexy forced herself to stay calm. Choosing her words carefully, she spoke softly and with compassion. "I understand that your marriage is important to you, but I'd be lying if I didn't admit that it hurts me to the core to lose that special bond we had."

"I know—I know. Please try to understand, I never meant to hurt you. But I feel like I done dug myself down into a deep hole and I'm scratching like crazy, tryna dig myself out."

"We're in that hole together. I care about you, Randy, and I know you feel the same."

"I do. I care a lot about you, but I love my wife, and I have to put her first. Cheryl said it's hard for a woman to get pregnant when she's under a whole lot of mental stress. I'm sorry, Sexy, but we have to break this off before it goes any further."

She sniffled and whimpered pitifully. "Are you sure Cheryl is trying to get pregnant? It's unusual for a model to deliberately mess up her body like that. Models are so obsessed with their looks, they usually don't start having children until they're in their mid-to-late thirties, and Cheryl's...what? In her late twenties?"

"She's twenty-four," Randy corrected.

Damn, she's got some mileage on her ass to be only twenty-four. That bitch looks like she's kicking thirty in the ass. "All I'm saying is that it seems odd that she suddenly wants to have a baby."

"It's not sudden. She stopped taking the pill months ago. She's giving up her modeling career and wants to commit herself to being a full-time wife and mother," he said defensively.

"Mm-hmm," she murmured suspiciously.

"You don't know Cheryl. All she's been talking about lately is how bad she wants to be the mother of my child."

Randy was so naïve. It was a shame the way Cheryl had him duped. She gave a long sigh. "Well, there's nothing else I can say except I wish you both the best."

"Thanks. Oh, by the way, you don't have to worry about me kicking you out of the apartment. The rent's paid up for six months, but after that, maybe you need to think about getting into that sports medicine school."

"Yeah, you're right. I suppose it's time for both of us to move on with our lives."

"That's what I like about you, Sexy," Randy said, sounding relieved. "You're so sweet and understanding. Now, I don't want you to have to worry about money or anything like that, so later this evening, I'll drop off a credit card for you to use for your daily expenses. It's probably best if I don't come upstairs, so I'm gonna leave the card with the concierge."

"I understand." Holding the phone to her ear, Sexy paced from room to room, trying to figure out a way to con Randy into stopping by to see her later on. If only she could get him alone with her, she'd make him forget that his lying-ass, phony wife even existed.

Running out of options, she had no choice but to resort to tears. "I can't believe I'm never going to be with you again," she blurted, sniffling and sobbing. "I realize it's for the best, but I miss you already." If Randy had been there in person, she would have flung herself into his arms and clung to him.

"Sexy?" he said in a whispery, gentle tone.

"Yes?" Certain that he'd had a change of heart, a smile spread across her face.

"Um, there's one more thing I have to say..."

"What's that?"

"I don't think it's a good idea for you to call me anymore."

Her shoulders sagged and her head dropped, as if she'd experienced a particularly vicious physical assault. "It's gonna be hard not being able to hear your voice, but I'll leave you alone if that's what you really want."

"That's the way it has to be."

"Okay, I'll delete your number," she said solemnly.

"I'm really sorry, Sexy."

"I know you are."

Once again, she simulated sobbing sounds, only this time, she was much louder.

"Please don't cry, Sexy. One of these days, you'll find a good man for yourself," Randy said, attempting to console her.

"No other man can take your place," she said shrilly. Realizing her voice had emerged high-pitched and indignant, she softened her tone. "You have no idea how much you mean to me, Randy. No idea how much I love you. But you won't have to worry about me contacting you again. Bye, Randy," she said, choking out the last two words and then hanging up abruptly.

Although she'd given Randy the impression that she couldn't bear to linger on the phone with the man she'd loved and lost, the truth was, she had to rush to the nearest Planned Parenthood center before they closed for the day. Sexy had one more trick up her sleeve, and to pull it off, she needed an extra pack of birth control pills.

A shiver of excitement ran up Sexy's spine as she bypassed the doorman by craftily blending in with a trio of leggy blondes who looked like a group of models as they entered the chic SoHo building where Randy and Cheryl lived. She made her way to the elevator, and the concierge, busy with a delivery person, didn't seem to notice her.

With the keys to the Alstons' apartment in her Prada bag, Sexy could barely suppress a smile as the elevator ascended.

Inside, she frowned as she took in the ridiculously large apartment that was decorated almost entirely in white. The stark white walls were adorned with white abstract prints. There was a white, L-shaped, sectional sofa placed on a huge black-and-white tribal rug. Oddly shaped white table lamps were set upon white tables. All that damn white was blinding. The only splashes of color were the overabundance of fresh-cut flower arrangements that were set in white vases throughout the apartment. There were so many flowers, the place held the heavy floral scent of a funeral parlor.

Sexy would have had more time to snoop and get into mischief if Randy and Cheryl were out of town at an away-game, but being that they were only as far away as the Bronx at Yankee Stadium, she couldn't risk dawdling and possibly getting caught.

Still, she couldn't resist taking a quick tour of the place, which was much larger and grander than the luxury apartment Randy had rented for her. Hmph! She'd make sure he made up for this slight in other ways.

The white theme continued in the master suite with a white chaise lounge and antique chairs in the sitting area. And of course there were bouquets of flowers on every available surface. *Geez! What is it with this chick and her obsession with flowers?* In the bathroom, the cavernous shower was tiled with pearly white marble, and a white, excessively fluffy, sheepskin rug was placed on the floor outside the shower and a matching rug beside the sunken bathtub.

Sexy took the pack of birth control pills from her bag and burst into laughter. Ironically, the ivory-colored birth control compact matched Cheryl's color scheme perfectly.

She considered hiding the pills in the medicine cabinet, but a cursory glance informed her that Cheryl would easily spot them inside the generously sized unit. She had to stash them in a place where they wouldn't be easily noticed. But first things first. She marched to the kitchen. The place sparkled with stainless steel, top-of-the-line Viking appliances. She scanned the contents inside the stylish French-door refrigerator, trying to figure out what food to spike with the birth control pills she'd crushed up before leaving her apartment.

But the fridge was poorly stocked with only low-fat yogurt, a few pieces of fruit, containers of arugula and other leafy greens, and a luxury brand of bottled water called Tasmanian Rain. Sexy sneered at the water that was packaged as attractively as an expensive bottle of wine. She'd heard about the trend among celebrities to drink pure rainwater, but Cheryl wasn't a celebrity and she had a hell of a lot of nerve trying to act like one. Before she'd hoodwinked Randy into marrying her, Cheryl had merely been one of thousands of unknown models. And Sexy was certain her tastes hadn't been so refined back when she was clawing her way through the competition to get the next moderately paying modeling gig.

Aggravated, Sexy slammed the refrigerator closed and began searching the cabinets. She spotted a dark brown bag with a label that read: *Ethiopian Fancy. Dark Roast Coffee.*

She recalled that this was the African coffee that Randy had mentioned when they were at the Empire State Building together. The same coffee that Cheryl was passionate about and drank several times a day. A sneaky smile crept across her face. *I got you now, bitch!*

After mixing the crushed pills into the coffee grounds, Sexy traipsed down the long corridor, admiring the lithographs on the wall as she made her way back to the master suite to plant the compact that contained the remaining pills.

T wo weeks later, Cheryl and Stephen were sitting in her living room sipping coffee and talking nonstop when Randy came in from the bedroom wearing his pajamas and robe.

"Hey, baby. It's about time you dragged yourself out of bed," Cheryl said cheerfully. "Want some coffee?"

"Cheryl, can I speak to you a moment?"

"Well, good morning to you, too," Stephen said irritably.

Randy didn't even bother looking at him. "Privately," he said, heading back to the bedroom.

Cheryl looked at Stephen and shrugged. "I'll be back in a minute, sweetie."

"Okay." Stephen looked at his watch. "I want to get to Bloomie's before the lunchtime rush."

Randy was sitting on the bed when Cheryl walked into the room. "What's up, baby? Something wrong?"

Randy stood up. "Cheryl, I was looking through your night table, and I found these." Randy showed her an ivory-colored birth control compact. "Do you mind telling me why you have them?"

"What? I don't know whose they are, but they're not mine." She took the compact from Randy and opened it. Six of the little yellow pills were missing. "Is this some kind of joke?"

"That's what I want to ask you," Randy said, a tremble evident in his voice. "All this time you told me you wanted a baby as much as me. Were you joking?"

"Are you serious? No, of course not," Cheryl said indignantly.

"So outright lying, huh?" Randy's voice was rising with each word. "Didn't want to ruin your beautiful body, huh?" He stood up. "But why didn't you simply tell me that, Cheryl? Of course I want to have a baby, but if you didn't want to, why didn't you tell me, you know? Why fool me like this?" He walked over to the window, and stared out for a moment before turning back toward her and shouted. "I guess you and your sissy friend out there have been having a big laugh over 'young country boy,' huh?"

"Randy, I don't know what the hell is going on, but you need to get ahold of yourself." Cheryl walked over and placed her hands on Randy's shoulders. "Where did you say you found these pills?"

Randy roughly pulled away. "In your night table, where you keep them, Cheryl. And if they're not yours, tell me who else keeps their birth control pills in *your* night table? I sure as hell don't use them."

"Well, neither do I!" Cheryl shouted, though she was still trying to keep her temper while she figured out what the hell was going on. "I don't know whose pills these are, I don't know how they got in my night table, but I do know I don't like being accused of doing something I'm not doing. Why would I tell you I'm not taking birth control pills if I really were?"

"To keep me in shackles."

Cheryl's mouth dropped open. "Randy, this doesn't even sound like you." *In fact, it sounds a helluva lot like that skanky-ass Sexy. I should have suspected that Randy was keeping in touch with that skank behind my back. What kind of shit has she been feeding Randy?*

"Why? Because I don't sound like, ya know, a pussy-whipped country hick? Someone you can twist around your finger? Someone you can keep using and using while you lie to me about wanting my baby?" Randy plopped down on the divan and cradled his head in his hands. "Cheryl, how could you do this to me?"

A pussy-whipped country hick, huh? Yeah, Sexy's gotten to him. "Baby," Cheryl said, dropping to her knees besides him, "you've got this all wrong. I haven't done anything to you. Randy, I want to have a child as badly as you. You know that."

"Then why are you taking those pills?" Randy demanded.

"I'm not taking any damn pills," Cheryl shouted. "Will you get a grip?"

"YOU have the nerve to get pissed off at me, now?" Randy jumped up. "I have to get the fuck outta here."

"Cheryl, sweetie," Stephen's voice rang out from the living room. "Sounds like you're going to be busy for a while so I'm going to go ahead and get out of here. Call me when you get a chance."

Cheryl watched Randy as he ripped off his robe, pulled off his pajamas, and threw on jeans, a shirt and sneakers, not bothering to shower, shave or brush his teeth. The pills weren't hers, someone was trying to frame her, and the only person she knew devious enough to do something like that was that damn Sexy. But how had she managed to plant the pills? She couldn't worry about that now, though. If Randy left believing that she had really deceived him, he wasn't coming back. But how could she prove she wasn't on the pill?

"Randy, I want a baby as bad as you, sweetie," Cheryl pleaded. "You know that. Why would I say I wanted a baby if I really didn't?"

"Because you're afraid of losing your figure," Randy shouted. "It's like Sexy said; you're more worried about your looks than about us starting a family."

"What does Sexy have to do with this," Cheryl stormed back. *Damn it, I knew it!*

"Nothing." Randy grabbed his keys off the bureau. "She doesn't have a damn thing to do with it. Except maybe she's finally opened my eyes. All this time you've been calling her a conniving slut, but now I see you're the one who's been doing all the conniving."

As much as she wanted to slap Randy for that statement, if she did, it was only going to hasten his departure. And if he left now, there was no doubt where he was headed, and she couldn't chance him heading there in the mood he was in. "Randy, listen, wait; how about I simply prove it?" she said as he walked toward the bedroom door.

He stopped and turned toward her. "How?"

"There's got to be some kind of blood or urine test I can take."

"You mean...you'd be willing to take one?"

The way he said that made the hair on the back of Cheryl's neck rise. He acted like he'd already thought about it, but had decided against asking her. But Randy would never think of something like that. Whatever...the test would prove she hadn't been taking birth control pills. Then she'd have to figure out how Sexy had planted the damn pills.

Three hours later, Cheryl and Randy sat silently together waiting for the results. Both of their arms were crossed, and both stared straight ahead. It had taken them only an hour to find a diagnostics lab that could do the tests, and an extra three hundred dollars on top of the usual one hundred-dollar fee to get the results immediately instead of waiting two days. *Boy, is he going to feel stupid when the lab tech comes back and tells him the results were negative. And as soon as we leave here, I'm going to find Sexy Sanchez and kick her little skanky ass.*

"Mr. and Mrs. Alston?"

Cheryl looked up, and Randy jumped up.

Two minutes later, Cheryl slumped back down in her chair as Randy stomped angrily out of the office.

S howing no expression, Sexy sat next to Randy on her expensive crocodile leather sofa and listened attentively as he expressed his hurt and disappointment in discovering his wife had pretended to want a child while secretly taking birth control pills.

"Like I told you on the phone, I found the container in her night table, and even though there was almost a week's worth of missing pills—pills that she had obviously taken while claiming she was trying to get pregnant with my child—she still insisted that she didn't know where those contraceptives came from." Grim-faced, Randy sighed. "She kept right on lying, even after we got the lab results that proved she took those pills. You were right; she'd been lying to me all this time."

Sexy slowly shook her head. "When you called me and told me, I wasn't really serious about you making her get tested. And I certainly didn't think she'd go for it, anyway."

"Getting tested was her idea! She offered to take a blood test, and that's what has me so baffled. I can't figure out why she'd take it that far, knowing she's guilty."

I can't believe the bitch played right into my hands! Sexy steepled her fingers in thought and then chose her words carefully. "Is it possible that she didn't expect you to take her up on her offer to be tested?" She peered into Randy's eyes, holding his gaze challengingly.

Randy thought about it, and then nodded slightly. "You might be right. Cheryl knows me well. She has me all figured out, and she knows I don't like to make waves in our marriage. Despite the damning evidence, she expected me to take her word for it, simply to keep the peace. She must have been shocked when I took her up on the offer, and even went so far as to go to the lab with her and wait for the results."

Sexy began to feel the early rumblings of excitement as she easily led Randy down the path of mistrust toward Cheryl. "She underestimated you. Thought she could manipulate you into going along with her bold-faced lies."

"The sad thing about it...I probably would have gone along with anything she said, except this. Becoming a father is dear to my heart. My father deserted me and never looked back. I learned from him not to take that role lightly. I'm going to be there every step of the way for my child...if I ever have one," he said glumly.

On cue, Sexy began rubbing his arm comfortingly. "You're still young. Of course you'll have a child one day. In my opinion, you're too young to be a parent. You need to get a lot more life experiences before you take on a serious role like that. In a way, Cheryl did you a favor by showing her true colors. It would have been a shame for you to think you were on the verge of fatherhood while she was playing you like a fiddle. You owe it to yourself to put your full focus on your new career. The Yankees are banking on you getting them to the World Series. My advice is that you work hard and play hard. Live life to the fullest, and when the day comes for you to put all your energy into Little Randy, at least you'll have a lot of wisdom to share with him."

"Little Randy," he repeated with a grin. "I like the sound of that. But I wouldn't mind a girl, either. All I want is to have a healthy child." He gave a little groan of despair and rubbed his forehead. "I'm young, but I was really looking forward to being called Daddy."

Sexy scooted closer, lightly caressing Randy's shoulder. "I heard some of the wives talking about how Cheryl made you over. Made you take speech classes to get rid of your Southern accent. They said she even changed up your style of dressing."

"She did it for my own good. So I could feel confident when I had to speak in public."

"How's that working for you—do you feel confident?"

"Not really. It's aggravating and makes me feel more self-conscious having to think about everything I say before I say it."

"I already told you that I like your Southern accent and that you sound a lot like T.I."

Flattered, Randy broke into a grin.

"That Southern drawl of yours is sexy. Turns me on. Listen, I don't want you to be guarded when you're around me, Randy. I want you to be yourself."

"Thanks. It means a lot to know you feel that way. I get so tired of pretending to be somebody I'm not. Cheryl means well, but—"

"No disrespect, but I don't think she means well, Randy. When you love somebody, you accept them for who they are. I believe that Cheryl was afraid to have your baby."

"Why would she be afraid?" Randy asked, frowning.

"You have to understand that someone as superficial and elitist as she is would believe that you'd produce an inferior child—a child with flaws," Sexy said, watching him intently as her words sank in. She saw the muscles in his face tighten; watched him flinch.

"You saying she was afraid she'd have a child who looked and acted like me?"

Sexy nodded grimly. "Cheryl is fake, Randy. Even her friendship with that gay guy, Stephen is fake. She's into trends after all, and every New York sophisticate has a homo friend these days. Being married to you gave her the money to live the lifestyle she'd dreamed of, but she didn't sign up to go as far as to bear your child."

Looking anguished, Randy grabbed his head and bent over, looking down at the floor. He stayed in that position for a few moments, and then sat up abruptly. "I realize that every word you spoke is the truth, but I'm so confused. I feel like I should be insisting on a divorce, but despite the way she tried to play me, Cheryl is my wife, and I still have feelings for her."

"You're too emotional to make a life-altering decision right now. Why don't you stay here with me while you try and get your head straight? Until you can figure out what you're gonna do about your marriage."

Deep in thought, Randy nodded mechanically. "I never dreamed she could be so underhanded, though."

"The more we talk about your wife's deceit, the worse you're gonna feel. So, on a different topic, how do you like the new place?" Sexy waved a hand through the air, indicating her newly furnished place.

"It's nice. You have good taste."

"I don't deserve the compliment," she said, laughing. "I couldn't have done this without the help of the interior decorator you hired."

"I did?"

Sexy feigned a worried look. "Don't you remember telling the realtor it was okay to send a decorator over here to help me? I hope you know I'd never spend your money without your permission. I'm not a gold-digger like Cheryl—"

"You said we were gonna keep her name out of our conversations?"

"I'm sorry. I didn't mean to mention her name."

He turned toward Sexy and offered a weak smile. "It's cool. It's not like we can pretend she doesn't exist," Randy said thoughtfully. "Anyway, back to the interior decoration…so much has happened in the past week, it sort of slipped my mind that I agreed to pay for that."

"Do you remember, now?"

"Yeah, I remember. And for the record, I would never call you a gold digger. You're the most honest and realest person in my life right now."

Sexy could feel the corners of her mouth twitching and threatening to spread into a triumphant smile. Suppressing the urge to gloat over her victory, she leaned in and covered Randy's lips with a big kiss.

"You haven't seen the finished bedroom, yet," she said with a sly grin as she led him out of the living room.

"It's nice," Randy said, admiring the Moroccan-themed room.

"I wanna show you something." Sexy picked up the remote and clicked on the wall-mounted TV. A famous reality-TV couple appeared on the screen—naked and in the midst of copulating. The camera panned in on the well-endowed man who pulled out of his girl's pussy and commenced to rubbing his thick dick all over her face, and commanding her to suck it.

"That's what I want you to do to me," Sexy stated. "I wanna get freaky with you."

"You want to act raunchy like that? You want me to treat you like a whore?" Randy sounded incredulous.

"Mm-hmm. That's exactly what I want." Sexy stood in front of Randy, rubbing her ass against the growing erection in his pants. She bent over, twerking in time to the music that played in the background of the sex tape.

It didn't take a lot of convincing for Randy to begin grinding on

Sexy's ass. Taking it a step further, he pulled up her body-hugging stretchy dress, and took a deep breath as he gazed at Sexy's bare ass.

Bent over, Sexy parted her legs so that Randy could get to her intimate parts more easily. And when he thrust a thick finger inside her, she gasped with pleasure. He slid his finger into her again and again and Sexy humped his finger, welcoming the delicious ravishment.

The tingling through her body was becoming more and more intense and she could tell that Randy's finger was soaked with her juices. "Smear it on my asshole," she invited.

"Huh?"

"Use my juices as a lubricant and fuck me in the ass."

"Are you for real?"

"I'm dead serious. Take your pants off and come get some ass."

Randy withdrew his finger, and his breathing was ragged as he stripped out of his pants. Sexy sauntered over to the bed and assumed a position on all fours. Wiggling her ass, she beckoned Randy.

"Um, I...uh, I ain't never done no anal sex before," he stammered. "I mean, we've talked about it before, but—"

"There's a first time for everything; now come on and get up in this, lover."

Randy gripped her slender hips and entered her delicately, but Sexy writhed and bucked. "Give it to me, Randy; fuck this ass the same way you fuck a wet pussy."

Goaded by Sexy's demands, he pushed in deeper, moved faster, his hands rocking her hips as he thrust his hard dick deeper than he imagined it could go.

"That's what I want. I want to feel that dick deep in my ass."

A primal groan emerged from the back of Randy's throat as Sexy bucked backward, her body jerking out of control. Caught up in what he considered decadent pleasure, he pushed her forward until her face was buried in the pillow, her ass tooted up in the air. On his knees and anchoring her body with his strong hands, Randy gave her a forceful thrust, his thick length filling her to the hilt. He fucked her hard and passionately.

"Damn, you got some good ass," he bellowed.

"Play with my pussy," she instructed, and Randy circled her clit with the pad of his finger, and then inserted his long finger into her juicy depths. Sexy's eyes rolled back in her head as the warmth of an orgasm bubbled up inside her. Lost in passion, Randy panted as he continued to desperately move in and out.

"Oh, my God," she shrieked as one final, hard thrust sent her body shuddering with a wave of ecstasy. Weak and spent, her knees gave out and she collapsed onto her stomach. Randy collapsed along with her, still stroking and groaning. He praised the goodness of her tight asshole moments before toppling into a blissful abyss.

"I don't care what you think, Randy; someone framed me."

Randy looked down at his clasped hands, then back up at Cheryl, whose red eyes were so swollen they couldn't produce or hold any more tears. "Cheryl, you know what? I actually want to believe you. But even if somehow someone did get past the doorman and into our apartment to plant a packet of birth control pills, how in the hell did they fix it that your urine and blood shows you've been taking the pills? And we've been to two different labs, Cheryl. Both of which you picked."

Cheryl rubbed her hands over her uncombed hair, then clutched her head and once again broke out in sobs. "I feel like I'm going insane. I don't know, Randy. I love you, and now I've lost you, and not because of anything I did wrong."

Randy slowly stood up, walked to the closet and pulled out a suitcase. "How can you say taking birth control pills behind my back all this time without telling me isn't wrong, Cheryl?" He started throwing unfolded shirts, pants, and underwear inside.

"But I'm not on birth control pills!" Cheryl started pounding the bed on which she was sitting. "I haven't used any contraceptive since we married. I swear."

"I don't know what to tell you, Cheryl. Like I said, I want to believe you, but at the same time, I can't let you play me like some country hick. Because I come from Alabama doesn't mean I don't mind being played the fool." He snapped the suitcase shut. "Even by a beautiful woman like you."

Beautiful? She thought back to the evening she and Randy had first met—the $3,000 Dolce & Gabbana white lace mini, diamonds dripping from her ears, and every hair in perfect place. Yes, she was certainly beautiful then. Cheryl looked up at the mirror on the wall opposite her. Her eyes were red and so puffy they were almost closed, her face was raw and swollen, and her hair was all over her head. She met him like *that* and he was leaving her like *this? No.* She shook her head furiously. *He's not leaving me. He can't leave me.*

But what could she do to stop him? And how the hell did all this happen? It had to be Sexy who put the birth control pills in her night table, but how could she prove it? And Randy was right; how was it that traces of the contraceptive were found both in her urine and blood? It wasn't like Sexy could have bribed someone at the lab; they didn't even know what lab they could use until looking a few up on the Internet. How did Sexy pull it off? She buried her face in her hands. That damn Sexy had finally snagged Randy for herself.

"Randy, can't we talk about this?"

"I don't think there's anything to talk about, Cheryl. I'll call a lawyer tomorrow to see about starting divorce proceedings."

Divorce? We haven't been married a year. We've not even celebrated one damn anniversary. "You know who did this, don't you?" she said, walking over to Randy who was throwing sneakers in a duffel bag.

Randy looked up at her, but said nothing.

"Your little innocent girlfriend, Sexy Sanchez," Cheryl said, venom in her voice. "Somehow that little bitch managed to get in here."

She looked at Randy through narrowed eyes. "I bet she stole your key and made a copy. She planted the birth control packet."

Randy laughed. "And then she stole the keys to every diagnostics lab and clinic in the city, and coated every single test tube with some concoction that, when mixed with your blood or pee, would show you were on birth control, huh? Do you know how dumb you sound, Cheryl?"

"How dumb *I* sound?" Cheryl looked at Randy while slowly shaking her head. "Did you actually say that to me?" She walked over to Randy and eased down on a chair. "You never would have talked to me like that before, Randy. I can't say it feels good to hear you talking to me like that now."

Randy shrugged. "Sorry if I hurt your feelings. That wasn't my intention. But now maybe you know how you made me feel."

"What?" Cheryl screwed her face up. "When have I ever made you feel dumb?"

"Oh, how about you when you insisted that I go learn how to talk? I have a Southern accent, but it doesn't mean I don't know how to talk."

"The diction lessons?" Cheryl sucked her teeth. "We talked about it and you agreed with me, Randy, and you know it! Neither one of us wanted you to sound as if you didn't know how to put together a sentence when talking to the media or making personal appearances."

"Yeah, well, some folks find the way I talk quite homey," Randy said sullenly. "In fact, some people think I talk like T.I."

"Well," Cheryl said, rolling her eyes, "if your only goal is to sound like a former drug dealer and second-rate rapper who's forever in and out of prison, then sure, the money we spent on diction was a waste."

"T.I. is not a second-rate rapper," Randy snapped.

"Oh, well, excuse me," Cheryl said with a smirk.

"And it wasn't money *we* spent on diction; it was money *I* spent on diction," Randy sneered. "I don't remember you contributing any money to the cause."

Cheryl's head jerked back in surprise. "Are you serious?"

"Oh, yeah, very serious! Like it was my money that bought all this." Randy waved his arm around the room. "It was my money that paid for this furniture, wasn't it? I don't remember you using any money from your modeling gigs to buy even the curtains. Or am I wrong?"

"Randy—"

"And who paid for this fancy apartment, your car, your clothes, for you to get your hair done, your furs, your jewelry—"

"Randy," Cheryl said through clenched teeth, "in case you don't remember, I had a place to live, my own car, my own clothes, jewelry, and furs before you met me."

Randy walked over and bent down so that his face was only inches away from hers. "But none were anywhere's near as nice as what you got now, right?"

Cheryl was speechless for a moment. Was this really the same man who swore he would love her forever? Who said he would never hurt her? Who said he wanted a woman like her whom he knew wasn't after his money? But then again, this was the same man who said he wouldn't cheat on her. And exactly how had that turned out?

"Randy," Cheryl said finally. "Maybe my things weren't as nice then as they are now, but they were mine. And I hate to remind you, but you were the one who didn't have a car, a real place to live, and barely more than the clothes on your back when we met. But I fell in love with you anyway. Or, should I say, the person I thought you were." Cheryl stood up and walked over to the window and looked out onto the city street. "If the person I thought you were met the person you turned out to be, he'd beat the hell out of you."

She was so lost in her thoughts that it took a good five minutes before Cheryl realized that her last words had hit a mark. That's when she realized that she no longer heard Randy talking, or moving around. She turned back toward the room to find him sitting on the bed staring at her. "What's wrong, now?" she asked wearily.

"Nothing. I... I..." He hung his head down. "I don't know. I can't figure out how we got here, you know?"

Cheryl gave a small smile. "I know."

"You didn't marry me for my money, Cheryl. I don't even know why I said that."

"I do. Because Sexy suggested it, right? She also said she liked your homey style and that I was trying to change you because I was ashamed of you, right?"

"Cheryl—"

"And, it was Sexy who first made you suspect that I was taking birth control pills behind your back, wasn't it?" Randy said nothing, confirming Cheryl's suspicions. "But," she continued with a sigh, "even though I wasn't, there's no way I can prove it. Sexy's winning this one. In fact, I'd say she's hitting it out the park."

Randy shook his head, but said nothing.

"Somehow, Sexy has arranged everything. What a smart little skank."

Randy bit his lip. "Cheryl, don't."

"Want a drink?" Cheryl stood up without waiting for an answer. "I want a drink. Scotch, in fact." She went in the living room and returned carrying a tray with a bottle of scotch, ice, and two glasses.

"Are you moving in with her?" Cheryl asked after she poured them both a drink.

"I don't know," Randy said in a low voice.

"You don't know. Hmm, that's interesting." Cheryl took a sip of scotch. "So, where, may I ask, are you heading to from here?" She shook her glass so that the ice tinkled against each other. "And tell me the truth, baby."

Randy downed his scotch in one gulp, and then lay down on the bed, his hands crossed behind his head, staring up at the ceiling. "Yeah, I told her I'd stay with her a couple of nights."

"I see."

"But, that ain't right, is it? I don't know what's wrong with me, lately," Randy said dismally. "I'll call her and tell her I've changed my mind."

"You've changed your mind?" Cheryl asked hopefully. "Are you serious?"

"Yeah, it's only right."

"Oh, Randy. Thank you, baby." Cheryl put down her glass, scooted closer to Randy and stroked his head. "Thank you."

Randy pulled her down to him and softly kissed her. "Cheryl, I'm so sorry I hurt you."

"And I'm sorry for any and everything I've done to hurt you, Randy." This time she kissed him—long and hard. "Randy," she said when their lips finally parted, "I would really like you to make love to me."

Randy swept Cheryl into his arms and carried her into the bedroom. As if she were capable of breaking, he gently laid her on their bed and slowly undressed her, and then removed his clothes. He embraced her, and Cheryl made a breathless sound, almost a whimper when their mouths touched. Lips and tongues fused, he caged her beneath his hard, muscled body, his soft lips and moist tongue now trailing down her neck while he gently squeezed her breasts. Cheryl's flesh tingled beneath Randy's soft kisses, and she gasped as she inhaled his familiar scent, so wonderfully masculine it made her dizzy with need.

"Oh, Randy, I miss you so much."

He didn't respond with words. He didn't have to. He released a groan as he buried his face in her bosom, rubbing his cheek against her dewy skin, kissing and licking her nipples until they tightened into hard knots of desire.

Cheryl clung to him, writhing and whimpering as the heat from his skilled hands warmed her. All the while, his erection pressed into her shaven mound with an insistent, grinding rhythm.

She held her breath until she could bear it no more and then let out a long moan as he touched her intimately. "I want to feel you inside me," she pleaded, aching to be filled with his hardness.

Lavishing her with all the tenderness he possessed, Randy caressed her face and whispered that he loved her as he gingerly entered her an inch at a time.

Cheryl's body clutched possessively at every delicious increment, and when he was fully inside her, she cried out, calling his name over and over as ripples of pleasure coursed through her. He made love to her slowly and with a gentleness that spoke volumes. Randy loved her as much as she loved him. His love was evident in every thrust—in every deep stroke, and the sensation that Randy was giving was unbearably intense.

Despite his deliberate and slow movements, Cheryl didn't last long. Pleasure throbbed through every limb, and to her fingers and toes. She seemed to be in an entirely different universe of dazzling sensations and powerful emotions. After receiving only a few excruciatingly pleasurable strokes, she felt an earthquake beginning to erupt inside her. And then, quite surprisingly, there was a catastrophic explosion that caused her to convulse and cry out in unbridled passion.

Eager to join Cheryl, Randy quickened his pace. "It feels so good to be inside you, babe. I love you, Cheryl, and I miss you like crazy."

He sucked in a shallow gasp, and then his body went momentarily rigid right before a blast of molten lava spurted, causing him to howl a torturous sound that seemed to emerge from the very depths of his soul.

It's all going to be okay, Cheryl thought as she dozed off to sleep. It's all going to be fine. Sure it wasn't going to be easy to get her marriage back on an even keel, but she'd put in the work. The way she figured it, God had decided to punish her for selling the baby by sending Sexy to destroy her life. But then God had taken pity on her when he realized how much she really loved Randy, and how much he loved her. And she was going to make things right. No, she wasn't going to tell Randy that she had sold a child, nor tell Sexy that she was her mother. And there was no use lying; she had zero maternal feelings for the girl. But she was at least going to try to be friendly to Sexy, and maybe become a good influence on her. After all, it was apparent the girl needed guidance. Imagine, seventeen years old and spreading her legs for anything in pants. Yes, she was going to take Sexy under her wing, and become a role model for the girl. God had saved her marriage, so it was the least she could do.

She didn't realize she'd fallen asleep, but she awoke when she went to snuggle closer to Randy and discovered he wasn't there.

"Randy?"

His clothes were changed, his face newly shaved, and he smelled like soap. And he sat down next to her and placed his hand on her face.

"I'm not sure how these things work, Cheryl. Divorces, you know? I, uh, guess until it's all done and final we'll be considered separated. I don't know how long or anything, but of course, you don't have to go nowhere. The apartment is bought and paid for, and even though it's in both of our names, I don't mind you having it."

Cheryl's eyes widened. Separated? But didn't Randy say he had changed his mind?

"Um, I know some guys do stupid things like cancel their wives' credit cards and stuff, but you know you don't have to worry about anything like that, right?"

But wait, Randy said he was going to call Sexy and tell her that he changed his mind. I know he did.

"I've called and made reservations at the Plaza Hotel, babe. You can reach me there if you need me, okay?"

He changed his mind about staying with Sexy, not about the divorce. She felt as if she'd been punched in the stomach, but she struggled to stop tears from falling once again or springing to her eyes. She'd begged. She'd pleaded. She'd tried to explain. If he was going to leave, then he wouldn't be leaving a groveling wimp; he'd be leaving the proud sophisticated woman he married.

Randy leaned down and kissed her, then stood up, picked up the suitcase and duffel bag, and headed for the door. Right before walking out, he turned around and looked at her. With tears in his eyes he said in an undeniably sad voice: "Bye, Cheryl. I want you to know I'll always love you."

"Bye, Randy. I hope she makes you happy." Cheryl responded. "And by happy, I mean I hope she gives you syphilis."

Sexy

U nable to get enough of Sexy's tight ass, Randy only stayed at the Plaza hotel for a week before moving in with her. Before long he professed his love for Sexy. Though admittedly, he still had feelings for Cheryl, he told Sexy he could never forgive his wife for duping him into believing she'd been trying to get pregnant with his child.

With the lucrative Coca-Cola deal and the Nike endorsement in negotiations, Randy had more money than he knew how to spend. Sexy, on the other hand, had no problem burning through Randy's wealth now that they were an official couple. Sure, he was still legally married to Cheryl, but that piece of paper was only a technicality. Randy was now Sexy's man and everyone knew it.

As an incentive for Randy to sign, Nike gifted him a beautiful Rolls-Royce Phantom, which he gave to Sexy. She seldom drove the car, however. It was terrifying the way New York drivers whizzed through traffic, making her feel as if her life was in peril every time she got behind the wheel. Still, it was nice owning such a super-expensive car.

But the biggest purchase she'd convinced Randy to buy was a seventy-foot yacht—a luxury vessel he named *Sexy*. The yacht soon became party central for the young and fabulous. When the news got out that Randy Alston named the yacht after his side piece,

Sexy's popularity spiked like crazy. The number of her Instagram followers went from 409 to almost 500,000, seemingly overnight.

When Sexy and Randy weren't sailing and partying on their yacht, they were hitting up the New York club scene where the paparazzi knocked each other over, clamoring for a shot of Sexy. As if she were an A-list celebrity, they yelled her name trying to get her attention, trying to goad her into looking at the lens of their cameras.

Sexy had quickly shot to fame simply for partying hard and dressing in the height of fashion. Blogs and other gossip tabloids mentioned her name on a daily basis, and often ran stories that linked her romantically with various high-profile male celebrities. Luckily, Randy didn't pay the gossip rags any attention. He knew his girl was true blue, and unlike his relationship with Cheryl, where he indulged in threesomes to keep things spicy, Randy had no desire for a third party to join him and Sexy in bed. Sexy, he often told her, was all the woman he needed.

Tall, lean, and shapely, Sexy was a fashion designer's dream. Perpetually swathed in couture fashion, she accepted clothing from top designers, but declined with a frown when the same designers requested she walk the runway garbed in their latest apparel.

In Sexy's opinion, models were empty-headed mannequins, and with her high IQ and sharp sense of cunning, she was far from stupid. Hell, she'd outwitted a grown-ass, well-seasoned woman and had taken her man. Not too many people had the brains to outsmart Sexy. Although snagging Randy Alston had been ridiculously easy, she considered it the biggest coup of her young life. She was completely independent now and no longer had to worry about her stingy parents trying to control her with the miserly amounts of money they doled out. Now that she had access to Randy's bank account, her lying, pretend-parents could keep their money and shove it up their asses!

Sexy sat on the bed watching Randy as he placed extra toiletries into his luggage. He was going to be on the road for ten days as the Yankees did a swing through the Midwest and California.

"I wish you could come with me," he said with a sad expression.

"I'm gonna miss you like crazy while you're away."

"Hey, I got an idea. Why don't you fly out tomorrow and spend some time with me? You know how much I hate sleeping in those lonely hotel rooms all by myself."

Sexy became pensive. It surprised her that a tough athlete like Randy could be so needy and childlike at times. The thought of spending time in Minnesota made her want to puke, but with Cheryl lurking in the shadows, wanting to get her hooks back into her husband, Sexy thought it wise to cater to any request that Randy made, no matter how absurd.

Her face lit with feigned delight. "Honey, it's so sweet of you to invite me. I'd love to join you in Minnesota, but are you sure I won't be in the way?"

"In the way?" he scoffed. "If anything, your presence is gonna help my game."

"Okay, if you insist," she said with forced cheerfulness. *Geez, I bet the night life sucks in Minnesota. The boredom will be so unbearable, I'll probably want to slit my wrists.*

Pleased by Sexy's seeming eagerness to join him out of town, Randy opened his arms, inviting her into them. When she stepped inside his embrace, he squeezed her tight and lifted her off the floor. "That's why I dig you, girl. You really know how to take care of your man, and I want you to know that I'm all in."

"You're my knight in shining armor, Big Daddy. And don't you ever forget it," she said as she rested her head against his chest. She'd discovered that calling him "Big Daddy" was a surefire way to get him aroused. Despite the fact that the team's plane was scheduled to take off in the next hour, Randy began tugging on the hem of her sundress, lifting it up.

"You're gonna be late," she whispered in a tone of concern, though she secretly enjoyed the idea of him wanting her so badly, he was willing to risk being late.

"I don't care," he murmured as he pushed her hair over her shoulder and peppered her neck with kisses. "That plane ain't leaving without me."

She held up her hand. "But babe—"

He grasped her wrist and kissed her hand, silencing her protests. He then licked the center of her palm as though it were coated with sugar. Sexy released a sigh and lifted her head to kiss him. Randy gripped her face in his hands and kissed her fiercely, his tongue sweeping inside her mouth, exploring relentlessly. His hands roamed freely over her body before resting on her ass. He lifted her sundress and squeezed her ass cheeks that were exposed in a skimpy thong.

He squeezed them, gently at first, and then with more force. Sexy rubbed Randy's crotch, urging him to get rid of his pants, and he quickly unbuttoned them, allowing them to drop. His black briefs could not conceal his obvious erection, and she slipped her hand inside and grasped his dick and slowly stroked it up and down, eliciting moans of appreciation from Randy.

Feeling his hard and heavily veined dick inside her fist aroused Sexy. Her nipples hardened and her breathing quickened, letting Randy know that her desire matched his, and that she was ready for him. In fact, judging by the dampened strip of cotton between her legs, Sexy was beyond ready.

Randy's hand wandered down to the elastic band of her satin thong. She gazed at him and recognized the intense yearning in his eyes. Randy formed a fist around the delicate fabric and tugged at it.

"Rip it off," she said in a rough voice, and as soon as she'd given the command, he tore the lingerie away from her body with one strong, sudden pull. She flinched as the elastic snapped, stinging her skin. Randy backed up and pushed his open suitcase out of the way and sat on the side of the bed. Slowly, seductively, Sexy removed her bra and then glided toward him. Naked, her pert breasts jutted outward. Her long legs, smooth as silk and athletically muscled, were made to wrap tightly around Randy's waist.

She straddled him, wriggling and moaning as she felt his dick brushing against her folds, the head parting them as it pushed inside, penetrating her slowly, giving her one exquisite inch at a time.

She gasped with pleasure. "Fuck me," she demanded, growing impatient. Giving Sexy what she wanted, Randy slammed into her, filling her completely and stretching out her pussy walls. The moment it felt as if it was deeply embedded inside her, he suddenly withdrew and then jammed his dick back in, giving her several more magnificent inches.

In a display of sheer strength and physicality, Randy delivered thrust after hard thrust into Sexy's drenched pussy, lifting her up a little and then proceeding to ram her with stroke after stroke of granite-like hardness. Sexy rode his dick, her hips swiveling in a manner that caused her clit to rub against his pubic bone. The pleasure was so intense, causing her to squeeze her eyes closed, causing her juices to pour out and trickle down his shaft. On the verge of an orgasm, she could feel her pussy walls begin to tighten.

"I'm cumming, Randy," she whimpered out the warning.

"Me, too, baby. I am, too," Randy grunted. His dick throbbed and twitched as he quickened his pace. His dick began to pulsate as Sexy's orgasm rocketed through her body. Joining her, he bellowed as his creamy liquid exploded inside her.

For a moment or two, Sexy felt lost in the cosmos, overcome by so much pleasure, she was barely cognizant. "Randy," she murmured as awareness slowly returned. "I love you."

"I love you, too."

"I want to get married," she purred while he was caught in a moment of weakness.

"We will."

"When?"

"Soon."

"How soon?"

"As soon as Cheryl signs the divorce papers."

"She's never going to sign them, Randy. You're gonna have to force her by taking her to court if necessary. You have to do something. I don't like being referred to as a home wrecker and a side chick. It's not fair."

Randy stroked her hair and tried to console her by suggesting she take his Black Card and go buy herself something nice at Tiffany & Co. And while Randy was in a giving mood, Sexy figured it was the perfect time to let him know about the party she planned to throw on the yacht to showcase an up-and-coming young rap artist.

"Yeah, baby, that's fine with me. What's the rapper's name?"

"Lil' Sizzler."

"Never heard of him."

"Not yet, but you will. I'm gonna help him make a name for himself."

"When you get to Minnesota, we can talk about some possible dates when we can host the showcase for the young rapper."

Sexy eased off Randy's lap. "You'd better get washed up so you can catch your flight on time."

Randy glanced at his watch. "Damn!"

Before he could rush to the master bathroom, Sexy grabbed his wrist. "By the way, I've already set the date for the showcase. It's at the end of the month." Her forehead creased with worry. "I'm so sorry, Randy. I made a mistake and planned the showcase during the week that you'll be in California. Several music industry executives have already confirmed the invitation to come and listen to Lil' Sizzler, and I can't ask them to change the date. So, is it okay if I throw the party while you're away?" She had Randy's back against the wall. He couldn't deny her, not when she was forced to play mistress while his conniving wife deliberately delayed their divorce.

Randy paused for a beat and then smiled at Sexy. "I don't have a problem with you having a yacht party while I'm away. That boat belongs to both of us and you don't ever have to ask permission to enjoy it."

"Thanks, honey."

He cradled her chin, lifting her head until their eyes met. "Cheryl is having a hard time accepting that our marriage is over."

"But she's the one who ruined the marriage," Sexy blurted with a great deal of hostility.

"I know, I know. But can you be a little more patient with her? Do it for me and I promise when we do get married, it's gonna be the wedding of the century."

Sexy nodded, but her mind had already strayed to a different topic. "Do I have to fly commercial to Minnesota?" she whined.

"No, of course not. Go ahead and charter a plane."

She broke into a big smile. "Aw, you're so sweet and you're so good to me, Randy."

"You may not be Mrs. Randall Alston yet, but that doesn't mean I'm not gonna do everything in my power to spoil you and show you how much I love you."

Sexy gave him a quick kiss on the lips and when he hurried to the bathroom, she mentally began planning her wardrobe for the rap artist's showcase. She'd probably change two or three times during the evening, and hopefully her hookup at Prada would send her everything she needed. If not, she'd reach out to Stella McCartney, who'd been dying for Sexy to wear her clothes.

It was too much trouble having to worry about her own glamour requirements while also planning a party. It was clearly time for Randy to let her hire a personal assistant. She needed someone who could help with nuisance details like contacting caterers and... hell, come to think about it, she could use an assistant at that very moment to take care of chartering the plane for her stupid trip to boring Minnesota.

"Babe, I just remembered something," Randy said as he picked up an invitation inside his luggage. "There's some kind of charity event in Saint Paul, Minnesota. My agent wants me to attend, so I need you to bring my tux with you and make sure you buy yourself a beautiful gown."

"What kind of gala?" Sexy inquired, dreading the idea of spending an evening with a bunch of stuffy, old fogies.

Randy read from the invitation. "It's sponsored by the Starkey Foundation."

"Let me see." Sexy reached for the invitation and perused it. "So The World May Hear Awards Gala? What's that about?"

"I think they provide hearing aids to deaf kids all over the world."

"Good cause, but it sounds kind of boring. Do we have to go?" She wrinkled her nose.

"I've already contributed some big bucks, so I might as well attend. There'll be a lot of A-list celebrities and the big bonus is that I'll get to show you off on the red carpet. With your fashion sense, you'll probably end up on the best dressed list featured on E! News."

Red carpet. E! News. A-list celebs! Okay, making a pit stop to the sleepy town of St. Paul, Minnesota was beginning to sound a lot more exciting. "Okay," Sexy agreed with feigned reluctance. "I'll go. But honey, I'm gonna need an assistant to help me juggle all these extra responsibilities."

Randy grabbed the handle of his luggage. "That's not a problem, Sexy. You can get all the extra help you need to make your life easier."

"Thanks." She gave him a quick kiss and escorted him to the door, where they kissed once more before Randy trotted down the corridor toward the elevator.

Smiling and waving goodbye to Randy, Sexy closed the door and rushed to her iPad to look for an agency that could quickly send over applicants to be interviewed for the position of personal assistant.

A top requirement of the applicants would be the ability to maneuver through Manhattan's crazy traffic while chauffeuring Sexy around in her Phantom.

Sexy had no intention of relying on Randy's handouts forever. She needed her own money, and representing desperate young artists seemed like an easy way to begin earning her own money. Who knew? Perhaps one day she'd become a powerhouse in the entertainment industry—a force to be reckoned with.

"Yes, Stephen, I saw it," Cheryl said wearily into the telephone.

"I'm only saying, that little skank has probably spent more of young country boy's money in a month than you spent in the eight months you were married."

"We're still married, Stephen, remember?"

"I'm not the one who needs to be reminded, honey," Stephen said with an attitude. "Someone should let young country boy know married men shouldn't be going around buying yachts, and naming them after their girlfriends."

"Yeah, I heard about that, too," Cheryl admitted.

"I bet you did. Especially since it was splashed all over Page Six of *The New York Post* when Sexy hosted a birthday party for some no-name rapper and the police had to be called because someone started shooting off more than their mouths." Stephen laughed. "Can you believe they're going to have to start putting metal detectors on yachts now?"

"Only yachts that Sexy gives parties on." Cheryl sighed and added: "Mila told me she ran into the little skank at Tiffany's. She was trying on a diamond necklace, but as soon as she saw Mila, she made a point of loudly telling the clerk that her fiancé would be stopping by in a few weeks to pick out an engagement ring."

"No!" Stephen exclaimed.

"Oh, yes." Cheryl examined her fingernails, noting it was time for another manicure. "Then she set aside five rings to show 'Mr. Randall Alston, the famous third baseman for the New York Yankees,' and then sashayed out the door without saying a word to Mila."

"Well, one thing you've got to give her, the girl got swag." Stephen laughed.

"Shit, the one thing I want to give her is a good swift kick in the ass," Cheryl retorted.

"But really, Cheryl, on a serious tip—what exactly do you think you'll get in the divorce settlement? You said there's no pre-nup in place, so I'm going to assume you're going to take him to the cleaners. The idiot is making it quite easy for you to do so, with him flaunting Sexy all over the place."

"Who said there's going to be a divorce settlement?" Cheryl said nonchalantly.

"What? Girl, don't make me run over there and slap you," Stephen said indignantly. "You are not telling me you're not going to get even a little something out this deal. You gotta get at least a couple of million. Shit, he signed that big endorsement deal with Coke, and then the Nike thirty-five-million-dollar deal. Don't be stupid!"

"Girl, please. If there's one thing I'm not, it's stupid." Cheryl rolled her eyes. "But I'm only saying there may not be a divorce settlement, because there might not be a divorce."

"What???"

"I'm only saying you never know," Cheryl said with a smile.

"Okay, spill it!" Stephen demanded. "What aren't you telling me?"

"Only that I occasionally get a call around two a.m. from a blocked number, and when I pick up the phone, there's only music playing in the background."

"And you think it's Randy?" Stephen asked breathlessly.

"I know it is," Cheryl said smugly. "The music playing is always the same song, Usher's 'Here I Stand.' The same song that was playing the day Randy and I met."

"Oh, my God," Stephen gushed. "And on your wedding day. That's so romantic!"

Cheryl was about to say something, but was interrupted by a buzzing sound. "Stephen, I gotta go."

"But—"

"Love ya!" Cheryl hung up, and walked into the bathroom and turned off the battery-powered time setting on top of the toilet seat, then picked up the white strip next to it. Looking at the blue plus sign in the little round window, Cheryl smiled and said:

"Bingo!"

It had to have happened that last night they'd spent together, when their lovemaking was exactly that...lovemaking. Cheryl felt warm all over simply thinking about the quiet passion they shared, and the way Randy had slowly kissed her over and over, telling her how much he loved her. What a wonderful night to have conceived a child. Tears sprang to Cheryl's eyes as she rubbed her still-flat belly. Sexy had better enjoy the money and fame that came with being Randy's side chick while she could because that bitch's days were numbered.

ABOUT THE AUTHORS

Allison Hobbs is a national bestselling author of twenty-five novels and has been featured in such periodicals as *Romantic Times* and *The Philadelphia Inquirer*. She lives in Philadelphia, Pennsylvania. Visit the author at AllisonHobbs.com and Facebook.com/Allison hobbseroticaauthor.

Karen E. Quinones Miller is the *Essence* bestselling author of *Satin Doll*, *I'm Telling*, *Using What You Got*, and *Uptown Dreams*. She has been nominated for an NAACP Literary Award. In addition, she is a literary consultant, CEO of Oshun Publishing Company, and a former literary agent. She lives in Philadelphia with her daughter, Camille. Visit her at www.KarenEQuinonesMiller.com or www.facebook.com/karen.e.miller.14